THE

Bamboo Blonde

by DOROTHY B. HUGHES

WILDSIDE PRESS

THE PRINTING HISTORY OF *The Bamboo Blonde*

Duell, Sloan and Pearce edition published July, 1941

1ST printing....................................July, 1941

Grosset and Dunlap edition published April, 1943

1ST printing............................February, 1943

Pocket Book EDITION PUBLISHED SEPTEMBER, 1946

1ST printing............................August, 1946

This Pocket Book edition is published by arrangement with Duell, Sloan and Pearce, Inc.

To BOY

HIS BOOK

CAST OF CHARACTERS
IN THE ORDER OF THEIR APPEARANCE

{ 1 }

CON was bored. If he hadn't been he wouldn't have prowled around the living room of their beach cottage, making more noise than the incensed roar of the waves. Below the fogged windows they shattered with nerve-jumping regularity against the sea wall. She liked the pound of the water at high tide. But she didn't like it tonight. Not with Con bumping against chairs, shaking the floor with his tread, pretending to fix the rented radio. He was bored and she didn't like it. He had said this would be a second honeymoon. It wasn't. It was exactly like the first.

"We're going to Long Beach."

He had announced that before they were two days in Hollywood, with parties scheduled for every party hour, and Griselda wanting to show him off to all of her friends and perhaps-friends.

When she protested, "But, Con, nobody goes there!" he told her, "You're nuts. Thousands of people go there. I can prove it by the Chamber of Commerce. The Navy's there."

The Navy wasn't; a part of the fleet was in the Far East, a part on the Atlantic, fending danger from America. Yet, surprisingly, there was a scattering of gray-towered battleships on the horizon. The papers didn't tell you that but there was.

They had come to Long Beach. And he was bored.

1

He was acting as if she were to blame that they were boxed in this old-fashioned wooden beach cottage instead of in the beautiful Malibu home Oppy had urged upon them. Con had been exuberant when they arrived; Barjon Garth was also in Long Beach. She hadn't liked Garth being there. She knew that there was good reason for his presence; foreign agents had been concentrating on the West Coast. It was to be expected in these times that the head of the X division, highest governmental secret service, would be on hand a part of the time. It was absurd to be uneasy about Con when Garth was in the neighborhood simply because he had once helped out the X chief. That was in the to-be-forgotten past. He had returned to his job on the air waves months ago with no hankering to continue the precarious sideline. Nevertheless, she had been relieved when she heard that the X chief was leaving. She didn't know then how Con would react.

Garth had sailed this morning on someone's exquisite and expensive yacht for a fishing trip in southerly waters and Con was left behind. It was a man's trip and this was a second honeymoon. He had to stay with her. But he was bored and Griselda was angry, sitting there trying to read, her nerves jumping with every crash of the waves and of Con. If she hadn't been angry she wouldn't have gone out with him and she wouldn't have seen Shelley Huffaker pick him up in the Bamboo Bar.

It was eight exactly by the rented clock with the bright blue ocean painted on its face. Con said, "Think I'll go out and buy a drink."

She hadn't spoken to him since seven o'clock, when he had ejaculated for the twenty-third time that day, "God, what I'd give to be with Garth right now!" She hadn't trusted herself to speak; the anger she'd been suppressing since she began to count the ejaculations was about ready to spill. At that point she was surer than ever that this was only the echo of the first honeymoon; then he'd kept wishing all over Bermuda that he were back at Tony's on Minetta.

She spoke now, spoke acidly so that he wouldn't know there was hurt as well as anger in her. "Don't tell me all those bottles are empty."

"My God," he said, "you don't think a bottle's an artesian well, do you, baby?"

He laughed and she was more furious. Drinks and fishing, that was all he cared about! But the fury vanquished the hurt with lucky immediacy. He was walking past her chair and he lifted her pale horn-rimmed glasses off her nose, bent his leggy length down to kiss her. She turned her cheekbone to him. She said, "I'll go with you." He didn't act as if he cared one way or the other.

She went into the one bedroom, slid her white polo coat from a hanger. The ancient cretonne of the wardrobe curtains couldn't have been any more attractive when new. It looked like pink fish climbing over faded black spots. At that, the cretonne was fully as pleasant as the other things in the house. She put the coat over her baby-blue slacks, took a quick glance in the mirror smoothing down the pale gold of her hair. Her eyes didn't look as watery as they felt. She returned to her husband.

"Let's go," she said.

He locked the door with the key. There really wasn't much sense in locking the cottage, a bent hairpin could have opened any door or window. As they started down the steps to the sidewalk garage she said, "Better let me have it, I may not last as long as you."

He laughed again, just as if he didn't know she was angry and could find out why by asking. But she was thankful he didn't ask. If he had, she might have capitulated against his blue shirt, and she didn't want to do that. She was too annoyed.

He handed her the key. "Oke, baby."

There was no reason for garage doors to scream like loons when they were opened. Even rust couldn't account for such ear-splitting disturbance. It was a part of the poltergeist atmosphere of the whole cottage.

The headlights of a car stopped where they spotted Con, not her standing in the mist shadows at the foot of the wooden steps.

It was a girl who caroled, "Con."

Griselda couldn't see her; she could only hear the voice. It didn't help matters that it was a voice that belonged with beauty; it had the poeticized sea-quality of softness, of lullaby.

Con turned. "What are you doing here, Kathie?" He sounded surprised and a little amused. He moved over to lean against the door of the open car.

The girl said, "I thought Walker might be with you."

"Didn't know he was on shore."

The gentle voice said, "Yes. I wasn't at the hotel when he came in. He left a note. I thought maybe he'd dropped in to see you. You're going out. I won't keep you."

"Just to the Bamboo for a drink. Won't you come along?" He didn't speak of a wife inconveniently in the background.

The girl said, "No thank you, Con. I'd better go back and wait for Walker. I don't want to miss him again." The car drove away and Griselda came forward. "Who was that?"

"Kathie Travis."

"And who is Kathie Travis?" She tried not to sound like a wife; she wasn't very successful.

"Mrs. Walker Travis. He's Navy. Lieutenant aboard the *Antarctica*."

She didn't say any more. He didn't mention that Kathie Travis was beautiful but doubtless she was. Con's bar acquaintances in women ran to beauty. If this one weren't bar, he wouldn't have mentioned the Bamboo so casually.

She had never asked him where he located the ramshackle coupe. It was keyed to a high-school sophomore's purse and choice, noisy and as disreputable, with its peeling black coat and red wire wheels. They could have had a choice of the cars in Oppy's garages at Malibu.

Disappointment blurred her eyes but she rubbed it away, pretending it was the night mist now dense on the windshield. He drove the five short blocks to the main street of Belmont Shores, parked the car directly in front of his pet, the Bamboo Bar. She hadn't been in it before. There was something ridiculously sinister in its look, like the opium-den sets in early movies. She cared even less for the interior; the greenish amber lights were too dim for seeing, especially without her glasses, and they made the color of flesh as ghastly as something photographed under water at sundown.

Con said, "Want to sit at a table?"

"I do."

"All right." He eyed the high bamboo stools of the bar with thwarted affection.

They took a table near the door. Con greeted the waiter fondly, "How you, Chang?"

The waiter didn't look as if his name were Chang; if it was, he'd changed it from Buck or Spike. He looked as if he would be a top sergeant in the tank corps if and when called for duty.

He returned the greeting lovingly, "How're you, Mr. Satterlee?"

All bar waiters were Con's intimates; all adored him. It wasn't because he bought so many drinks; it was just something about Con, his nice horsey face, his gray eyes that could be careless or keen with equal lack of effort. She adored him too, but she was nothing but a wife. Her adoration didn't matter to him.

Chang-Buck took the order for two Scotches and rolled with a prizefighter's gait over to the bar. He hadn't acquired the cauliflower ear from palming trays. Probably one of Con's lame ducks from past newspaper days. Probably too he was the attraction at the Bamboo Bar, the reason Con couldn't go by it without stopping for a drink. She could just hear them with Con's Scotch as a wailing wall, remembering Tony's and the good old Prohibition years. Not tonight they wouldn't! Her fury hadn't abated one jot. She sat stiffly, her eyes beginning to accustom themselves to the lack of light.

The room was almost empty. There were two couples, from Kansas or Iowa if looks were honest indication, having a devilish good time at one table. There were two men in the far corner, attending to the business of drinking. And perched on a stool there was a blonde girl. She was all alone and she'd evidently been there for too long a time. She was slumped forward on her elbows, her head bent over the flat top of the bar. She wore the inevitable California slack suit; it looked a sickly green-gray in this light, but so did Griselda's own. Her face wasn't visible.

Chang brought the drinks. "How's tricks, Mr. Satterlee?"

"Can't complain. How's with you?"

"Okey-dokey with me." His voice had a rasp to it, as if his throat had a touch of prizefighter's resin in it.

"Travis been in tonight?"

"Not tonight, Mr. Satterlee. His wife was here earlier."

Griselda put a stop to them, asking frigidly, "May I have a cigarette, Con?" She didn't care to hear about this Kathie.

Chang or Buck went away. There was an annoying amusement and sympathy behind his unexpressive face as if he well knew wives on rampage. It didn't help Griselda's temper. She didn't feel like crying now; she felt like smashing things.

The man who started away from the far table looked as a gentleman should. Even in this murky light his brown jacket was the right color and cut, his lighter colored slacks tailored deliberately with casualness. She looked at him again; something about the short crop of his brown curly hair, about the way he moved, straight and secure, was familiar. His head turned back to his companion and she saw the mustached profile.

She cried out in delight, "Con, it's Kew. Kew Brent." No wonder she hadn't known him immediately; he wasn't the man to sit drinking in imitation opium dens; you only met Kew in the right places, escorting important men or beautiful women.

"Pretend you don't know him," Con muttered, and then groaned, "Oh, my God," for Kew had caught sight of them or had heard her exclamation. He came toward them, settling his ascot as he moved.

Con muttered again, "See you later, baby."

"Con, you can't," she began, but he could. He was already walking bar-wards rudely, not even waiting to speak to Kew. Her anger rose impotently. There was no reason at all why Con should behave that way about Kew, simply because Kew liked to dress as a gentleman instead of in dirty old sneakers, antediluvian gray trousers, not deliberately casual, but impossible to be anything else; a brown coat that didn't go at all, a blue shirt with neither tie nor ascot to give it shape. Kew was originally Con's friend not hers, dating back to the newspaper days before Kew became the featured Washington correspondent of the greatest news service and Con the crack news commentator for the greatest broadcasting company. He was one of the few remnants from Con's early days who wasn't thoroughly disreputable. That was probably why Con couldn't stand him.

Kew greeted her, pleasure printed all over his square browned face. "Griselda, this is a good surprise. I thought you were in New York. Where's Con off to?"

She put her hand in his. "Grand to see you, Kew. It's been too long." And she shrugged, laughing to hide her displeasure. "You know Con's thirst. He'll be back." She didn't have the least assurance that he would, but one had to pretend; if he had no manners or bad ones, she must cover up for him.

Kew asked in surprise, "But what are you doing in Long Beach? I understood you were the particular bright-haired child designer of the studios. I should have expected to run into you at the movie hideouts, not here."

She said simply, knowing it would explain all to one who knew him, "Con wanted to come," and she added, "We're married again, you know." He probably hadn't heard; he'd known them in their first two-year attempt, and she had met him once or twice during the four-year divorce desert.

"Congratulations?" he grinned.

But she didn't answer. She was looking toward the bar. The bleached girl had moved to the stool next to Con. He was lighting her cigarette. Her face was still hidden.

Kew's eyes followed hers. "Who is it?"

"I don't know." She turned back to him, picked up her tasteless drink. "I've never been here before." But she couldn't keep from looking again at Con and the blonde. She knew how Lot's wife must have felt; it wasn't being curious; it was urgency.

And she heard the bartender say, "I'm sorry. I can't give her another one."

Con's voice was deceptively mild. "I said I'd buy the lady a drink." Every word was distinctly audible in the small, quiet room.

The barman repeated with unshaken stolidity, "She can't have no more."

"No?" Con put his hand on the girl's arm. "Come on, honey. I know where they'll sell us one."

Griselda's eyes widened. She saw Con help the girl away from the bar, brush past Chang-Buck's attempted words, start with his companion across the room. The blonde had a short coat over her arm and she held it with her free hand.

He didn't stop at Griselda's table but he slowed enough to wink at her in passing. Her hands clenched. He couldn't do this, not on their honeymoon. She remembered to close her fish-wide mouth after they disappeared through the door.

Kew was watching. He smiled. "Same old Con," and then he must have noted the distress she was trying unsuccessfully to hide. "I'm sorry, Griselda. You know he'll be right back. You know how Quixotic Con is. He'll take her home and be right back."

She looked away from him. "I won't be here."

He said, "Could I run you home?" His watch was crystalline copper. "I'd ask you to do something better than that but I'm late for an engagement now."

She answered, "No, Kew. Thank you. But it's only a step."

She wouldn't go with Kew. She didn't want to make a fool of herself to Con's friends. She'd wait until she could leave alone with no one to look boredly sympathetic if her eyes were moist. She wasn't sure she could pretend to be a casual modern wife even for five blocks—she wanted to howl and kick her heels.

He said, "Tell Con I'll drop by tomorrow. I'm at the Villa Riviera. Give him a ring."

She watched him disappear behind the presumedly artistic doors of swinging bamboo. The now solitary drinker at the table where Kew had been, finished his stint and prepared to leave. He hesitated crossing to the door and her eyes were enormous when he stopped at her table. She'd never seen him before.

He introduced himself sparsely, "Mrs. Satterlee, I am Major Pembrooke."

She had met many of him in London, on the continent, in kinder days. The bulldog British breed, stocky rather than tall, red-faced, with a sand-colored bristle mustache beginning to gray; hair, the same, beginning to recede. She had never met one wearing so cold a mask, almost a brutal face. She didn't like him. Instinctively and with no reason for it, she feared him. He had no business knowing who she was. Kew hadn't told him; Kew hadn't seen her until he was leaving that table.

She acknowledged the introduction as sparsely as it was given.

He was standing there looking down at her but he wasn't interested in her. That wasn't in his face. He announced, "I will escort you home, Mrs. Satterlee."

She was suddenly furious at him, a stranger daring to intrude, the straw at the breaking-point of this insufferable day. She jumped up, said with more anger than hauteur, "You will not escort me home. I am not accustomed to being escorted by strangers. Good-night, Major Pembrooke." She strode head high out of the place, regretting that swinging doors could not emphasize a point.

Con had, of course, taken the car as well as the pick-up blonde. Griselda was always nervous walking alone after dark; short as the distance to the cottage was, she dreaded to turn from the lighted main street for the final two blocks on the one closed to traffic. There was the night-lonely beach of the bay on one side, the drawn blinds of white apartments on the other. She walked in the center of the wide pavement.

It couldn't be that she heard footsteps falling accurately in hers. It was nerves, her usual night nerves. She could glance over her shoulder and make certain it was only imagination but she didn't. She hurried her steps and the relentless echo-steps paced faster. She strolled now; whoever it was behind her could pass easily, she'd rather have it precede her than follow. But the sound steps retained their metro- nomic mimicry. Without willing, her eyes slid left to the bay and she saw the shadow of a man, not far, not far enough from her own shadow. Her feet began to move swiftly, blindly, forward. She could hear her breath come and go, louder than those insistent pur- suing steps still behind her as she began to climb the long stairway leading to the catwalk porch and her front door. She was near hysterical laughter listening

—one-two-three-four—those last steps thwarted, silenced, not accompanied by hers. She didn't know
who or what she expected to see but she couldn't
turn. She stood there breathing.

And then the voice spoke, stones dropped on the
cold gray of the Pacific beyond. "I would have preferred to escort you home, Mrs. Satterlee."

She turned slowly. The fear she had smelled on
seeing this man in the bar was tangible now. There
were no neighbors to hear a shout for help. The sea
wall extended about the left, the other side of the
house. The cottage a sand lot away on this side was
unoccupied. She stood at the head of the steps, hoping he would climb no further, hoping she might continue to bar his way. She had her voice now. "What
do you want? How did you know I was Mrs. Satterlee?"

"Mr. Brent told me who you were." That was a
lie; Kew hadn't even known she was Con's wife
again until she told him.

She wanted her heart to stop pounding so hard
that it hurt to breathe. She asked, "Are you a friend
of Kew's?"

"I knew him in Washington. I didn't know he'd
come to the West Coast until I ran into him tonight.
I was pleased to find him here. I was also pleased to
learn that Con Satterlee was here."

She questioned, "You know my husband?" She
wasn't surprised at that; Con was always pulling some
astonishing creature out of his bag of acquaintances.

But he said, "No, I wish to meet him."

She stated firmly then, "I'm sorry, Major Pembrooke, but Con isn't here. And I don't know when he
will return. If you will call some other time—" It was
dismissal but he didn't accept it. Not even his eyes

moved. They retained their cold expressionlessness against hers. He said, "I presume Mr. Satterlee is here for the same purpose as Mr. Brent."

She could speak up now and she did. "Then you are quite mistaken, Major Pembrooke. My husband is here on his honeymoon. I doubt very much that Kew's presence in Long Beach is for the same reason." She actually smiled. The darling bachelor Kew wasn't to be caught by matrimonial entanglements.

Pembrooke was silent for the moment. "Mr. Satterlee is not here seeking Mannie Martin?"

Amazement must have been wide in her eyes. She could feel it there. "Seeking whom?"

"Manfred Martin. Mannie Martin. You know him, of course."

"I have never heard of him." She repeated definitely, "I have never heard the name before."

"Con Satterlee has heard of him," the Major stated.

"Possibly." She didn't know half of Con's freaks.

"Con Satterlee knows him. Martin has been production director of the West Coast division of the broadcasting company."

She remembered then. But she had never met this Martin. Con hadn't even looked him up in Hollywood. Why should he be seeking the man here? Her face must have been a question mark.

Major Pembrooke said, "Mannie disappeared two weeks ago Monday." He explained before she could protest, "It hasn't been in the papers. The studio didn't want publicity unless they were certain it was not a self-induced disappearance. By now, however, not having heard from or of him in that time, his associates are becoming nervous." His mouth was scornful. "By now the trail is cold."

She picked her words icily, "What has this to do with my husband?"

The Major ignored her ill humor. "I was certain Con Satterlee came here to trace his friend. Even as Mr. Brent has come."

She took a deep breath for courage. "What is it to you?"

"Mr. Martin was entering into a partnership with me. The contracts are ready but I can do nothing until he is found. And my backers are becoming impatient."

It sounded harmless enough but she didn't want Con drawn into anything that this stone man was a part of. In fact, she didn't want Con engaged in anything now, harmless or not. This was a honeymoon.

She spoke with a forced brightness, "Well, you've made a mistake, Major Pembrooke." Her laughter sounded shallow, ha-ha. "Con isn't here for any such reason. He hasn't even mentioned Mannie Martin. I would advise you to go to the police with your problem."

This time he accepted the dismissal. "The police have been informed," he stated. He turned to descend. "You will tell your husband I called and that I wish to see him. About the letter."

"What letter?" Major Pembrooke must be crazy. But he was leaving.

"The letter Mannie sent him before he disappeared."

Con hadn't mentioned a letter. There could have been one. Neither of them pried into the other's mail.

"I am at Catalina, rather, off Catalina. *The Falcon.* I can't delay longer. I have guests there. You will tell your husband."

She didn't speak. She would tell Con nothing. It

would be just like him to take up a wild goose chase like this one to thwart his boredom. And even now that the Major had proved himself legitimate, she didn't like him. She called after him, "If you want to see Con again, please don't follow me. I don't like it."

He apologized without moving a muscle of his face. "I wished to make certain I could speak to you tonight. And you had made it definite that you did not care to be escorted."

She frowned to his receding steps, then fumbled for her key, the kind you bought in the five and ten, rattled it into the lock. She wasn't frightened; she was just cold from standing long in the damp dark.

She locked the door after her, then unlocked it; Con had no key with which to get in. It would serve him right to be locked out but she didn't want that. She wanted him with her. She left the living-room light burning, went into the bedroom, and undressed. She wasn't afraid; there was nothing to be afraid of. There had been no harm in those echoing footsteps, her nerves alone had translated them as such.

She put on the pink-sprigged dimity nightdress that made her look like a Kate Greenaway illustration. Actually there was no point in looking like anything except a deserted wife. She turned out the bedroom light, climbed into bed, and put her face into his pillow.

A fine honeymoon, going to bed alone.

2

Con said, "Are you awake?"

It woke her. He was standing by the bed, his hands jammed into his pockets, rattling something. But he wasn't smiling. The light from the living room made half-light here; she could see the disturbance in his frown. And a little fear without reason came into her heart.

"Yes, I'm awake." She pushed over halfway to her own side of the bed. He sat down on the edge, pulled his hand out of his pocket. She saw what had made that rattling. On his palm lay a half dozen shells, not the kind you gathered on the beach, the kind that were put into revolvers for lethal purpose.

"Con!" She gasped it, moved back close to him. "Con—"

He said, "Want to hear what happened?"

"Yes. Con—" She stilled the quaver of her voice. After all there was no reason to be panicky just because once before he had been in danger. He wasn't now, not here on vacation in Long Beach. Not with Garth safely gone. She spoke easily, "Give me a cigarette first."

He lit one for each of them and began talking. She could see it as it unfolded.

He'd helped the girl into the old coupe, said cheerily, "We'll go where we don't have to be insulted. What do you say?"

She'd been drinking but she wasn't drunk. She spoke without inflection, as if he were a cab driver. "I want to go to Saam's Seafood Place."

"O.K." He'd started the noisy motor. "Where is it?"

"Down Seal Beach way. I'll show you."

They drove across the bridge, on down the San Diego highway. He tried to talk to her but she was silent. And then Con wanted another drink as Con usually did. Saam's Seafood hadn't appeared but other places were handy. He slowed at one, said, "Let's have a snifter before we go on. What do you say?"

She said, "All right."

It was then that her coat fell to the floor. It made more noise than a light green fleece should. She picked it up quickly, got out of the car quickly, and so did he. He didn't know what it was all about, and, being Con, he wasn't going to let her escape until he did. But she wasn't running away. She went into the little place, took a seat in the second booth. He sat opposite her.

He ordered two beers, and eyed the girl. "Now what's it all about?" he demanded. He had an idea maybe she was running dope. There was something dopey about her, he told Griselda. She acted as in a trance. But that didn't disturb him; he was never afraid, not even when he should be. That was why he got involved in things; not scrapes that you could laugh at later, but serious trouble where death whispered, and which you tried never to remember after.

She did show some spirit now. She said, "I told you to skip it."

"I'm not skipping it." He waited until the beers were set down and paid for, then he said—Griselda could see him lolling back and saying it— "It's a long walk back to town, sister. Either you'll tell me what's up or you can prepare to spend the night right here in this dump."

She wet her lips, looked out again at the opposite booth, and quietly showed him the gun in her coat pocket. She said, "I'm going to blow myself out tonight. But I'm not going alone."

Con said, "Oh no, you're not." He told her, "It isn't that I give a damn if you blow yourself out or how many you take with you, but you're not going to do it tonight. Too many people have seen you with me. I'm here on my honeymoon and I can't be bothered hanging around inquests and spouting a lot of fool testimony. Give me the gun."

They sat there arguing, fortified by beers. How long Con didn't know. The girl and he were both adamant. She wouldn't give up the gun; he wouldn't drive her to Saam's until she did. He could have reached over and taken it but he was afraid she might get it first, he said, and choose him to accompany her on the voyage out.

Finally he compromised. "I can't sit here all night. I have a wife waiting for me."

"You actually remembered me?" Griselda asked. But she didn't say it acidly. She was holding tight to his hand now, pressed close against him.

He kissed the top of her head. "I never forget you, kitten."

He told the girl, "I'll take you back to town if you'll let me hold the baby until we get there. Then I'll give it back to you. You can get someone else to drive you to Saam's joint."

She agreed to that. "I'm going to powder my nose first." She was a little unsteady when she stood up.

He waited for her to reappear. When she did, she had the coat on and he could see the gun wasn't in her pocket.

He demanded, "What did you do with it?"

"I flushed it down the toilet," she said.

That made him mad; it might have been the beers but he was mad. He said, "I may look like a cretin but I'm not. That's scientifically impossible."

He marched into the Women's Room without any bones about it. He found where she'd hidden it, beneath paper towels in the wastebasket. He didn't know why or what she'd hoped to gain by it, but he unloaded the gun, put the shells into his trousers pocket, the gun into his coat pocket.

She was waiting docilely by the door when he returned. She said without spirit, "You will give it back to me? I was afraid you wouldn't; that's why I hid it. I have to have it."

They went out to the car. He asked, "So you can kill yourself and some rat?"

She said, "It's none of your business," and she didn't say any more on the ride back.

He let her off where she directed on Ocean Boulevard, handed back her gun, said, "Good night," and drove away, leaving her there on the walk.

"Then I came home to you, baby," he said.

That was Con's story.

3

Griselda breathed again.

Con stood up, yawned, said, "Mind the light?" turned it on, flung the shells on the bureau, and began unbuttoning his shirt.

She asked blankly, "But what was it all about, darling?"

"Damned if I know." He yawned again. "Screwiest performance I ever heard of."

Griselda wondered, "What was her name?"

"She wouldn't answer that one."

She shook her head hopelessly. "Was she pretty?"

"Might have been on the Congo. I've seen too many of her lately. Blondes like that are a dime a dozen in Hollywood. You know. She didn't even have a mole to distinguish her."

Griselda shook her head again. "Why do you do these silly things, Con? Why did you go out with her?"

He laughed. "I don't know. Curiosity, I guess. Ye olde newsy instinct. I couldn't understand why

Bennie refused to serve her. I know now, of course. He'd seen the gun."

She said soberly, "Some day you'll get yourself in a mess."

"Won't be the first time, angel face."

He creaked down on the bed to untie his sneakers. "What did your fancy friend Kew have to offer? What's he doing here?"

"He's your friend, not mine," she said. "I don't know. He's coming by tomorrow, and Con, you have to behave. After all he is your friend."

He said sleepily, "I'll hide first. I'll dig a hole down to China. I'll lie about my age and enlist. I'll—"

"Con!" She broke in sharply, sitting bolt upright.

He turned to put an arm about her. "Aw, I'll be good, honey."

But it wasn't that. It was fright that had come over her, rational fright now. "Con, if she should do anything—your fingerprints would be all over that gun!"

His voice was uninterested. "I thought of that. But I figured it was too late for her to get any more shells tonight. And even if she should, she'd have to get someone else to drive her out to this Seafood dump. There'd be someone seen with her later than I—" The phone in the living room began insistent ringing. Con said, "What the hell—" Sock-footed, he padded to answer.

Griselda remained bolt upright in the bed. Con had accuracy in getting himself involved. She couldn't let him step into danger again when he was only so recently free of it. Tomorrow she would insist they leave this place, return to Hollywood's civilized community. Deliberately she had refrained from mention of Major Pembrooke. Con had done enough to conjure trouble tonight without adding a disappearing man to the brew.

She waited sleepily for the conclusion of the telephone call. Con was using his newspaper voice; she couldn't hear what he was saying. He returned whistling and he didn't look pleased. He picked up his shirt from the bureau, began buttoning it on again.

"Con—" she cried it. "What—"

"Simmer down." He came over to the bed, pushed her onto the pillow with his right hand. But his left hand was fastening buttons even when he kissed her. "Got to go out for a little."

"Why, Con?" She wouldn't be treated like a small child, put in her place with no explanation.

He grinned. "If you must know, there's a fellow coming in to town that won't be happy until he sells me a dog." The grin was gone. "Darling, it has nothing to do with the blonde business, I assure you. I'll be back in an hour."

He kissed her again and was gone. He hadn't said it had nothing to do with a frozen Major Pembrooke or a missing radio executive. She couldn't ask him that. She couldn't introduce those names until she was certain they were not unknown.

She tried to sleep but the ocean was making so much thunder it was hard to hear other sound, a door that might be opening, footsteps that wouldn't belong in this beach cottage.

She listened until she was certain; someone noiseless was in that next room. She faltered, "Con—" She had forgotten the vagaries of this bed; it clanked as she stirred. There was deeper silence preceding rustle. A door clicked.

She didn't dare move. There was no use trying to

pretend she wasn't scared now; she huddled under
the covers, counting not sheep but steps that came
endlessly, ruthlessly after her. Who had entered the
cottage, stealthily, left with stealth? She didn't know
why anyone should be trailing her; she hadn't done
anything to anyone.

CON hadn't returned. It was nine and the sun
was quick on the deceptive peace of the Pacific.
She must have slept or morning wouldn't be here.
Her heart was clenched within her, wondering where
he might be. One radio man had already disappeared.
And then she heard his voice.

There was no accent of trouble in it; she'd been
worried over something she herself had invented.

"Of course you'll have dinner with us. Sure you
will. Meet you at the Hilton at seven, Kathie."

That Kathie again. She called out, "What's it all
about?"

He came into the bedroom. He hadn't slept; his
eyes were weary. He wore an old checked cardigan
over bright blue bathing trunks, the same dirty sneakers, and carried a tall glass of orange juice.

"For me?" she asked.

"Hustle your own." But he handed it to her, kissed
her nose, and said, "Made a date for us tonight with

the Travises. I want to see Walker. You'll like them."

He was himself this morning, not alternately jittery and deceptively quiet like the ocean outside. He said nothing of where he'd spent the night, stretched himself long on the bed. "Your turn to get me a glass."

She ignored him blissfully. "Give me a cigarette. What makes you think I'll like the Travises?" She doubted it very much.

"You will. I like them. So will you." There was something in the way he spoke made a small frown on her forehead. It wasn't optional that they like the Navy Travises. That much was clear. She asked, "Where did you meet them, Con?"

"Garth knew them," he said.

Why hadn't he mentioned them before? But she hadn't time for further questions. Someone was rapping at the door.

She pushed Con. "That's probably Kew. Entertain him while I shower." She whispered, "And be nice."

He growled something but she heard his greeting through the closed bedroom door and it was hearty. "How you, Kew, old man? Come on in. Great to see you," more of the same.

Griselda showered quickly, put on the white satin bathing suit with the magenta fish splashing on it, purple clogs on her feet, her gilt hair smoothed back of her ears. The shells patterned on the crocheted dresser scarf. She brushed them into Con's handkerchief drawer before she went into the living room. Con was on the couch reading the morning paper, Kew in the chair. Both held glasses but it was only orange juice. She hoped only orange juice; it was too early to put gin in it.

Kew was *Esquire's* best again, the rough white terry robe and scuffs, the white trunks against the

California golden brown of his body. He greeted
Griselda the special way he always greeted pretty
women, an under-ripple of tenderness. Doubtless another of the reasons Con didn't like him.

Con said softly. "Well, what do you think of
that?"

Griselda looked at him quickly. She knew that
voice. "Con! What?"

"A murder in our peaceful little town."

She knew she went whey-colored. Why she should
have connected it with last night she didn't know.
But she was frightened.

She took the paper from him. Woman's body
found in Bixby Park. Dressed in light blue slacks. College boy returning from his job as night soda jerker
about one-thirty A.M. saw the girl's body under a
tree. She was identified as Shelley Huffaker visiting
from Hollywood. There was a picture. A pretty
blonde girl. "A dime a dozen in Hollywood." Griselda
hadn't seen the girl's face. It had been only midnight
when Con said, "Are you awake?"

She wasn't going to be disturbed about it. Even if
it should turn out to be the same girl, Con had nothing to do with it. Someone would have been with her
later. Someone would have been a murderer, would
have taken pains not to be seen! She wouldn't worry
about Con. He could take care of himself. She laid
down the paper as if it didn't matter. "Shall we
swim?" and then she noticed the two men. Behind
cover of their orange juice, their casualness, they
were watching each other. Kew was looking at Con
in just the way that Con was looking at Kew. They
didn't seem to have heard her.

Con asked, "Did you know her, Kew?"

He laughed without really laughing. "Of course
not. Whatever made you think I might?"

Con tapped the paper. "Says Hollywood. Understand the studios have been bidding on your pen."

Kew almost seemed to flush. "Nothing so attractive, I fear. Only a nibble." And then he set down his empty glass on the table, reached out for the sheet. He studied the cut. "She looks rather like the girl you took home last night from the Bamboo. She isn't the same one, is she?"

Con said easily, "Yes, she is."

Griselda didn't breathe. She'd known it but she didn't want to hear it said. She watched him lounge across the room as if it weren't important, open the old-fashioned music cabinet, take out a bottle that wasn't water. He'd had plenty in the house last night then; it had only been that he was restless, wanted to go out. He poured lavishly into Kew's glass and more lavishly into his own. Kew hadn't spoken; he had dropped the paper to the floor. He didn't look surprised or curious; there was no expression save handsomeness on his face.

Con added orange to Kew's glass. "But I didn't take her home."

He shouldn't be telling this, not even to Kew. The brown eyes opened wide.

Con grinned at him. He said, "She didn't want to go home. She wanted to go to Saam's Seafood Place. Ever hear of it?"

Kew smiled tolerantly, "Afraid not."

Griselda noticed again, they were still watching each other behind their eyes, their smiles, their words. And she knew for the first time with startling certainty that Con hadn't come to Long Beach aimlessly. He was here for definite purpose. That purpose, insanely enough, was mixed up with a murdered girl and Kew Brent. That purpose might well be mixed up with the missing man a British officer was seeking. She shivered. More bitterly than ever she knew that Con was marching into the teeth of danger.

Kew repeated, "Afraid not," and took a scroll of white plastic from his pocket, extracted a cigarette mysteriously from its narrowness. "What's it like?"

"Like any other beach dump," Con said. He was Jesuitically lying to Kew; she didn't know why save that Kew was newspaper and Con evidently didn't want the truth to be published.

"You left her there?" Kew asked as if amused.

Con said, "Well, I couldn't stay out too late, could I?" He put his hand on Griselda's knee. "The little old lady wouldn't like it if I stayed too long with a beauteous blonde, would you, baby?"

She tried to smile, a sickly imitation. But she put her hand over his tightly, as if by so doing she could hold him to her side and away from this new menace in which he'd involved himself.

Con reached for his glass. "Drink it up, Kew, and I'll get you some more orange juice."

Griselda pleaded, "Not so early, Con."

He patted her leg. "Read in the papers where you can't be over-vitaminized. California. Land of oranges. Got to be loyal. How about it, Kew?"

He said, "I'll take another." They were pretending they weren't conscious of each other now. Con shuffled into the kitchen, returned with a milk bottle more than half filled with orange. "How about it, Grizel? Want to sit in this time?"

"Without the gin," she told him.

He said, "Women are peculiar people," and to Kew, "You haven't told me, friend, what you're doing in this neck of the waves."

Kew took the glass. "Well, I can't exactly say." He spoke as easily as did Con. There was no reason not to believe in their careless vacationer act but she didn't. Even if Major Pembrooke had not told her why Kew was here, she would have been certain they were playing a game. It couldn't have been for her benefit; certainly they were not fooling each other. She didn't comprehend; at this moment she couldn't stop to figure it out. She could only watch and listen.

Kew said, "One thing, I was hoping to see Garth."

"Postman's holiday?" Con asked.

"Maybe," he smiled. "I've got a couple of able subs on my column but Garth is always good for a yarn—and hard as the devil to nab these days, even in Washington."

He might have said, " . . . and even by Kew Brent." His expression seemed to say it. Griselda wasn't certain she liked that; in her meetings with Kew, there were always these moments when she wasn't sure that she liked him, when maybe Con was right in his anti-Kew attitude. But when you were away from him you forgot those moments, remembered only his mental keenness, the wit and the brain, the handsome arrogance, the suggestion that you were the most attractive woman he'd ever met—one word covered it, his charm.

"I suppose you've seen him?" Kew asked.

"Yeah. He was here when I came. I ran into him."

It was more falsification. Con might have run into Garth but he'd been closeted with him for days before the yacht trip came up; she had taken it for granted it was renewal of a friendship and the gathering of broadcast material. It hadn't occurred to her then that Con had known Garth was in Long Beach before they arrived, and that Garth had expected him. Real fear trembled Griselda now; if Con were working for the head of the X service again, there was reason for fear. The foreign agents concentrated on the coast were known to be important, to constitute a real menace. She suddenly was cold. If Mannie Martin's disappearance were connected with that—she hadn't thought of it that way. She must speak to Con. If that were it he definitely mustn't look for Mannie.

She couldn't be certain that he wasn't pledged to Garth again, not with these half-lies to Kew. And this fear dwarfed the one that he might become involved in last night's murder.

"Garth's gone fishing," Con told.

"Fishing?" Kew seemed incredulous.

"Yeah. He needed a vacation badly, y'know. He's been on day and night shift since Poland. Some big boy steamed in on his yacht and rustled up a fishing party. I couldn't go. Stag."

Griselda caught her lip. He was still regretting.

Kew asked, "Where are they cruising?"

"Down in Mexican waters, I gathered. They were heading southerly." Why was he giving Kew all of this information and withholding other seemingly more harmless?

Kew said quietly, "Another reason that brought me here was an invitation from Dare."

Griselda cried it: "Dare Crandall?" She couldn't stand that; she'd thought Dare was out of their lives. She hadn't seen her for years, not for more than four years. It was Dare more than any one other thing that had caused the break-up of their marriage the first time she and Con tried it.

Con asked as if surprised, "Is she here?" but Griselda wasn't fooled. He knew Dare Crandall was in Long Beach; he had known it all along; perhaps he had even seen her. He might have been with her last night.

Kew said as if imparting important news, "Yes, indeed she is."

Con said, "What will they think of next?" He drank. "What's she doing here?"

"Some connection with the Navy."

Griselda couldn't help saying it, "I suppose you mean she was barred from the Brooklyn yards."

Both men looked at her. Their amusement wasn't amusing to her. Con said, "How you talk, Griselda!"

No one had to break the silence. The phone did that. Con answered.

She said to Kew then, in apology, "What is Dare actually doing here?"

"She's making over a house for an Admiral's daughter, I believe. You know she's taken up decorating now."

She didn't know.

"It's to be all Modern Norse and Chinese Ming and will probably take all summer to fit. She has an apartment on"—he managed to recall the street—"on Junipero until September. I haven't seen her yet. I only came down yesterday morning and she was out all day. Her man said she'd gone to"—again he recalled—"Avalon on some party."

Con was standing in the middle of the floor now, thumbs in his sweater pockets. They both looked up at him. "That was the Chief of Police," he said. "He's on his way out to see me."

The silence was so utter, you could hear the sound of the water shivering across the pebble sand.

Kew finally smiled. "There goes our swim. I'd better run along."

"Not at all. Not at all." Con finished crossing the room, drained his half-filled glass. "I told him we'd be out on the beach and to holler when he arrived."

2

Captain Charles Thusby was fuzzy bald and por-
poise fat. His right leg was wooden. It was not disguised by modern craft but a delightful replica of the
kind pirates wore in childhood story books. He
should have been dressed as a seaman; he was instead excessively official in his policeman's blue serge
and gold buttons.

He stood on their cat-walk and hollered, "I'm here,
Satterlee."

Con yelled back, "Be with you right away." He
didn't seem nervous but then he wouldn't be. He enjoyed scrapes. To him, obviously, this business was
no more than one. But to Griselda it was frightening.
Her teeth clicked, and Kew said, "I'll go along."

"Nothing doing." Con put a wet arm around Kew's
shoulders. He was overdoing friendliness today.
"Come up and have a snort to warm you up. Besides
you ought to meet the folks."

The captain was in the easiest chair when they
dripped in. On the couch in policeman's uniform was
an extra-gangly, long-faced lad eating peanuts, putting the shells neatly into his upturned cap. The chief
said, "I'm Cap'n Thusby. This is Vinnie. Brought
him along to drive the car. I don't drive. No, nothing
to do with the leg, ma'am."

She had inadvertently glanced at it and it did look
exactly like Long John Silver's.

"Never could learn. Can't teach an old dog new
tricks." His face regarded his leg with creased pleasure. "Shark took it off down around Hatteras. Neat
as a whistle."

Vinnie said, "Now, Pa," but the captain disregarded him.

"Wasn't much older'n Vinnie here when it happened." His face was smiles but his faded denim eyes were sharp as an aching tooth. "Which one's Satterlee?"

"I am." Con touched Kew's shoulder. "This is Kew Brent. You've heard of him."

"Heard of both of you." He rubbed up his curly halo.

"And my wife, Mrs. Satterlee."

Griselda acknowledged the introduction and said, "I'm freezing. I must get into something warm." She knew that she must before her teeth chattered out loud. It wasn't only from the wet bathing suit.

She heard Kew say as she went toward the bedroom, "And I'll have to run along. I'll take that drink another time." He was determined now, making his gracious good-byes. She could hear Thusby as the outer door closed. "Now about this murder, Mr. Satterlee," and she went swiftly into the bathroom beyond to rough herself warm with a towel. She did it quickly; the voices were silenced in this room, and she was trembling with anxiety. Con's prints were on that gun. The police couldn't know it yet they'd come already to him. For him? She dressed rapidly, pullover beige sweater, brown wool slacks. But she took time to open Con's drawer and wad handkerchiefs over and around the shells.

Con was telling his story, " . . . and I didn't even know her name until I read it in the paper this morning. I simply offered to give her a lift and when she changed her mind about going to this Seafood place I brought her back to town."

He wasn't telling all of it. Griselda emerged to

sit quietly beside him, between him and Vinnie.

"Mighty funny," Captain Thusby was saying.

"Yes, it was," Con agreed. "She didn't give any reason for it. Of course she'd been drinking."

Thusby asked, "Did she have a gun then, Mr. Satterlee?"

Now it was coming. Griselda waited, hands unclenched but tight as guitar strings.

"That's strange. Why do you ask?"

Thusby said, "On account of her being killed by her own gun. Or at least one she'd brought with her from Hollywood. And so far as anyone knows she hadn't been back to the apartment after you let her out. Where'd you say you let her out?"

Griselda wanted to warn Con to be careful. She was being absurd; he was always aware. You couldn't trap Con.

He said now, "I didn't say, Cap'n. But I can tell you. It was on Ocean by that park."

"Bixby Park," Vinnie supplied and flushed at the unexpected sound of his own voice. It was a tenor toot compared to his father's foggy horn. He put another peanut between his teeth.

"East or west end? Junipero or Cherry?"

Con figured it out. "The Belmont side. That'd be east."

Thusby nodded. "Junipero."

Vinnie wasn't as startled this time. "She was found on the Cherry side, Pa."

"I know it," Thusby said placidly. He was as garrulous as the son wasn't. "This kid, Tip Thenker, has been squirting sodas up a ways on Cherry at a drug store. He goes to college." That evidently impressed Thusby. "He and a friend were on their way home, going to cut across the park, when they saw her foot there in the shadow under one of those fat palm trees. It sure scared those kids." He chortled and then his eyes fixed. "They ought to been scared. It's a wonder they weren't mowed down too. Whoever killed her couldn't have been far away. The blood was still running."

Griselda asked, "What time was this, Captain Thusby?"

"About one-thirty, ma'am. One-thirty-three when they called us. And they didn't waste no time doing it." He chortled again.

Con was safe. Even with his fingerprints he was safe. He'd been home by midnight. But she didn't know how long the blood would run. And he'd gone out again; where, he didn't say. She moved closer to him. "How did you happen to come to talk to my husband about it?" She didn't want them to get back to the gun.

He was very polite. "Trying to trace what she was doing last night, ma'am. She left the Bamboo Bar with him. Mr. Alexander Smithery told us that."

"Chang," Con informed her, and explained, "I call him Chang."

Thusby came in again. "Where was that place you stopped?"

"I couldn't tell you the name," Con repeated. "On the way to Seal Beach. Ed's or Ray's or Andy's—something like that."

Griselda inserted, "He was at home by midnight." She wouldn't even think of his being called out later.

Both of the Thusbys took that in silence, and the father asked again, "Now about that gun?"

"She had one, yes," Con admitted. Griselda tightened. "Are you sure she was murdered?"

"Sure," Thusby stated. "Why?"

"Because she was going to kill herself last night."

Griselda hadn't been mistaken in the captain's eyes. They could snap like mouse-traps. They did. And then he was mild again. "Well, she couldn't have, Mr. Satterlee. You don't shoot yourself through the back. Can't be done."

Con lit a cigarette easily. "Who identified her?"

"Her cousin. There was a porter first said he thought it was this girl visiting in his apartment house and turned out he was right. We got hold of the cousin and she finished up the identification for us."

Con let out three perfect smoke rings. "I'm an old newspaperman, Cap'n, and sometimes I get kind of wondering about things." He drew in smoke again. "Why wasn't the cousin's name used in the newspaper story?"

Thusby said, "Admiral Swales asked me as a favor not to give it out. No reason to. She wasn't here and couldn't have done it. It wasn't the kind of publicity the Admiral would want."

Vinnie's cocker ears were ruddy. "She's new here, doing interior decorating stuff for Admiral Swales' daughter."

Griselda cried it for the second time that day: "Dare Crandall!" and then she stiffened and felt her heart turn over bitterly. They were all looking at her, three pair of eyes, and none of them were mild.

"That's the name." Captain Thusby's eyebrows were fuzzy gray as his half-moon hair. "You know her, Mrs. Satterlee?"

Griselda nodded. She couldn't speak.

"And you knew Shelley Huffaker?"

"No." She denied truthfully but too quickly. "No." She spoke for Con, too. "We've never heard of her." And she added, "We used to know Dare. We haven't

seen her for years." Neither officer believed her. She
herself didn't know if it were true for Con.

Thusby asked, "But you knew she was in Long
Beach?"

Before she could explain, Con was speaking. What
he said kept her mouth open. "Yes, we knew that."
No more. She didn't continue her explanation of Kew
Brent only this morning informing them. For some
reason Con didn't want that mentioned. He'd stepped
in to keep her from saying it. She didn't know why.

"But you didn't know Shelley Huffaker was visiting
her?"

Con shook his head. He answered firmly and his
eyes didn't move from Captain Thusby's. "We didn't
even know of Shelley Huffaker's existence. We haven't
seen Mrs. Crandall. She's been on a party at Avalon."

Thusby kept saying, "Yes." No more. But he knew
more than that. Maybe he even knew that Con had
seen Dare. Then he said, "Long Beach is a law-abiding town, Mr. Satterlee. Don't suppose I've ever had
a real grade-A murder before to deal with. Hardly
know how to go about it. I don't read detective magazines like Vinnie here. I prefer Dickens for my reading, always have. Bet I know Little Nell by heart
almost. Can't teach an old dog new tricks."

He stood up and tapped his peg-leg on the floor.
"Don't suppose you knew Mannie Martin either?"

Griselda hoped that none of them was looking at
her. She hadn't controlled herself when that name
was spoken. And she was ice when Con answered,
"Yes, I knew Mannie."

"Figured you might," Thusby said. "But you didn't
know Shelley Huffaker?"

Con said, "No. I haven't seen Mannie." But he'd
given it away that he knew this Martin was missing;
he'd used the past tense to speak of him. "I came to

California on pleasure, not business. Haven't gone near a studio." He asked then, "What's the girl got to do with Mannie?"

Thusby's eyes half-mooned. "Don't know that yet, Mr. Satterlee. But her getting killed and him missing —things like that don't happen around here every day."

His voice suddenly boomed out and Griselda started. Con put his hand on hers. "Fixing to stay here for your vacation, Mr. Satterlee?" He didn't wait for an answer. "That's a good idea. No prettier place on the southern coast than Long Beach."

He wasn't doubling for the Chamber of Commerce. It was warning not to leave. Her hand under Con's was cold. She didn't move when he went with the police to the door nor when he returned, opened the music cabinet, clattered forth a whisky bottle, poured himself a sturdy one. He finished it, looked across at her and stated, "Sometimes you don't have a lick of sense."

"Con—" She wanted to tell him he was in danger of arrest; he was innocent but he was involved. He knew it but she wanted to emphasize it, to make him be careful. She only said, "You shouldn't mix gin and whisky so early in the morning."

He didn't pay any attention to her remark. He sat down beside her and eyed her coolly, steadily. "You're young enough to stick to being seen and not heard."

She shook her head, puzzled, trying not to be hurt that he was relegating her to being no more than a doll wife again, just as he had when they were married before. "What did I say wrong? What did I do?"

He raised an eyebrow. "Why didn't you let me do the talking?" And then he stared at her as if something had just occurred to him. "My God, baby, you didn't think I came to Long Beach for my health, did you?"

She didn't answer right away. Then she said, "I thought we came for our honeymoon."

He waved an abstracted hand. "We'll take care of that later."

She knew then, knew what she had been fighting to keep from knowing all through the sleepless hours of the early morning. Con was working with Barjon Garth. Con was getting into danger. Panic was in her voice. She couldn't quell it. Nor could she keep from asking stupidly, "Con, you didn't kill her?"

"Kill her?" He came out of his fog on that. "Kill Shelley Huffaker? God, no." He put his arm around her. "Are you going nuts, baby?"

Her cheek touched his sleeve. "I knew you didn't. But who did? Why was she killed?"

"I don't know the answer to either of those. I'm going to find out." He took his arm away, went over, and poured another. "Don't tell me it's too early," he warned the look in her eyes. "I'm thirsty and nobody but a native son could stomach the fish juice that comes out of those taps." He swallowed, said, "I'm going to find out. Who and why."

It was necessary that she speak now. The man who had introduced himself to her last night could have killed Shelley Huffaker in cold blood, deliberately and with less emotional reaction than he would scratch a horse at the paddock. She asked, "Do you know anything about a Major Pembrooke?"

He turned on her quickly. "Who's been talking to you about him?"

"I met him last night."

He looked at her disbelieving, and then he repeated, "You met him last night? Where? How?"

"He was at the Bamboo Bar."

He was wracking his brains, unsuccessfully.

She said, "The man with Kew at the far table."

He was quick. "How did you know that was Pembrooke?"

"He stopped to talk to me. After Kew left."

Con sat down then too quietly. He didn't touch his glass. He said to himself with disappointment, almost anger, "I could have met him if I hadn't been so damn curious about that blonde." He doubled up his fist and thumped his forehead.

She spoke with hushed insistence. "You don't want to meet him, Con. He's—" She searched for a word. "He's—ugly."

Con looked at her under his scowl. "You think I've been inhabiting that bar to improve my mind? It's Pembrooke's favorite hangout."

Difficult as it was, she kept her voice quiet, not frantic, "And who is Pembrooke?"

He didn't answer. He was thumping again, muttering, "What a dope I was! Could have met him."

She didn't hide the franticness now. "Con, why do you want to meet him? What have you to do with him? Who is he?

He said, "Pembrooke is a British officer." He hesitated, "I can't tell you much, Griselda. It isn't permitted. But I want to meet him."

That made it definite; he was working for Garth. There was sickness inside of her. "Kew can introduce you."

"I don't want a planned meeting. It wouldn't—look right. Last night would have been perfect if I hadn't been playing the fool." He seemed to see her now. "You mustn't be involved in this. That's one thing I won't have."

"Con." She had to swallow to make her voice audible. "Con, Major Pembrooke was here last night."

Con's eyes were hard and bright. "What for?"

Her voice was weak, "Evidently he wants to meet you as badly as you want to meet him."

"But he knew I wasn't here. Kew's back was to us. Pembrooke must have been facing the door. He'd have seen me leave with the blonde."

She nodded, holding her hands tightly together. She didn't ask how Pembrooke would know Con when they had never met. He had even known her.

"That wasn't it. Why did he come? What did he want?"

She could hear the cold voice. She shook her head. "I don't know. Maybe—" She thought hard. "He said you were in Long Beach to find Mannie Martin. He said you and Kew came for that. He wants Martin found. They were to be partners in some business. And his backers are impatient because the contracts can't be signed with Martin missing. He said you had a letter."

"Thorough cuss, ain't he?" She didn't know that fighting-mad expression on Con's face. "Listen. Pembrooke came to you to find out what you could tell him. But you couldn't because you didn't know. I'm going to keep you out of this."

Her voice faltered, "Con, you didn't come here looking for this man, did you?"

He said briefly, "I'd like to find him."

"Con." She went over to him and put her arm tightly through his. "Con. I'm afraid. Let's leave. Let's go up to Malibu."

He only said, "You don't think old Cap'n Thusby was just playing polite host, do you? He's a smart old geezer no matter how he looks. Used to be in Naval Intelligence."

"If he's smart he knows you didn't kill that girl."

"He knows I was out with her just before she was killed. He probably doesn't have the touching faith in my innocence that Garth would have." He finished his drink and started to the bedroom. "Got things to do. I'll get dressed."

She walked to the far end of the living room, stood by the bay window staring out at the gray waves pushing at the beige beach. There must be some method to get Con away before he was—hurt. Someone else could help Garth; Con wasn't a part of the organization. It was dangerous to remain here, dangerous for both of them. And she didn't like danger. It made her feel sick, the way she was feeling now.

She stood there until he returned. He was dressed up and she was surprised. He didn't look like work; he looked like a party. He was wearing the natural camel's-hair sport jacket he'd bought at Desmond's under protest, the pale natural and white-checked flannels. She would have to change. In an old sweater she couldn't go out to lunch with him in his grandeur.

He came over to her and kissed her. "If anyone should drop in, be as dumb as you ought to be with those looks instead of as smart as you are." He kissed her again. "I'm going to see Dare."

She didn't have any answer; her mouth stood open. That casually he said it and went away. She waited until he was gone before she let herself think. He wasn't rushing to Dare because he wanted to; it was because of what had happened. She wouldn't let Dare ever be important enough to her again to disturb her. There was enough trouble here without Dare. But why did she have to decorate Long Beach houses? And why did she have a blonde cousin? Damn Dare Crandall!

3

The afternoon wore on, so long and so dull, that she would almost have welcomed some sinister stalker of Con to whom she must play dumb. But no one came, not until almost four and then it was only Kew. He was perfection in blues. "Sorry to bother you again, Griselda. I thought maybe I left my cigarette case here. Have you seen it?"

"I haven't." She looked in the chair, by the table where he'd been, but it wasn't there. "Won't you have a drink while you're here?" Now that he had come, she knew that she had been hoping he would; she wanted to find out what he knew about Major Pembrooke.

"You'll join me?"

She nodded.

"I'll fix them. How about a Tom Collins? Limes?"

"In the box."

He went into the kitchen and she followed with the gin bottle.

"Con out?"

"Yes. You might have dropped it on the beach."

"Dropped—my case. Perhaps. I'll probably find I mislaid it in my room."

They returned to comfortable chairs with the cold glasses.

"Where is Con? I thought maybe you two might join Dare and me for dinner."

She stated into the liquid, "Con went to see Dare."

He didn't look sympathetic but he did look too kind. "How about tonight?"

"We can't. We're having dinner with some friends

of Con's. I don't know them." She recalled the name.
"The Travises."

He looked up then. "Not Walker Travis?"

"I don't know. Maybe that was the name. You
know him?"

"No. But you know who he is, don't you?"

She said lazily that she didn't.

"Walker Travis is the naval radio expert." He
added, "I've been wanting to do a story on him."

"He's Navy. Con said so." She wasn't very interested. There was something bigger than radio experts
filling her thoughts. Kew could have read a part of
them.

He asked, "What did the police want with Con?"

"It was about that girl who was killed last night.
Shelley Huffaker." Of course, he must know that.

"Why come to Con?"

"Because"—she could have wailed over Con's head-
strong curiosity—"because he was with her, that's
why."

"And how did they know that?" He shook his head
as if disbelieving.

"Evidently his bar friend, the one at the Bamboo,
the one he calls Chang, volunteered the information."
She said, "It's so stupid. Con didn't have anything to
do with it. He didn't even know her. And now we
can't go to Malibu. We can't leave here."

"Can't?" His dark brows were perplexed.

"Captain Thusby won't let us. Con said so."

"He's not under—" He didn't finish.

"Oh no!" She stressed it. "Oh no, of course not."
She finished lamely, "But they might want to ask him
some more questions."

His dark eyes smiled into her blue ones. "Selfishly
I'm glad of that. Glad you won't be running out on
me for the movie paradise."

Of course, he meant nothing personal but Kew always made it sound that way. That was why women liked him, why men did not. But she wasn't interested in him the way other women might be. She didn't know exactly how or what to say of the major. The man might be Kew's friend. She continued speaking, waiting for a bypath.

"Kew, the cousin who identified Shelley Huffaker was Dare." And then she realized, this couldn't be news to him. "But you knew that."

"I didn't." He was thoughtful, then spoke again, "I still haven't seen Dare. I spoke to her on the phone but she said she was busy this afternoon."

Not too busy to see Con. They were both thinking that.

He was finishing his drink. She had to blurt it now, "Kew, who is Major Pembrooke?"

He set down his glass. He didn't look at her. "Why do you ask? Have you run into him out here?"

She didn't explain. She said, "Yes."

Kew's eyes were steady. "He is a British officer."

"Con told me that." It was surprising that you could speak when you were so cold you trembled without willing it. Whatever his title Major Pembrooke was a dangerous person; that was written on him. She asked, "Are you here looking for Mannie Martin?" She added hurriedly to the flash in his eyes, "Major Pembrooke said that you were."

The flash had faded. He answered as evasively as Con, "I wouldn't object to finding him." He held out his hand. "I must go. Maybe we'll see you tonight anyway. Where are you dining, the Sky Room?"

"Yes. I suppose so. We're meeting them at the Hilton."

"We may run into you."

She asked curiously, "Is Dare going to be with you?"

"Yes." He repeated, "We may see you. Unless Dare decides not to go out."

She had little hope that Dare would make that decision. Not the Dare she remembered. She watched Kew's roadster, handsome as his face, make a turn toward the city. She would have to dress with competition in mind. It was ridiculous to have to compete for your own husband but there was no faint hope that the leopard had changed her spots in the intervening years. Con had been gone too many hours for that.

He didn't return until after six-thirty. He was jaunty as he'd always been after seeing that woman, and he was slightly alcoholic. He didn't notice that she was wearing the pale blue swiss, wide ruffles to the waist, a tiny ripple squaring the neck; he didn't know the dress was a dream, that she'd designed it for Oppy's favorite ingenue, and that it looked better on her than on the slightly bawdy young actress.

All he said was, "Hello, hon. Ready to go?"

She nodded. "Aren't we a little early?"

"Thought we might stop for a drink on the way."

"You've had enough as usual." He wanted to go back to that truly sinister bar; even an afternoon with Dare hadn't made him forget Pembrooke. She prayed the major wouldn't be there.

He was whistling by the window when she returned with her army-brown silk duster. "Any callers?"

"Only Kew."

He twirled. "Only Kew!" He seemed suspicious and then he was casual again. "What did he want?"

"He wondered if he'd left his cigarette case."

"An ancient stall."

She shrugged. "Maybe. Why should he need a stall?

He could come any time without it. He's a friend of
ours."

"Yours. Did he find it?"

"No. We looked. He decided maybe he'd dropped
it in his room."

"Probably in his pocket all the time." Con was dis-
gusted. Was it that he thought Kew had come to see
her and didn't like it?

She hoped so. It would serve him right. She smiled
in the darkness as the uncomfortable coupe rattled
across the street fronting the bay. "We may see him
tonight."

She saw Con's face turn to her in the street light. It
was expressionless. That meant he was angry. She
didn't know why.

"Does he know where we're going?"

"Yes—" she began.

"You told him."

"Yes." She defended herself. "I couldn't help it,
Con." He'd stopped the machine in front of the Bamboo Bar. "He asked us to join him and Dare at dinner. What could I tell him?"

He stated, "I suppose you also told him who we
were dining with?"

"Yes." She knew she'd done wrong but not why
or how. "What could I say?"

He started the car again, swore at the traffic light
snapping red, and said above the noisy coughs of the
engine, "You could have told him we were busy and
let it go at that, couldn't you? I asked you not to talk.
Do you think I want him scooping me? Wives as a
rule don't help out their husbands' business rivals."

She hadn't thought of their being in competition.
Con must be after a story too on this Travis. She said,
"I'm sorry."

He shot the car ahead at the first warning of green,

quickly leftwards into Ocean Boulevard. "Maybe we
can beat him there and sneak the Travises out somewhere else to eat."

It was no more than ten to seven when they reached
the Hilton, but the Travises were seated there waiting. Walker was a skinny young officer with a round
preoccupied face, pale sandy hair plastered above a
recessive forehead. He didn't look like a bright boy.

Kathie was beautiful. Even the white chiffon dress,
obviously made over and without style; the blue street
coat over it with the big pink fish pin on the lapel,
didn't diminish her beauty: the soft soot hair, the sad
contour of her face, and her eyes, blue as early night,
soot-lashed. The pin might have served as model for
the bulbous examples on the beach-cottage cretonne,
pink, with black spots superimposed on the enamel.
No one with any taste could have selected, much less
worn it. It wasn't hideously smart. It was hideously
banal. But fish or no fish, Kathie was exquisite.

Griselda looked at Con. He too knew that Kathie
Travis walked in beauty. It had been too much to
hope that he wouldn't.

He was smiling at the girl, "I thought we might—"
and then he broke off. Griselda saw where his eyes
had strayed. White-linened Kew rising from one of
the period chairs. He raised a friendly hand and
started toward them. He was intercepted. Without
her glasses Griselda couldn't be certain, but it looked
as if the man patting Kew's sleeve was Sergei
Vironova, Oppy's favored foreign director. She'd done
costumes for one of his pictures.

Con put his arm through Kathie Travis's. "We'll
eat in the Sky Room. O.K.?"

Her smile was even lovelier than her quiet face.
Griselda followed to the elevators with the dull lieutenant. It wasn't fair that Kathie Travis should exist

with Dare already here. In the stereotyped beauty
land of movie stars, Griselda wouldn't have been disturbed by any or all women. But Kathie didn't need
the Westmores or Griselda Cameron Satterlee. And
Dare didn't need anything. With gloomy foreboding
Griselda watched Con bend down to the slight girl's
words as the elevator rose swiftly to the roof.

They sat on the terrace looking out at the sea that
moiled in twisted currents to a once mythical East,
land no longer of cherry blossoms and delicate things,
land of drawn sabers and crashing bombs. A low parapet protected the diners from a sheer drop to the
Pike below.

Con suggested the menu, said, "We should have
stopped at the bar first. Care to investigate it, Kathie?"
He had said he wanted to see Walker Travis; it
seemed he'd mixed up the forenames. Griselda wasn't
surprised.

She was left with the negative little officer. She
didn't know how to make conversation with him;
when she spoke he was a rabbit peering insecurely
from a safe dark hutch. The weather, the night, Long
Beach—he scuttled from each topic back into his hiding place. And then she stopped trying, watched silently the approach of Kew and Dare Crandall.

They came directly to her. Dare kissed her, crying,
"Darling, I'm so glad to see you again! I told Con I
was just furious that he didn't bring you along this
afternoon but he said you had other fish to fry."

Dare hadn't changed although she had let her hair
go back to neutral. It looked as brown hair should,
shining as if light were upraised above it. Her body,
draped in white wool jersey, would alone make
women distrust her; it had, as Griselda remembered,
the sleek lines of a polo pony. She was talking to
Griselda but the slant green eyes in her almost ugly

face were looking at Lieutenant Travis. And Griselda could have cheered. After thirty-odd years, Dare had met her match. Walker Travis wasn't any more impressed by her than if she were a waiter. He was peering into the lighted main room where his wife and Con were laughing at the great bar.

And Con saw him. Quickly he returned Kathie to the table, said bluntly, "Hello, Kew. Hello, Dare." With incomprehensible rudeness he shouldered them out of the way to give Kathie her chair. When he sat down, Lieutenant Travis did too. It was obvious that Con wasn't going to make introductions; Kew and Dare knew it.

Dare said, "We must see a lot of each other while you're here, Griselda. It's been so long—" They moved beyond to an unoccupied table.

The husky sweetness of Kathie's voice was relief after Dare's pseudo-British shrillness. She asked, "Who are they?"

Con said wickedly, "Friends of Griselda's. The girl's quite a decorator. For fame, not nickels. She was married to a mint, son of the tobacco Crandall. He was killed in a plane wreck. Before that she was the damn best newspaperwoman ever worked New York." He added disinterestedly, "The man is Kew Brent, the Washington columnist."

Travis's eyes colored in recognition. "I read him," he said, as if he read nothing else in the paper.

"Too many people do." Con was enjoying himself. "That's why he exists. Mrs. Crandall is here to decorate the Swales's house."

"Admiral Swales?" Kathie raised her eyes.

"Yeah. The daughter."

Kathie said, "Oh," and her head turned slightly to where she could see the other couple, there where the low wall made an angle. She said softly again, "Oh.

The Swales are terribly rich." She was like a naïve child. "She'll make their house beautiful, won't she? It's that big white one on Ocean. It has private steps to the beach. I was there once at a tea. I'd like to meet that—Dare." She sounded wistful.

"Some other time," Con replied promptly. "Not tonight. I've spent the afternoon with her. That's enough."

"You don't like her?"

He laughed and he had the grace not to look at Griselda. "I might like an electric current but I couldn't stand it crackling in me twenty-four hours a day."

The small lieutenant emerged from his silence temporarily. "You understand, dear, don't you?"

"Yes, I understand." Her expression didn't change and her voice was gentle, but there was irritation gnatting behind the words. She devoted herself quickly to Con. "You've known her long?"

"Yeah. Pretty long."

Walker Travis spoke up, "Why are you so interested in her, dear?"

Kathie hid the irritation this time. She said, "She sounds wonderful. She's rich, and she makes money besides, and she has beautiful clothes. She's really good-looking too, in a queer sort of way. She has everything, hasn't she?"

Con said, "Uh-huh," not very interested; and Griselda to herself said, "Everything but Con." Nor was she going to have him. This time she'd fight Dare, foul or fair, preferably foul. She hated her being in Long Beach.

Con began to entertain. It was deliberate, and if the Travises but knew, it was a rare compliment. Griselda herself hadn't heard these tales of Ethiopia, of Spain, of France..Whether or not they were true, they

were exciting. She scarcely remembered that Kew and
Dare were on the roof. And then he eyed the table
sprawling with empty dishes. "Let's go somewhere
clean." He grinned. "Some place where we can have
a drink." He took Kathie's coat to help her but he
didn't. "Where'll we go? Any suggestions? I'm afraid
if I ask you out to our trailer we'll have drop-ins.
Griselda and I seem to be awfully popular this sea-
son."

Walker Travis spoke as if it were prearranged, "We
could go up to our room." He looked for approval to
Kathie but it was not forthcoming.

Again there was no change in the Madonna face,
the gentle chime of her voice. But her, "Oh, no," was
definite as concrete, and her deprecating, "Hotel
rooms are so dreadful," sealed her decision.

Con stood up. "I like hotel rooms. I'm never really
happy except in a hotel room."

The fine chiseling of Kathie's chin wasn't soft.
"They depress me." She turned her smile on him.
"Let's go some place where it's fun, Con."

Dare and Kew were preparing to leave too. It
might have been that they'd only come to watch Con's
party. Griselda knew that was absurd, quite naturally
they would finish, even as they'd started, at approx-
imately the same time.

Con delayed. "We'll find something to amuse you.
Now if it were New York . . ." He beckoned the
waiter.

Kathie moved to the parapet, stood there looking
over at the dark tumultuous waters beyond the
crowded Pike. Griselda shivered from a safe distance.
The girl turned her head. Her eyes were shining as if
lighted by the stars. "Look!" she whispered. Her hand
pointed, a white tendril over the sea.

Griselda shook her head. She said, "It would make

me dizzy to stand there and look over." Saying something prosaic took away the gulp at the idea.

Kathie's eyes were wondering. "Really? I love it." Her voice was shiny too. "It makes me feel as if I have wings."

Walker sounded anxious, "Come, dear. We're ready to go."

Again there was the faintest displeasure under the outline of her face but she obeyed, walking not to her husband but to Con. And the undercurrent had been swept away before he saw her face.

CON said, "I'll get the car," and Griselda smiled. Kathie wouldn't be so eager for Con's company when she viewed that model.

They stood there, not long, but conversation languished as always in idle waiting. She shouldn't have heard what Kathie said to Walker; Shelley Huffaker's headline in the night's paper had sprung at her, and she stepped to the newsstand.

But Kathie had spoken too soon, too hurriedly, before Griselda was out of earshot. "Remember. Don't mention her." It wasn't spoken gently, even her voice seemed changed, harsh.

Griselda didn't hear the lieutenant's answer. When

she turned back, paper under her arm, Con had come through the door and Kathie's window was again dressed.

They went into the always misted night. Con flourished, "Madame, the Duesenberg." Kathie didn't care for the form of transportation, not even when Con herded her into the center place leaving Griselda to sit on top of the lieutenant, to be bumped on knees and skull. Griselda presumed there was reason for all, for the Travises, for an afternoon with Dare, even for the horrible little car. She knew one thing. There must be explanation soon or her namesake's virtue wouldn't be one of her qualities.

Con stopped at the Bamboo. "This is the best place I've found for fun." He was that determined to find the major; even a social evening couldn't give way for it. She wanted to speak to him; she had thought she glimpsed Kew's car following them as they drove out Ocean, not that there weren't other lean black roadsters in town. But Con gave her no opportunity; he was hanging on to Kathie as if he'd won her in a lottery.

Griselda followed hesitantly; tonight, haunted by the memory of the blonde girl, the green shadows were not amusingly sinister. Major Pembrooke was not lurking in them, and Chang displayed no conscience about throwing Con to the Thusbys. He came happily to the table.

"Drinks all around, Chang, and don't spare the bottle." This still wasn't Con, this hyper-gay spiriting; it was imitation of some of his newspaper colleagues in their cups, not Con with Barjon Garth's business on his mind.

Without surprise flecking anyone's lips, not even those of Chang, Kew and Dare walked in. There was no eluding them this time. Dare's narrow wrist, gemmed with marquise diamonds, rested on Con's shoulder. "Are you preceding us, darling, or vice versa?"

Kew had hands on two neighboring chairs. "Don't mind if we join, do you?"

This time Con had to make the introductions. "Lieutenant and Mrs. Travis, Mrs. Crandall, Mr. Brent."

Mrs. Travis knew Mr. Brent. She acknowledged the introduction but when their eyes met there was a secret, a delightful secret, hidden in hers. Kew, at some time during his two days in Long Beach, had evidently made yet another conquest. The rabbity husband wasn't to know; that was the why of the pretense here and earlier. It lifted one care from Griselda; she wouldn't have to worry about Kathie Travis chasing Con, her starry eyes encircled Kew alone.

Dare wedged herself between Kathie and Con, not adeptly but with arrogance; Kew sat himself by Walker Travis. Griselda between the Navy couple was in observation post. She heard Kew working toward a column on naval radio, even while Dare's narrow jade eyes posed on Kathie.

"I've seen you before, haven't I?"

Kathie murmured, "Perhaps. We were at the Sky Room tonight."

"I don't mean that." Dare's pointed elbow lay on Con's coatsleeve. She put a slender cigarette into her mouth, pressed her naked shoulder against his coat, tilted her head to him for a light. When she exhaled smoke she turned narrow eyes again. "You're Shelley's friend," she stated.

Griselda waited, startled into immobility. Dare's statement was more than definitive; it was almost accusation. And then she noticed that she wasn't the only one waiting that answer. Con's lids were down, his ears up, and he wasn't drinking. More surprising, Walker Travis was ignoring Kew, and he seemed to want to say something but he didn't know how.

Kathie's little laugh sound was obviously a play for time. And she asked stupidly, "You mean Shelley Huffaker?"

"Certainly I mean Shelley Huffaker." Dare was brazen. She didn't make any attempt to keep her words to this table, and she was insolently amused by Kathie's scarcely hidden discomfiture.

Again Kathie didn't seem to know what to say. She was hesitant. "Yes—I—we—I met her in Hollywood." She glanced around the circle, began again with apparently aimless volubility, "I hardly knew her. I hadn't seen her for months."

Dare struck. "You had lunch with her yesterday." She said it without her usual triumphant arrogance; she said it almost quietly but it might have been a dart transfixing Kathie's security. No one spoke. Griselda was certain Chang—Mr. Alexander Smithery—wasn't hovering for reorders. He was listening as eagerly to the conversation as was Con, and Kew pretending to be engrossed by his cigarette.

And Kathie denied it, denied it barefacedly, in that too sweet, soft voice, "No, I didn't."

Dare persisted, her lizard eyes watching Kathie with unwavering certainty. "You called her the night before, at about six. You asked her to meet you for lunch at the Hilton."

"Yes," Kathie agreed. "I called her. But I didn't lunch with her. She didn't show up."

Chang moved one step to Con's shoulder. "Another, Mr. Satterlee?"

"All around," Con ordered. And he turned to Kathie. "So you knew Shelley Huffaker."

"Very slightly, Con. I hadn't seen her for the longest time. I didn't know her well, anyway." Her great eyes were an epitome of harmlessness but she had warned her husband not to mention a her, a her who could only have been Shelley.

Dare wasn't satisfied. She glistened when she said, "If you knew her so slightly, Mrs. Travis, how did you know she was in Long Beach?"

Kathie answered innocently, "I noticed it in the paper. And I just thought I'd call her and see if she'd have lunch with me." She leaned across Dare to lift her dark lashes to Kew. "There was nothing wrong in that, was there?"

Again Dare answered, "Nothing wrong at all." Her laugh wasn't pleasant. "Save that she'd only just arrived and no one but myself knew she was in Long Beach. She particularly didn't want it known."

Kathie was sweet but stubborn. "Some reporter must have found out." Her voice expressed her awe of the gentlemen of the press.

Kew moved words between the contestants. Con had done nothing to alleviate the tension; he might have been egging the women on, sitting back there with that enjoying smile around his mouth.

Kew spoke with such nice matter-of-factness, "The papers are saying she was your cousin, Dare. I never heard you mention her."

"But, darling," she shrilled with delight and was her normal self again, "I don't go about mentioning my relatives in civilized society. You've never heard me mention Uncle Ebenezer or Aunt Jerusha or Cousin Marmaduke, I'm certain."

"Of course, he's heard of your Aunt J'ushy, Dare," Con helped out. "You remember the time she brought her old Tom in the canary cage—"

They were off again, Kew and Dare and Con, the

three. No matter what worldly ladders they had climbed since their days on the old *World,* there would always be the past, delightful hare-brained past, linking them. And as always when they were off again, Griselda felt left out and lonely. But tonight they did not retain the mood. It did not interest them. The reason was obvious. It was the mild naval lieutenant sitting there, quite frankly not understanding, and feeling sheepish because he didn't belong. All of them, even Dare who had no business with him, were there because he was present.

And when he said, "Kathie, we must be going. It's late," Griselda knew that the evening was practically over.

Kathie didn't want to leave. She protested, "It's barely eleven, Walker," but this time he didn't give her her own way. He was already on his feet. "We have taps early in the Navy, you know. I'm tired. And I haven't been feeling well."

Con said, "I'll run you down."

"No reason for that," Kew inserted. "I go that way." He attempted to rise but Con, standing, pushed his hand on his friend's shoulder.

"You keep an eye on Griselda until I get back and we'll think of something to do with our money. The evening's young."

Kew needn't have wasted words; when Con was decisive he didn't fall back. Travis kept trying to protest, "You needn't bother," but his voice was lost in the discussion. Kathie did not assist. She powdered her nose complacently, watching Kew under her curled eyelashes.

Con's fingers lay on her arm as they left the table. He called back, "Bring another round, Chang. I'll be with you before you get 'em poured."

Dare watched the exit with slit eyes and calculating

mouth. As the bamboo door swung behind them, she turned to Griselda with deliberate malice. "Well," she demanded, "what do you think of Con's most recent acquisition?"

Griselda could have told her where Kathie's interests lay but she didn't. Not with this opportunity to warn Dare to stay on her own side of the fence. She thought her reply carefully. "Just what I've thought of all of them. They don't know Con very well."

Kew said, "*Touché*," and moved his chair beside hers. "You asked for it, Dare."

"Deliberately, and with careful consideration of the chances," she replied easily. And she looked with steady eyes at Griselda. "But if I were you, darling, —if you'll excuse my offering advice—I wouldn't let Con get too involved with this one."

"Why not?" She hated Dare, cool, insolent, so sure of herself.

"Because—" She hesitated before continuing. She looked at Kew rather than at Griselda. "Because she is dangerous."

Kew laughed out loud. He didn't seem to notice Chang wiping the dry table next to theirs. "Ridiculous. Dare darling, are you seeing sheets for ghosts? That timid girl, that creature steeped in an inferiority complex, dangerous?" He laughed again as if he were enjoying himself hugely, as if he'd only met that girl for the first time an hour ago.

Dare spoke directly to Griselda. "Because she is dangerous. That quiet voice and those innocent eyes and that damn cloying sweetness—it's a wonderful game. It's even taken Kew in, you see. And Kew isn't half so curious about the female intricacies as Con."

Dare had no business saying that. It wasn't true. She was trying to use Kathie as a red herring to mask her renewed attachment to Con. And perhaps her nose was out of joint because Con had left her temporarily. Yet there was something false in Kathie Travis. Griselda herself had sensed that.

Dare went on. "I have never met a woman any more certain of herself and so determined to have what she wants."

"And what does she want, Madame ZuZu?" Kew asked. He winked at Griselda.

"She doesn't want what she has." Dare smiled now. "And she does want what we have."

She gestured vaguely but Griselda knew that Dare was right. Kathie's want for Dare's air, for clothes and jewels, for moneyed things, hadn't been disguised at dinner.

"For one thing," Dare laughed a little, "she doesn't want that funny little Lieutenant Travis." She lit a cigarette slowly.

Again Dare was right. Kathie's irritation with Walker was constant; women weren't that way with men they wanted.

Dare laughed again. "She'll trade him in at the first chance. She had one before Walker, you know, a farmer. He was considerate, though. Left her a widow so she could climb up in the world on Lieutenant Travis's shoulders. But she'd like to climb a little higher. And I'm afraid the lieutenant won't do as well by her as his predecessor. The Navy watches its men too closely."

Kew said, "You seem to have a bit of information on someone you never met before."

"Darling," she droned, "I'm working for the Navy. And the Service does gossip." She approved the narrow length of her parrot-red nails. "But even you should have recognized that Kathie Travis is a damn liar."

Con had returned, slid into the chair beside hers. "You've decided."

"I knew. Kathie did lunch with Shelley yesterday. The Hilton maître-d'hotel told me this morning. He remembered Shelley with her pictures slattered in all the rags. Moreover, he knew Mrs. Travis very well. She and her husband stay at the Hilton frequently."

Kew made a sound like hmmm. Con murmured, "Incredible, Dr. Watson."

Dare continued, "Moreover, there wasn't one line in the Long Beach papers about Shelley being here. She'd have yelled if there were. And she went over them inch by inch as if she were looking for something lost."

"Why did Kathie lie?" Kew seemed puzzled.

Con shrugged. "Perhaps she doesn't want to get mixed up in it. The Navy's almost as particular as a boarding school some ways. Perhaps she's allergic to the police. How would we know why she lied? Maybe she's just a psychopathic liar. Some women are."

Kew asked then, "Was Shelley really your cousin, Dare?"

She eyed him almost in disgust. "Of course, she wasn't. Do I look as if I'd have that sort of cousin?"

His eyebrows rose quizzically. "Why the disguise?"

"It seemed—wiser. Better than trying to explain." She moved her hands. "I knew her in New York, slightly. One of my lame ducks perhaps you'd call it. It doesn't matter. She hasn't been around for some years, not since she left to try Hollywood."

Con asked, "Was Hollywood avid?"

"Rather not. But such trifles would never faze a Shelley Huffaker. She hadn't much ambition. All she wanted was a golden bed to lie on."

"She found that." Con stated it.

"Doubt not. Shelley knew her way around as far as that was concerned."

Dare held long fingers for a cigarette. Griselda noticed they were not controlled; they rattled like bones. "Monday night she telephoned me from Hollywood. How she knew where I was, where to reach me, I hadn't a notion. She wanted to know if she could come spend a day or two with me."

"You accepted her invitation."

Dare said, "I couldn't do anything else on the spur of the moment. It was a demand in her own inimitable blatant fashion. And remembering her, I knew it wasn't I she was interested in. She either wanted a place to hide out for a few days, or she wanted to make some contact through me. I suspected Navy."

"And it was that?" Con's eyes were keen now.

Dare shrugged. "I never knew why she came. She arrived Tuesday morning in a cab, a local one. She said she'd traveled by interurban. Simply incredible, if true. She preferred a good Duesenberg any hour. She didn't go out at all that day, just puttered around in some black chiffon she called a wrapper. And I left for Avalon Wednesday morning. That's one reason I let her come. I knew I wouldn't have to endure her. I told her on the phone I had the yacht-party thing on my hands."

Kew put in, "She must have had something to say to you if she was underfoot all day Tuesday."

"But I wasn't there," Dare rebutted quickly. "I left almost as soon as she arrived. I was with the Swales all morning, lunched with them, and most of the afternoon. I saw her when I went back to change for dinner."

Con drank. "How do you know she didn't go out if you weren't there?"

"My China boy told me."

"But maybe she used the phone."

"She did. But to no avail. According to Bing."

"Bing?"

"After his hero." She said, "I've had him two years now, ever since I came to California. He wouldn't lie to me."

Why had Dare made these inquiries of her servant concerning her guest? She must have known something of Shelley Huffaker's purpose in coming, more than she admitted. At least she had, by tacit admission, been suspicious.

"The only call we know that she had was from Kathie Travis while I was dressing for dinner."

He was quick. "Was that what she had been waiting for?"

"I don't believe so." Dare spoke thoughtfully. "If so, she put on a good scene. She didn't want anyone to know she was in town and some way this girl that was always bothering her to meet Hollywood nabobs had found out. Now she'd have to waste time lunching with a woman and getting rid of her afterwards. A long dull tirade to which I didn't listen." She shrugged her uncovered shoulder again. "That's all there is. I went to Catalina. Came back when the police called me."

Kew insisted, "You never ran into Shelley at all in Hollywood?"

She protested. "I'm speaking God's truth, Kew. I'd not heard her name in years." That was possible, even probable. The multitudinous cliques in the cinema capital seldom overlapped.

Con asked, "You don't know who she'd been golden-bedding it with?" Dare shook her head. Con's eyelids dropped. "Could it have been Mannie Martin?"

"No." It was Kew who answered. "He lived alone

and played the field. That's been doubly checked."

"Shelley would insist on steady employment," said Dare. "And get it." She looked at her mouth in an enormous circlet of mirror and white jade. It was early, barely midnight. But she said, "I'm tired. Take me home, Kew." She stood.

Kew covered her with the flaming wool.

She laid her gems against Con's cheek. "Busy tomorrow?"

"Yes. Tied up all day."

Kew grinned deliberately. "Lunch tomorrow, Griselda?"

Her answer was as deliberate: "Delighted. It's going to be awfully dull tomorrow at the Satterlees."

Even Con laughed. But he put his arm about her in possession. "She is stuff, isn't she, Kew? Don't blame you for wanting her. But she's posted, you know."

They all laughed again. But Con wasn't laughing as they trailed the others to the street. He was ironical. "You don't think Kew's asking you out because of your bellissima eyes, do you, baby?"

She looked at him curiously. It wasn't like Con to be obvious about anything, even jealousy.

He wasn't smiling. "It's to keep tabs on me," he said.

He started to help her into the shabby car while Kew was helping Dare into the far from shabby one parked in front of theirs. But Dare was hesitant. She waved her escort aside, came along back to Con.

She said quietly, "I'm going to Avalon tomorrow. There was a wire at the apartment."

Con didn't say anything but his look was significant. Griselda put two with two and the answer left her shaken. Dare wasn't mixed up with Shelley's death alone; Major Pembrooke was returning to Catalina the night of the murder; he had mentioned waiting guests; Dare had been on the island.

Dare's lashes unveiled the green eyes. "Why don't you come along? Albert George would welcome a diversion. Although he won't be there until evening."

"What about Kew?"

"I'm not telling him." Her mouth was small. "I don't want an argument tonight. He's always so particular about what I do. And he doesn't care for the major."

Con yawned. "Regrets to the deah fellow but Mr. Satterlee is in partial custody to that worthy son of the sea and land, old Cap'n Thuṣby."

Dare laughed, "You want me to relay that?"

Con threw back his head and crowed. "Don't care if you do. Or tell your friend I'm honeymooning and don't like crowds."

Griselda murmured, "You'd never guess it."

Con grinned at her.

Dare asked, "You mean you won't go?"

"I mean that. Doesn't interest me." Griselda froze as he belied the truth. "Where is said house party held?"

"On his elegant yacht, *The Falcon.* Lying at anchor just off the coast of Catalina—St. Catherine's Landing. Manned by the duckiest Oriental navy. The kind that fine-comb your luggage—so sorry."

Con's mouth pursed. "If I should run over to the St. Catherine for the week end, how do I get hold of you?"

"Telephone from the hotel." She turned, hesitated. "I've been thinking about it. Shelley might have been killed because she was with you. It might have been to put you away safe for a couple of months."

Con's face was dark. Then he rejected. "No one would kill an innocent girl to strike at me." He was

looking at Griselda, staring at her. If it had been anyone else she would have said there was horror dawn-
ing on his face.

Dare said, "I'm sending Bing to Hollywood tomorrow. He needs a vacation."

Griselda wouldn't let Con send her away; she didn't
want to be safe if he weren't. Without further words,
Dare wheeled abruptly, returned to Kew. Con
watched the big car slide away. He had that scowl
still between his brows as he took her arm, put her
in their car.

She spoke urgently, "Con, Con, you don't have to
be in on this, do you? You don't know anything about
that girl?" If he'd only be willing to leave now, tonight.

He stepped on the starter. "It's a dirty trick on you,
angel, but we'll get that honeymoon yet." She knew
by his voice that there was no hope he would agree
to departure.

If she had to endure this new danger she must
know more about it; she must have information for
a shield. She insisted, "I want to know all of it, Con,
everything. What are you planning to do? You
mustn't treat me like an idiot child."

He didn't look at her. "I don't think you're either
idiot or child, but I won't have you in this thing."

That darkness had shadowed his face again and
now the horror came into her being. Stupidly she
hadn't realized it before. If a strange girl had been
threatened by being seen with Con, how much more
did she, his wife, stand in danger? But he was wrong.
Why couldn't he see it? She couldn't protect herself
without knowledge. "You can't keep me out of what
you're mixed up in. I'm your wife. It's better to know
than go around this way, hearing patches of it, guessing. Isn't it?"

His reply was quiet but she heard it as if it were shouted above the fuming engine. He said definitely, "No, it isn't."

2

Griselda opened one eye the smallest crack possible. Something had waked her and she didn't want to wake; she was sleepy. She opened the eye wide, the other eye wider. She was right. Con was out of bed. She called tentatively, "Con," louder, "Con." The silence of the cottage closed in on her. For a moment she lay there in unreasoning fear before she caught up the golden fleece of her robe. He wasn't in the living room; he wasn't in the kitchen. His dinner jacket wasn't in the wardrobe behind the curtain of pink fish. His bag wasn't in the corner by the bureau.

She knew it last night. She knew it when he told Dare he wasn't going. But she hadn't wanted to know. She didn't want him to go to Catalina.

She couldn't let Con walk alone to meet possible danger. Her place was beside him. The clock said noon. She would take the afternoon plane and find him.

She packed like an automaton, swiftly but with slight realization of her movements. Evening clothes. The black froth of lace. She could face Dare in that without qualm. Her canary flannel suit and crimson sweater to warm her. She drank coffee while she packed. Two cups. Then a third. The sound of steps on the creaking porch froze the steaming cup in mid-air. She moved warily into the living room where she could see out. It was Captain Thusby's apple face, his knuckles on the door.

She opened it, spoke more cheerfully than she felt, "Good morning."

He looked at the crimson hat flaring on her head. He looked at the cup in her hand. "Morning, ma'am. Mr. Satterlee here?"

"No." Wisdom crowded in on her and it didn't give her reassurance. Thusby had told Con not to leave Long Beach. She must speak carefully. "He isn't in now."

He couldn't know Con had left, that she was planning to follow. A woman would dress to go into town shopping or for lunch.

"Figgered maybe neither one of you was here. Tried to call earlier but there wasn't any answer. Thought I'd just run up and find out. Vinnie might as well be sitting out in the car reading his Superman as in the office."

And if neither had been here, what would he have done? Sent out a short-wave call for them as if they were criminals? She stiffened but she smiled at him. "The phone evidently waked me but too late."

Her half-packed grip in the bedroom suddenly loomed so large in her mind that she wondered he could not see it printed on her face. She didn't know if it were visible from the chair in which he was and she didn't dare turn to see. She knew she'd left the door ajar; she always did. She could hear time ticking away on the bed table.

She sprang up. "Won't you have some coffee with me?" The percolator was on the bureau. She could let the door follow her carelessly when she came out.

He said, "No, thanks. Never eat between meals."

She couldn't suggest another cup for herself, not until this was downed. And she couldn't swallow now. She sat down again.

He rubbed his fuzz. "Funny about all you folks knowing Mannie Martin."

She said defensively, "I didn't know Mannie

Martin. I'd not heard his name in ages until—" Until Major Pembrooke spoke it. But she didn't want to mention that. She said honestly, "I wish you'd tell me about Mannie Martin." She felt a little sorry for herself. "I don't know what's happened to him or why everyone's so interested in him or anything."

Thusby said complacently, "Nobody knows what's happened to him. And I don't know myself why everyone's so interested. I only know why I am. The Los Angeles police have asked all the lower coast towns to keep an eye out for him."

She wondered. "Where did he disappear?"

He grimaced at her. "That's kind of like losing the dollar, ma'am. If I knew where I'd lost it, I'd go get it. Nobody knows exactly. The police weren't called in on it until the trail was cold."

Major Pembrooke had said those very words, said them with scorn.

"He took his boat—a speed launch—from the Santa Monica Club Monday afternoon. Two weeks ago last Monday. It was found at Navy Landing, across the bridge down here, the next morning. Hadn't any business being docked there but it was. Nobody's seen him. At least nobody's said anything about seeing him around here. Nobody's said why he'd want to disappear either."

She forced brightness into her voice again. "Well, we couldn't have seen him, could we, Captain Thusby? We didn't come to Long Beach until a week ago. And Kew's only been here a few days." She didn't mention Dare; she didn't know.

He was calm. "None of you further away than Hollywood. And seems like you all moved in fast enough when the investigation started."

He couldn't, actually he couldn't, believe any of them had caused a man to disappear. They weren't

magicians—or murderers. Her heart beat more
quickly. He had connected Con with the blonde's
murder; he might incredibly extend it to this other
unsolved case. He couldn't; it was rank stupidity;
she wouldn't allow it. But she must get rid of him
and find Con. Con must know about this visit.
Pointedly she looked at her watch.

He rose to the hint. "I'm keeping you, ma'am.
You don't know where Mr. Satterlee is, do you?"

She said, "No." That was truth. "He went out before I wakened."

"Don't matter anyhow. Tell him I'll drop by tonight to see him." He rolled jauntily away.

She sank down again on the lumpy cushions. He
had checkmated her departure. He had seen the
preparations. She moved to his chair. There was no
doubt. The opened grip was framed in the doorway.
She'd have to be here tonight; give some explanation for Con's absence. She'd have to stay, not knowing what danger Con was forging into. She felt so
futile; her hand holding the cup trembled.

She wouldn't sit here in the cottage all day alone.
Inaction would be insufferable. Her nerves couldn't
stretch to it. She must find out more about the missing man, what made him secret and important to
Con and Kew, and, she was certain, to Dare. Con
wasn't going to tell her. They'd talked over her head
last night; furthermore, he was not here but in Avalon. Kew had definitely been noncommunicative.
There was one person who might know something,
who had been here two weeks ago, who would at
least have heard gossip. A young Navy wife with
time on her hands wouldn't scorn gossip. And Dare
had suggested that Kathie had avid interest in Hollywood; it was possible the girl might even have
met Martin.

Griselda's spirits lifted. She would go see Kathie. If she broke the jesting lunch invitation of Kew's, it wouldn't matter.

Mrs. Travis was in. Griselda used the Hilton house phone. Kathie's voice was mildly surprised. "Yes, do come up, Mrs. Satterlee."

It was an average hotel room, neither the best nor worst in the house. Kathie was untidy in negligee. Her dark hair tumbled to the limp shoulders of the bright pink stuff. There were even brighter pink marabou feathers flittering at the neckline.

She slid back into the unmade bed. "I'm just having my breakfast." She had a wistful smile. "When Walker isn't here I sleep mornings." The tray held the deep brown of hot chocolate flanked by a round silver bowl of whipped cream, sugared strawberries, and some incredible rolls with pecans studding the burnt sugar icing. Griselda hoped she wouldn't have to design for her in twenty years.

Kathie said, "Won't you have something, Mrs. Satterlee?" She was not quite at ease, her eyes were watching the cut of the canary suit, the infinitesimal diamond chain on Griselda's wrist, even the expected black and white spectator pumps.

Griselda was looking at the pink-fish monstrosity fastening the maribou. The girl wore it even in bed.

Kathie noticed. She might even have seen the faint distaste beneath Griselda's polite face. She fingered it with echoing distaste. "Walker gave it to me for a present a couple of weeks ago. He's so particular about my wearing it when he's around—you know how husbands are about their presents." She had unfastened it, tossed it carelessly on the bed table.

Griselda really laughed. "Do you know, I don't remember my husband ever giving me a present save on the prescribed occasions." It never occurred to Con. "You're fortunate to have such a thoughtful man."

Kathie absently dipped a roll in the whipped cream. "Yes, I am, I suppose."

Griselda didn't continue on the subject. She hadn't come to put this girl at ease in the presence of a better groomed woman. She had come because she must find out important things, and obviously must find them from unexpected sources. She asked, "Did you ever know a man named Mannie Martin?"

Kathie's eyes were wide and her voice eager, "Yes, I did. He is a friend of Walker's, a very good friend of Walker's."

Griselda breathed more easily. She actually would learn something here. "Did you know that he's disappeared?"

"He has?" The deep blue eyes widened. "That's why he hasn't been around lately." She looked at Griselda. "Maybe that's why Walker's been so worried. Mannie was supposed to meet him two weeks ago Monday and he didn't show up. They'd been working together on something." She shook her head slowly. "And he's disappeared?" She dipped into the swirled cream again.

"What were they working on?"

"I don't know. Some radio thing, I suppose. That's all Walker's interested in. He doesn't like to dance or go on parties or anything—just radio." She looked at Griselda again. "Mannie was in radio too but not the Navy." Her nose disparaged the Service. "He made lots of money. He had a perfectly wonderful house in Brentwood. That's part of Hollywood. It had a swimming pool and oh—just everything." Her eyes were shining. "He had an English butler and a German chef and Jap houseboys and—it was wonderful. Walker and I have stayed there several times."

"How did you happen to meet him?" She asked it casually.

"Oh, Walker's known him for years. They were at Annapolis together." The narrowing of her nostrils was barely perceptible. "But Mannie had sense enough to resign and make something of himself."

Griselda didn't envy Lieutenant Travis although his wife was more beautiful than any woman she had ever seen, including those myriads clamoring to climb on the Hollywood auction blocks.

Kathie was continuing complaint without the least inflection of it spoiling the cadence of her voice. "I didn't even know that Walker was a friend of his until this spring."

It might be important. "How was that?"

"Oh, Walker never tells me anything." Her slender hands stirred. "And he'd never think of looking anyone up. But Mannie looked Walker up." She was proud of that. Lieutenant Travis had for once proved the worth of his existence.

"When was that?" She still sounded casual.

"In March. We've seen a lot of Mannie' since."

"Was he—do you know if he was interested in women?" Thusby might have had reason, not hunch, for coupling the two cases.

Kathie's eyes rounded in surprise. "I suppose so. He was a bachelor."

"I don't mean it exactly that way." She asked outright, "Did he run around with women or do you know?" She made it plain. "Did he know Shelley Huffaker?"

"That's where we met Shelley Huffaker. At the broadcasting studio."

"He introduced you to her?"

"I don't remember who introduced us." Her eyebrows thought about it. "It was months ago."

Griselda persisted. "Was she—do you know—" She
fitted her vocabulary to Kathie's probable understanding, "Was she Mannie's girl friend?"

"Oh no." Kathie laughed at that. "No. Of course
not. He was too important to waste time on someone
like Shelley Huffaker. She was terribly common, you
know."

Griselda said, "I didn't know her. I only saw her
once and I didn't know who she was." She gathered
her bag and gloves in one hand. "Did you ever meet
a Major Pembrooke in Hollywood?"

Again Kathie's eyebrows drew together. "No. I
don't remember anyone of that name. Walker might
know him. He never tells me—"

She left Kathie to her dubious comfort of a slov-
enly bed. The fresh sea air of Ocean Boulevard was
good in her lungs. She hadn't learned anything of
value, nothing to give reason for this Martin's disappearance and the seemingly unrelated murder of
Shelley Huffaker. It was four o'clock before she returned dispiritedly to the cottage. There was yet the
long evening to endure. She didn't know when the
captain would arrive, what she could say to give
apparent innocence to Con's absence. If Thusby
would come early enough it might be possible to fly
to the island tonight. That was stupid. She couldn't
risk rushing from him to the air field. Thusby was
smart; he would anticipate the move if he had the
least suspicion that Con was not in town. She mustn't
seem even to be considering it.

She replaced the suit with white slacks and jacket;
it would be a simple matter to make the exchange
again after he left, if it were urgent that she carry
word to Con.

He didn't come early. Dark and mist had covered
all but the sound of the sea before she heard his

irregular rhythm on the catwalk. She opened the
door for him.

"Mr. Satterlee not back yet?"

She laughed and evaded. "It's difficult even for a
wife to catch him in when he's on vacation, Captain
Thusby. He seems to think it paramount that he
personally inspect all the bars in the area."

He laughed with her but she wasn't certain that
he was fooled. "You weren't asleep when Mr. Satterlee came home Wednesday night?"

"No." She amended, "I was but his coming woke
me. It was midnight." She waited stiffly for what
was to come.

"Didn't go out again, did he?"

She couldn't lie. That was how criminals were
trapped, separate stories that didn't agree. He might
reach Con before she did, learn the truth. She had
hesitated; now she answered. "Yes, he did. Someone
phoned him." She pushed time forward frantically.
"It was at least one-thirty before he left. He couldn't
have done anything to that girl." She begged him to
understand. "He wouldn't kill anyone, Captain
Thusby. He isn't that kind of a man. Even if he were,
he couldn't have done it. He was with me from twelve
to one-thirty."

He held up a worn palm. "Whoa!" He chuckled
mildly. "I'm not saying he killed anyone. You're
way ahead of me, Mrs. Satterlee."

She'd been wrong to mention it. Her breath came
back. But he wasn't looking for Con to sell him a
ticket to a policeman's ball.

"Who'd you say called him?"

"I don't know. He wouldn't tell me."

Suspicion canceled mildness in those old blue eyes.
"What time did he come in after that?"

She answered slowly. "I don't know. I didn't wake

again until morning. He was dressed for the beach
at that time."

Captain Thusby chewed his underlip. "Didn't
tell you nothing about where he'd been?"

The truth of her words was like a chime, even to
her own ears. "He hasn't had a chance yet, Captain.
Things have been happening too fast."

He laughed again over that. "Well, you tell him
I'm wanting to see him soon as he gets in. He can
call me."

"It may be late."

"If it isn't too late, you have him call."

She listened to his steps fade. She wondered if
Vinnie were reading Superman in the dark. It was
nearing ten. She could leave now but it was better
not. Better to be here if the chief took it into his
head to telephone or drop in again.

She turned off the lamp and her eyes met the win-
dowpane. There had been a face outside, an animal
face. She waited tense, listening, but there was no
sound save the relentless ocean beyond pounding on
the breakwater. She didn't move. The pane was
without portrait now.

The sibilant tap on the door was as thunderous as
a battering ram. She didn't know what to do. A bent
hairpin. She had to move her feet some way, to put
her hand on the key and turn it, open to the unknown terror outside. There was no porch light for
warning. She didn't know who was standing there
until the opened door flung yellow from the room
upon the ugly face. It was Chang.

His rasping voice was polite but he came in without invitation. He said, "I want to talk to Con."

Her hand remained on the doorknob. She said,
"He isn't here."

The face was suddenly belligerent. If he'd thumped his chest and bellowed, it wouldn't have surprised her. He demanded, "Where is he?. He didn't tell me he was going no place."

If she hadn't been alone with him, she would have answered with spirit. There was no reason to be frightened of a bar waiter. But pyramiding him on to what had already occurred in two days left her shaken. She answered without irritation, "I don't know where he is. I didn't come in until four and he wasn't here."

Chang muttered but she heard. "He oughtn't to do it."

"Do what?"

"Go off not letting anyone know where he's like to be. Not letting on to anyone that he was going off."

"He hasn't gone off!" she denied hotly. That mustn't be said, not with Captain Thusby so recently in the neighborhood, not with Thusby suspecting under his acceptance that Con wasn't returning. And she recalled with sudden fear, Chang was the Mr. Alexander Smithery who had given Con away to Thusby in the first place. This might be a police trap; Chang might be a stool pigeon. She explained, "He has old friends here. He was with some of them last night. Doubtless he is with others tonight." She couldn't keep some scorn out of her voice. "Shall I have him call you, too, when he comes in?" Con report to an ex-pugilist.

He said, "Never mind. I'll find him."

At least he had gone. And if his final words sounded menacing to Con, she could do nothing now. Anything Chang said smacked of menace. That was the rasp in his throat.

3

The rattling car jerked over the morning road to Wilmington. Griselda felt heavy as a cold potato. No plane seats available until afternoon; some floral-sounding convention had reserved all the morning places. The voice on the phone had been obnoxiously regretful. Had she but called sooner. The boat took longer but it would get her there by noon. She would certainly be able to locate Con before nightfall. She didn't want to endure another night alone.

She parked in the official garage, checked her bags with the attendant, and went into the raucous crowded terminal. There was a half hour before sailing. She bought her ticket, returned to stand docilely in front of the restaurant booth, her eyes resting without interest on the scurry of motley persons.

A prim high-pitched tenor said, "Griselda Satterlee. I didn't expect to see you in this place."

She didn't know which one it would be until he came around the corner of her yellow coat. So many Hollywoodans had that same voice. It was Sergei.

She said, "Hello. Catalina bound?"

He didn't look like a famous Russian director. He looked like a cloak-and-suiter on a holiday. There should have been a bowler and a box lunch, a fat wife, and six or seven greasy children with him. There wasn't. And if anyone had been with him, it would have been a blonde.

He wiped away the heat from his neck. "Yes. A little vacation is what I need. I need a rest. I've been so perturbed." He squealed on about his needs while she listened vaguely. She tried to interrupt the prattle and dismiss him, moving to the gangplank. But

he walked alongside her canary sleeve, his head no
higher than her shoulder. And all at once she realized
what he was saying.

"Of course. Of course. You are Con Satterlee's
wife. Of course. I had forgotten." He smiled sweetly,
all across his narrow blue jaw line. "You are going
to Catalina to join your husband? And you will be
taking the boat? What a coincidence. So am I. I must
get my ticket. Of course. Perhaps we shall meet on
the boat." He went hurrying toward the ticket window.

Griselda murmured, "Not if I see you first." She
found a place on the top deck next the rail, on the
port side well toward the bow. She watched the
shuffling file of passengers on the gangplank. But
she didn't see Sergei among them. It looked as if he
were going to miss the boat. She sincerely hoped so.
She didn't want to listen to his perturbations all the
way to Avalon. She had plenty of her own.

The voyage was too short. She stirred as the boat
approached the sheer cliffs upraised in the falsely
calm waters at St. Catherine's Landing. The little
speedboats were circling the ship, sirens blowing,
passengers screaming welcome. She walked the gantlet
at Avalon, down the roped-off path where masses
of faces pushed laughter upon the newcomers. None
was familiar to her. Whatever Con was doing here,
he was not playing at tourist. She walked to the
St. Catherine cab. Con always chose the best. If he
were not there, she at least would have comfort until
he was found.

He was registered and she convinced the clerk he
had been expecting her arrival. She hadn't expected
to find him in. His room was old-fashioned but you
could see the bright green terrace and the blue-green

ocean beyond. She flung off her hat, rumpled her smooth golden hair. It might be a long wait. She opened her bag, lifted out the blue mull negligee. She could catch up on sleep; there might not be an opportunity soon.

He was singing, "The life on the open wave, tra-la," off key and misworded, when she opened her eyes.

"You're certainly noisy."

He put his head out of the bathroom door. "And what do you think the teeny-weeny bear found in his bed?" He returned the head. "How'd you know I was here?"

"I'm psychic that way." He was shaving without being told and he had his white dinner jacket laid out. "Successful afternoon?" She knew it was from the lustiness of the song. Only Dare gave him this lift and only for Dare would he dress to the gills. "Are we dining with her?"

"Who?" He made sounds scraping his upper lip. He wiped the razor carefully on a towel before his pretense went out in a sheepish grin. "Yeah," he admitted.

She yawned and stretched her arms up to the headboard. "That means the black." She was right to have brought it. It fitted her like cellophane and the clouds of fluff were no less flattering. No glasses on her nose at night. Straining her eyes made them look bigger and brighter anyway. With Dare present she needed every advantage.

She asked, "Why didn't you tell me you were coming to Catalina?"

"Didn't know it till I landed here. Too much orange juice."

She hardened her calm chin in her hand. "Not good enough, Satterlee."

"Do you want it straight?" He looked out at her. She said yes.

"I didn't want you along." Perhaps he was frowning at the microscopic cut under his chin but she didn't like that faintly troubled voice, and she went swiftly into the bathroom, touched his side. "Con, I want to help you. What can I do?"

He turned slowly to her. His voice was level. "You can stay out of it. Don't ask questions of me or anyone. If you don't know anything, no one can hurt you." He put his hands on her shoulders. "I involved you in a mix once but never again. You understand. Never." His voice was sharp but his look was deep in hers. "I'd saw off my right arm with a damn rusty saw before I'd let anything happen to you."

It was so seldom that he slipped the casual front, allowed her to see the real feeling behind it. Her lids stung with unexpected tears. If he'd show her the real more often, she'd know, not have silly feminine qualms about Dare and other beauties.

She said, "Darling," and then, "It can't be that dangerous."

He said soberly, "It is," and she thought of the blonde girl who'd been seen with Con before she lay in the palm shadows of Bixby Park.

Con shook her a little. "Sweet child, don't be curious. Promise me you won't do a Pandora."

She said, adoring him with her eyes, "I'll do anything you say, Con."

He nodded. "Then just go along as if there's nothing up. So far as you're concerned, nothing is up, understand?"

She was hesitant. "But—Shelley Huffaker?"

It was as if he'd just remembered her, as if it had nothing to do with him. "Let Thusby worry about that." He kissed her, a quick one, gave her a shove. "Go on and get dressed. We'll be late."

"Oh Con!" Her face was patched with shaving soap.

He was jauntily scraping again. "That's what gals get who invade men's bathrooms."

She was firm. "I gave you an electric razor. If you'd use it."

"Never could stand vacuum cleaners. My face is no rug."

He was dressing quickly. She wasn't surprised when he said, "Think I'll go down and have a quickie while you're finishing up. How do I look?"

"Elegant." She watched him survey himself in the mirror. "You ought to try store clothes more often." She dodged. "Go on and drink. I'll get along faster without you. Where do we meet?"

"On the terrace."

She took a last survey of her hair and lipstick by the deepening twilight window, and she saw Con's length below on the path behind the bushes. He wasn't with Dare. She leaned out. It looked amazingly as if he were with the dreadful Mr. Smithery. But surely it couldn't be he. Chang would have to be on duty at the Bamboo Bar on a Saturday night.

She caught up her evening coat, locked the door after her. The corridor was dim lit, down one angular flight to the first floor. She had to cross through the glassed supplementary dining room to reach the terrace. She thought she recognized the figure standing there outside. Sergei wore his beret at that angle. And Sergei would wear that navy beret even with dinner clothes.

He piped, "Griselda!" as if he were surprised to see her but he wasn't. He'd been waiting for her to come out. "Griselda, I missed that dreadful boat and had to come over by the plane. I had planned we would be friends on the boat. Make the trip go so fast with talk. Traveling perturbs me. It is so endless."

There had been no available plane reservations; he had had his when he spoke to her at the Terminal. He had never intended to take the boat; he had only wanted to make sure she was taking it. But why? It made her feel faintly uneasy. She turned away. "I must find my husband."

"He is down below there." He waved a gesture to the beach. He had been watching Con, too. Was this all a maneuver to meet him?

He said, "You and your husband will have dinner with me, yes? I should like to know him. He is the unusual young man, yes?"

"I'm sorry." She wasn't. "We're dining a friend of Con's."

"Such an unusual young man. I would know him."

She was disturbed. No one thought Con unusual. "He's a good newspaperman who's turned into a good air reporter."

"Not that, not that!" His hands fluttered. His eyes in the twilight seemed sharp, prying. "It is not that I mean. Of course that is very fine. But he is the confidant of Barjon Garth, the great Barjon Garth who directs the great X division. That so fine organization who protects your country, my country to be."

She put her hand on his arm and laughed out loud. "Sergei, you're incredible. Con knows Garth but as for being his confidant—" Her laughter rolled merrily as if it were real. "Imagine a newspaperman

being in the confidence of the head of the secret
service!"

He pouted like a hurt child. "But I was told,
Griselda."

"Someone was ribbing you, Sergei." She let her
laughter run lightly down the terrace; it had reached
Con; he was materializing before her.

He asked, "What's the joke?"

She took his arm, not answering, murmured introductions, and led him firmly down the terrace away
from the sulky face. She didn't want to talk longer
with Sergei. She'd never cared for him, for his in-
satiable taste in tawdry girls.

"Where'd you find that and why?" Con asked.

She shook her head helplessly. "It found me."

"Which wholesale house is he with?"

"He isn't. He's one of Oppy's directors. You know.
Sergei Vironova."

Con stepped back and stared into her face. "My
God, why didn't you say so?"

"I did," she retorted.

"You mumbled." He took her arm again. "So that's
Vironova."

She looked at him out of troubled eyes. "Yes."

He had stopped walking, was watching the silhou-
ettes back there on the terrace, particularly one small
one with the round shadow of a beret. "Why didn't
you ever tell me you knew Vironova?"

She said, "I don't really know him. I just know all
of Oppy's hired hands, that's all."

"You've never mentioned Vironova."

She touched his arm. "Darling, if you really want
me to, I'll take a couple of days off and tell you
everyone I know in Hollywood. Or it might be
more amusing if we'd run up to Malibu and I could
introduce them to you."

He wasn't listening. "Maybe he'll join us later."

Sergei's interest in Con evidently was mutual. She tried to speak as if she weren't nervous about it. "I hope he doesn't. His perturbations don't amuse me."

"He has perturbations?" Con's eyes were narrowed on his cigarette. "What about?"

"I didn't pay any attention. I suppose his latest blonde walked out on him." She was sharp now. "Con, why are you interested in him?"

He didn't answer.

She said, "He's interested in you," and she caught her breath. "He thinks you're in Garth's confidence. He wants to know you."

That was why Sergei had been waiting for her. She knew that definitely now. Sergei had not ever trailed her at the studios. She was blonde, yes, and thought beautiful by some; but she wore horn-rimmed glasses while she worked, and she was always at work. She wasn't a Hollywood blonde who sat around and looked sexy and didn't need to work. It was Con, who had no connection with the pictures save by remarrying her, that Sergei Vironova was fishing for at Catalina.

Con said, "Forget it. He isn't important."

"Is he in on the party tonight?"

"Not yet." He whistled. "You can never tell what the night will bring."

A tender was landing a party there at the far end of the pier; Dare's shrilling came heightened by night and sea. Con, surprisingly, turned on his heel. He moved Griselda toward the hotel, took a seat at a table on the upper terrace, and beckoned a boy. Sergei wasn't in sight. "Rum and gum. What about you? Dubonnet?"

She sipped it watching Dare and a man come

nearer. Sipped it as if it weren't connected with death in a quiet park.

Dare cried, "Con, my love," pretending that she didn't know he would be waiting for her. She wrapped one diamond arm about his shoulder, said, "Griselda, how nice to see you." She didn't expect to see Griselda; shadowed by moonlight, the green glint of her eyes told that.

Con came to his feet without disentangling her. "Griselda thought she'd try a week end, too."

She waved an arm at the shadowy mass of her escort. He closed in. "Of course, you'll join us for dinner. We've reservations."

Con said quickly, "Defer introductions until we're surrounding a table. I like to meet people where I can see them."

Dare shrieked again, "Isn't he wonderful, Albert George?"

She led with Con. The stone-faced major watched them go in a thoughtful and terrible silence. Then he turned to Griselda. "Shall we follow, Mrs. Satterlee?"

Evidently, Con was having it as he planned, meeting Albert George Pembrooke without seeming prearrangement.

She didn't speak. She went with Pembrooke as if she were walking to her doom.

MAJOR PEMBROOKE'S table was in a favored spot, the waiters were deferential. Griselda sat beside him in well-mannered docility, ate and drank, listened and spoke. She didn't want to. She wanted to clutch Con's hand, make him run, swim, fly with her away from the macabre reverberations there at the St. Catherine. But Con didn't notice her; he was not wasting charm on a wife that night. Nor did he pay any attention to the man he had traveled to meet. Pembrooke should have been harassed at having his companion taken over completely by Con. Actually he wasn't, Griselda realized. It was because he was waiting for something, for someone else.

When Kew entered the dining room with Kathie Travis on his arm, Griselda knew what that something was. She knew with such certainty that there was no amazement in her at Kew being there, nor at Kathie being with him, not even at Sergei Vironova following sadly in their wake.

Con saw them, too. He laid his fingers on Dare's arm and shouted, "Look what's here!"

Dare put her other hand on Albert George's red-haired wrist. "There's Kew Brent and Kathie Travis. Shall they join us?"

Griselda was certain this had been staged. More than ever she resented being on the outside, being relegated to busboy intelligence. She knew wheels within wheels were revolving, revolving with rapidity and precision; she didn't like not knowing the

motive nor the goal. It left her nerves too tight for
comfort.

Dare signaled, crying, "I didn't dream you were
coming over, Kew. Why didn't you tell me? And
you, Mrs. Travis. Of course you'll join us."

She made introductions. Sergei Vironova stood
back, wetting his sad lips. Kew remembered him,
"You know Vironova, Dare, the director."

She broke in, "How d'you do," as if not interested
but her eyes measured him. Albert George was curt
to the little Russian. Sergei knew it. He cringed. But
he had accomplished what he was here to accomplish.
He wedged in now beside Con, made his chair closer
than need be. He was afraid of Albert George. He
glanced in the major's direction and quickly again
at Con's shoulders as if these were bodyguard. Con
ignored him.

Griselda sat quietly in that group encircling the
table of shining glass and silver and white napery,
her scalp prickling. She knew that she was dining
with Death. She was conscious of only one person,
the reason that each of the others was present. He
bulked there, certain of himself and his power.

Why was Kew here? Was it to give Kathie a taste
of the luxury that grimly, sweetly, she was determined to attain? Would he do that much for a
woman? Or had he brought Kathie to deliver her
over to Major Pembrooke for some unknown purpose?

She heard him say, "Mrs. Travis's husband is Lieutenant Travis, Major."

The silence was brief but it was pregnant. Un-
consciously Griselda glimpsed over her shoulder for
a hovering Chang Smithery. He alone was missing.

Kew's repetition was distinct. "Lieutenant Walker
Travis of the *Antarctica*."

Major Pembrooke laughed. "Indeed!" His laugh didn't belong to him; it was pleasant, disarming. He seemed to thaw all at once but it was mere external radiance. There was still the mouth, the icy brain beneath the suddenly warm face. "Where is the lieutenant tonight, Mrs. Travis? Could he join us?"

"He didn't come to the island with me. He was on duty."

"A shame." His voice leaked fatherly kindness. It was stark travesty; anyone would have known; even Kathie should have known. The legend of the ravening wolf with careless lamb's wool hung on his haunches was being enacted before their very eyes.

"And your week-end vacation must be enjoyed alone?" She wasn't alone; she had Kew and the trembling Sergei. "I am so anxious to meet Lieutenant Travis. He is the naval radio expert, is he not?"

There was no necessity for Griselda to stiffen, to wish to warn the girl to tell this man nothing, no matter how harmless it seemed. For Kathie wasn't interested. She said, "I guess so."

. The major tried again. "He was a friend of Mannie Martin, wasn't he?"

She brightened at that although she still wasn't interested in Pembrooke. He wasn't handsome and glamorous like Kew. She evidently hadn't heard about the yacht. She said, "Yes, he's Mannie's best friend."

Kathie shouldn't have said that. Mannie Martin was missing. Major Pembrooke wanted to find him. And by now Griselda was certain in her bones that his purpose in finding him wasn't harmless. Nothing that the major did would be without harm.

Kathie was continuing as she had in her stuffy bedroom. But the pink fish wasn't goggling on her tonight. She must have known there was no chance of meeting her husband. "Mannie and Walker have known each other for years—"

Sergei shouldn't have said anything. He hadn't been invited; he was on the outside; he had insinuated himself in some manner upon Kew in order that he might sit at the table, but he should have had an intuition of the necessity for his silence.

He began, "I hear—" but his peep was not audible over the orchestral rhumba, laden trays, and parakeet conversation. He repeated, "I hear—" and a third time with clarinet shrillness, "I hear—"

The major recognized him. "Yes?"

Sergei rubbed his tongue over his lips. He didn't know where to put his eyes. "I hear Mannie has been found." In the silence he made the mistake of letting his eyes meet those of Albert George. They were held fast hideously as by snake-hypnosis.

Kathie's soft words released him from the spell, "Found? Really? Where is he?"

But Sergei offered only anticlimax. "I do not know. They are saying this in Hollywood. At the studio."

Kew explained, "Mr. Vironova directs the Masquers on the air, too, you know. He tells me that the rumor is all over the broadcasting studio."

The major said with his teeth, "I trust it is true. I am very anxious for Mr. Martin to return. It is a matter of marking time for me until he does."

Con broke in rudely, lightly, "He won't return."

Griselda held tightly to the edge of the table. The major's gritty eye was on Con now. "What do you mean, Mr. Satterlee?"

Con didn't tremble as Sergei had. He said blandly, "He can't. He's no Lazarus."

Again there was silence in the midst of sound. And then Kathie's mouth whispered, "Con—is Mannie dead?"

He wasn't rude to her. "He wouldn't have been gone this long otherwise, Kathie."

"You know that?" Pembrooke demanded.

Con actually smiled into the terrible mask. "Sure, I know it. I've known Mannie ever since I've been on the air. And I know he wasn't a guy that'd walk out when he had"—his smile was impudent—"an important deal on."

Kew asked quickly, "You don't really know he's dead, do you, Con?"

Con took a drink. "What do you think?"

"Well, I didn't know him." Kew was evasive again. "I'd met him, that's all. But—what could have happened to him? If he'd been in an accident, it would have been reported long ago. If anything had gone wrong on his way down from Santa Monica, the boat wouldn't have been tied up at the landing. Boats can't tie themselves, Con. And he was alone. The attendants at the Santa Monica Club are certain of that. I can't see it any other way than a disappearance for his own purposes."

Major Pembrooke spoke coldly, "I am afraid that Mr. Satterlee's supposition is superior to yours, Brent. Martin had an appointment with me here at Avalon on the night he disappeared. He was bringing the final and complete plans for our deal. He never arrived. I remained here at the St. Catherine until after one in the morning before returning to *The Falcon*. He sent no message. It wasn't like him."

Was he offering an alibi for the time of the disappearance or murder?

Kathie's eyes were enormous. She shivered, "Oh, don't let's talk about him like this. We don't know that anything happened to him. Walker was with him the night before and he was perfectly well."

Albert George put down his cigar. "You're right,

Mrs. Travis. This sort of conversation is only depressing and sheer guesswork. A dance perhaps?"

He would dance heavily; he was heavy. But Kathie couldn't refuse. The relief at the table was almost startling as he moved away. Sergei's breath came out of his mouth in a rush. He said, "I get me fresh air." He was the color of his cigarette ash as he weaved away.

Con pointed to his receding back. "And when did you gather the little red flag to your heart, Kew?"

Kew's nose wrinkled. "He intruded. God knows how he does it. I'd only just met him in Hollywood but you'd think I owed him money the way he's hung on. Short of punching his nose I couldn't get rid of him."

"What does he want?" Dare asked it lightly.

"God knows."

Con snickered. "Maybe he'd like to take Kathie over."

Dare's voice lifted mockingly, "How did you entice the little princess to Avalon, Kew? You didn't tell me you had a rendezvous."

Kew was on the defense. "I'm not here with Kathie if that's what you are suggesting, Dare. I ran into her on the plane yesterday. That's all." He came around the table, touched Griselda. "Come on, darling. Dance. I don't like your husband or his friends."

He had rescued her from Con and Dare's joint happiness. But it was not that she might enjoy a moment of relaxation. For he asked almost at once, "Has Thusby any more on Shelley Huffaker?"

She almost started at the name. She'd been trying not to remember it tonight. Just as everyone at the table who knew had taken pains not to mention the case. She said, "No."

Even more startling came the next question, "You've been around Hollywood quite a bit. What do you know about Vironova?"

Con was right; Kew wasn't interested in her beauty; he was a newsman pumping. But she made her answer thorough, "Very little, Kew. I worked on one of his productions. He is a crack director, one of Oppy's best. But I just don't like him. I've never cared for the type."

"Intuition or reason?"

"Both. Intuition strong. Reason—I don't like flashy bleached girls who endure anything for a screen test. And I don't like reptilian males who trade screen tests for flashy bleached girls."

His mouth said, "One of those." And then he asked, "You've never heard of him being tied up with Mannie Martin?"

Everything went around a circle and returned neatly to the missing man. She said, "He must have been. Sergei's radio play hour has been a feature for several years now."

"I mean more than that kind of deal." He was a superb dancer.

"I didn't know Mannie Martin. You know Hollywood. I'm one of the set that doesn't go to cafés or premières or even stay home entertaining my hundred most intimate friends in my marble cottage."

Kew interrupted, "Everyone eventually turns up at the Derby."

"The day I go there is the day everyone else stays home. Or I'm at the Vine when they're at the Beverly. In other words, I never know the latest, Kew. A costume designer isn't much more important than a writer."

The music stopped its din. She put her hand on his arm. "You don't mind? I'd like a breath of fresh air." She didn't want to return to the major. She did want to talk with Kew. They walked out on the terrace. The moon was pointing one shimmering finger over the dark waters. She said slowly, "Tell me, why is Mannie Martin's disappearance so important?"

He flared his lighter for their cigarettes. Only men like Kew had handsome cigarette lighters that behaved impeccably. She was apprehensive from his expression that he would evade but he didn't.

"Because Major Pembrooke came west to make a deal with Martin."

She asked again as she had over and over, it seemed, but she kept her voice stifled and looked over his shoulders before speaking. "Who is Major Pembrooke?"

"A British officer—"

She broke in, "I've heard that one."

"There isn't another. He is in this country in the interests of a Pan-Pacific network, jointly held by Britain and us. Monitoring and field stations to be included. It would be important if the war moves to the Far East. Major Pembrooke has been studying our stations throughout the country, their working plans with the major networks."

She asked, "And Mannie Martin?"

"Pembrooke had offered him the management of the new network."

"Why did you come out here, Kew? Was it because Mannie disappeared?"

He shook his head. "I was here before that happened. I came to get a story. I don't like to be scooped, even by governments. I heard about the Pan-Pacific deal in Washington. But I couldn't get a line on it from official sources. I knew Mannie slightly so I thought I'd trek out and he'd give me some dope." He frowned. "He wasn't talkative."

"You saw him?"

"Twice. I lunched with him the day before he disappeared. He said he wasn't ready to give out yet. He said stick around a few days and I'd get the whole story." He shrugged. "I'm still sticking." He leaned across the table. "Con heard from Mannie before he disappeared, didn't he?"

She couldn't say no. She wasn't certain. She shook her head.

Kew asked, "Are you sure? Mannie's copy of the contract is not in his office. I thought he might have sent it to Con for a checkover. He knew Con was close to Garth."

And Kew knew more than he was saying. He had reason for believing that Mannie had communicated with Con. He wasn't merely guessing. Fact was on his mouth.

She said definitely, "No. Con didn't hear from Mannie." Her hands didn't relax. She willed the tremble from her voice. "Why would Mannie want Garth to look over a business contract, Kew?"

He didn't answer but he said, "There isn't a note —not a line—dealing with the Pan-Pacific deal in Mannie's files."

"How do you know that, Kew?" She asked it quietly.

"Pembrooke told me." He looked squarely at her. "I believe that disturbs him more than Mannie's absence. I'm guessing now."

He knew. He was a newspaperman and always they knew; their nostrils recognized the smell of the truth.

Her words were distinct, "You think Con might have them?"

"I think Con might have whatever missing document it is that is worrying the major."

"He hasn't." She could speak with certainty. Con left packing to her. She'd know if there had been contracts, documents, somewhere. He left his papers flung about, not filed as a businessman would.

Kew grasped the certainty. "There are only two answers. Either Mannie gave the stuff to someone or it was stolen from the office. If so, it was a deft job. The secretary swears not a paper clip is out of place."

She seized solution. "Why couldn't Mannie have given the stuff to Walker Travis?"

"He could have," Kew admitted. "Travis reports not." His voice was even. "The fact that the stuff hasn't turned up makes it pretty conclusive that Mannie didn't want it to turn up. It was given in confidence."

"Or stolen."

"Yes." He was thoughtful. "I'd like a look at those contracts and notes."

She asked, just as if she didn't realize he knew Pembrooke too well, "Why don't you try to examine the major's copies? Dare could help you."

He spoke slowly, "I don't trust Dare."

She was silent. She didn't herself but it was startling to hear it said, and by Kew.

He said, "They're coming out now. Nice weather we're having."

Dare called, "You ran out on us," and Con added, "Wife-stealer."

His hand caught Griselda's and she smiled at him. "The ocean's out here, not in that stuffy room."

Kathie was standing beside Kew, looking at him. She slewed her eyes to Griselda in suspicion. Sergei was again at Con's sleeve, almost touching it.

Dare cried, "Major Pembrooke has invited us all to cruise a bit about the island. Isn't that divine?"

Kew didn't move. "Awfully good of you, Major, but I promised Kathie some dancing tonight. It's Rob's farewell at the Casino, her favorite orchestra. Unless she wants to change her mind."

Kathie's enamored look was on Kew. Griselda had a fleeting pang of feeling for the poor little lieutenant on guard on a battleship. His wife said, "I don't care what we do. But I've never been on a yacht."

Sergei, suddenly courageous, squeaked, "Let us all go to Rob's. Yes, we must go dance with Rob. I have promised him personal. Any time we can yacht."

Griselda laughed silently. It was as if to him yachts were a dime a dozen—like blondes. But she had no intention either of getting on that yacht. Her laughter ended in a shiver. For Con announced, "Rob will be at the Ambassador next week. We'll make up a party. Tonight we all sail in the moonlight."

He had his hand on her arm. He must have known it trembled. But he led the way jauntily toward the dock and even Sergei, with drawn face, followed.

2

The Falcon didn't look peaceful lying at anchor. Her lines were too dark and swift; the face at the top of the ladder wore the malicious gravity of a heathen god. He spoke in his own tongue and the major answered in kind before turning to his guests. "You will excuse me a moment." He followed the short white-duck legs.

The lights of Avalon across were not Japanese paper lanterns at an old-fashioned garden party, but they were as evanescent and as far distant. The deck here was as non-sinister as any floating playground. The ducky Oriental navy Dare had mentioned was moving without sound within the lighted salon; its mouse pattering ran all over the ship.

Griselda managed to reach Con's arm for one moment before Dare coiled there again. Under her breath she pleaded, "I don't want to cruise in the moonlight."

He said out of the side of his mouth, "You won't," and to Dare's approaching nearness, "You couldn't find that little guy who mixes the Planter's Punches, could you? I'm thirsty."

Dare said, "But, of course, darling." She went to the door of the salon.

And Griselda heard the tender sputtering away into the night. Sergei stood by the rail watching wishfully. Kathie alone was unreservedly content. Her fingers touched the chromium; her eyes licked the moon-white lounging chairs. She liked yachts. She didn't care who owned them or what he wanted with this group. Kew watched her.

Albert George returned. His mouth was grim. "I'm afraid my invitation was premature. I'd forgotten it was Saturday night. My captain and first mate evidently shared the popular desire to hear this Rob. I have sent for them. Meanwhile—"

"I've ordered drinks, darling," Dare told him.

Con said, "Hope you didn't mind, old man. But my tongue was hanging out for your specials. I sampled them yesterday afternoon when I barged in on Dare."

You didn't barge in on a yacht; you took special steps to get there.

Dare cried, "We had a grand session about old times. I'm sorry you had to be on the mainland, Albert George. You'd have enjoyed it."

Kew spoke flatly. "He'd have been bored stiff." He
walked over to Kathie, slid his palm against her arm.
"Like it?"

"It is wonderful." Her eyes were aglow.

"I'll show you around after a bit, Mrs. Travis," the
major said.

The Planter's Punches arrived. Everyone drank
but Griselda. Maybe she was behaving as absurdly
as Con's eyebrows seemed to point out. But this
wasn't a pleasure visit.

Nor did the pretense of it remain on the surface
for long. There was a second round of drinks. And
the major asked casually, but it wasn't casual, "I believe you mentioned that your husband saw Mannie
Martin the night before he disappeared, Mrs. Travis."

Con took Griselda's second untouched glass. That
made four for him; two up on the others. "Thought
we weren't going to talk about Mannie."

Albert George wasn't pretending now. He was
military. "As a matter of fact, I suggested this re-
treat in order that we might discuss the problem
without the infernal din." He waved his cigar at the
hotel across the waters.

"Let the police find him," said Con. "We're not
detectives."

"The police have not been effective," Pembrooke
said. "Against my better judgment they were not
consulted until too long after the disappearance. I
spoke to the studio officials the morning after Martin
did not keep his appointment with me. I suggested
then that they report to official quarters. They
didn't."

"If I told 'em once, I told 'em—" Con quoted
broadly at Dare. "Let's have another set. What's
your hurry, Major?"

He answered with distinct control. "You should

realize that it is necessary for our governments
jointly to speed the Pan-Pacific network, much as
the Pan-American network which has recently been
inaugurated commercially was arranged. Perhaps you
realize that it is necessary to speed the plans, not
knowing from one day to the next what will occur to
thwart them, or to make such a network of supreme
importance. My hands are tied awaiting Martin's return."

"Why wait for him? Why not forge right along?
Serve him right."

"I need him," Pembrooke admitted brusquely.

"Why?" It was unusual for Kathie to be interested. She doubtless sniffed more kudos for the fam-
ily friend.

"I need him or I need your husband, Mrs. Travis.
I was told in Washington that there were only two
men capable of planning this system." He smiled at
her. "Unfortunately the lieutenant couldn't help
out because of Navy regulations, although Mannie
did confer with him on some technical matters."

Her eyes were wide. "I never know anything
about Walker's business. He never tells me. He
knows I'm not interested."

"Just like my wife," Con interjected loudly.

Pembrooke ignored him. "You wouldn't know
then, Mrs. Travis, if your husband kept a memo-
randum of the work he and Martin did?"

She shook her head helplessly.

"You can see why my hands are tied. I don't have
the data. We believe that Martin was bringing it to
me when he disappeared. It isn't among his papers.
There is nothing I can do until he is found. That,
Mr. Satterlee"—he spoke with ironic deference to
Con—"is why I asked the question of Mrs. Travis.
I feel that there may be some piece of information

that has escaped the police in their broader search, something that might lead us to Martin. Do you know, Mrs. Travis, if Martin told your husband that Sunday night anything about his plans for the next day?"

The wind stirred her dusky hair and she was beautiful. And stupid. "He was going to see Walker the next day. He was going to meet him at seven-thirty at Navy Landing. But he telephoned before dinner and postponed it until later. And then he didn't show up at all."

Griselda was watching her. It might all be lies, even as she had lied about Shelley Huffaker. She had spoken then with that same sweet quietness. Mannie had liked women. Kathie liked men. She was impressed by the radio executive's belongings. She might have had a private friendship with the man, know much more than she was saying. But her heart was so obviously on her sleeve for Kew. Another man didn't belong. And even if she had played a game with Mannie, there was no reason for her lying now. Unless . . . Griselda winced. Unless Walker Travis knew what had happened to his friend. Was Walker as hard under his rabbit front as Kathie under her seeming softness? Could he have wanted to supplant Mannie in this new deal, gather to himself some of the things his wife clutched after? A man could resign from the Navy. If Mannie didn't reappear, Pembrooke would move mountains to retain Walker's services.

The major had turned to Con. "Mannie didn't send you his notes, did he?"

Con roared happily. "For God's sake, why would he send them to me? I'm a commentator not a technician. I wouldn't know a kilowatt from an antenna."

Pembrooke wasn't amused. "He did write to you.

His secretary mailed the letter. But it wasn't dictated to her."

"Oh, that." Con beckoned the attending boy. "That was personal."

"You did receive a letter?"

"Yeah. I didn't get it till after Mannie'd flown the coop. He sent it to New York and then it had to travel way back out again to Hollywood. If he'd known I was in town he could have called me up and saved postage."

"Do you have the letter with you?"

Griselda waited tensely.

"Never keep letters." Major Pembrooke couldn't know that Con's suits resembled a newspaper wastebasket until cleaners' day. And that there hadn't been need for cleaners' day these past weeks. Con must still have the letter. Was that what the intruder had been after Wednesday night? She looked at him. He was leaning back in his chair content in the acceptance of his lie.

"Do you remember what he had to say?"

Con sat straight and scowled. "I told you it was personal."

"Con." Dare laid her hand on his arm. "Don't be that way. Can't you see Albert George is just trying to get any slight lead as to where Mannie might be found? Any small hint—"

Con waved his glass in apology. "Sorry, old boy. I don't remember anything about it. Something about a fishing trip or a fish or something. Nothing important. Nothing about taking a powder." He held Dare's hand, rubbing his thumb over the smooth black-red polish of her nails. He spoke as if the major had vanished. "Anyhow, darling, Albert George is asking the wrong questions of the wrong guy. Sergei's already told us that Mannie is found."

Sergei shrilled nervously, "I told you I do not know. It is the rumor I hear." His hands deprecated it. "That Hollywood, so much always the rumor, never what has happened."

Kew interjected gently, "Perhaps if they find the murderer of Shelley Huffaker, they'll have a lead on Mannie. Kathie met this Huffaker girl through him. It is quite probable that she knew Martin too well."

Kathie shook her head softly. "I told you she wasn't his girl, Kew. She wasn't his type at all. She was common."

"I know, darling." He turned back to the others. "But she might have run into some information about this deal which someone wanted to suppress."

Dare broke in, "Your assumption, Kew, is that Mannie was suppressed to keep the deal from going through? At any rate at this time?"

"What else?"

Pembrooke admitted, "It is that which I fear. It is for that reason that I pleaded with his associates to call in the police at once."

Con passed his glass. "You can relax, old boy. Cap'n Thusby is on the job now. He'll find Mannie for you."

The major eyed him. "You said earlier that Mannie would not return."

"He won't. But Thusby'll turn up the cadaver. Probably have all the papers you want in the pocket. And you can make new plans."

Griselda wondered—did the major really want Mannie found? The man was worried about something; that couldn't be an act; it sweated from every pore. It was these papers, written information of some sort. Did he believe, as Kew did, that they had been turned over to Con or to Travis? Was that why they were here on *The Falcon?* Kathie in her hus-

band's place because Walker was regulated by the
Navy? Was the major that determined to regain this
information? Griselda sat tensely on guard waiting
for the return whir of the tender and for the throb
of the engines below deck.

Kathie protested, "I don't want to hear about bad
things. Please let's not talk about it." She raised her
lashes. "You said you'd show me around, Major Pembrooke."

"Delighted." His cigar circled the semi-dark.
"Would the rest of you care to come?"

He'd rather they wouldn't but each one accepted,
even Sergei. Griselda alone remained on the deck,
the one small hand against the dike. She tried to
think about what had happened, what was happening. Somehow, somewhere, Shelley Huffaker's death
must be a part of Mannie's disappearance. If it were
entirely unconnected, a happening that had nothing
to do with the Pan-Pacific network, the police might
involve Con merely to solve the murder. They
couldn't do it. Even if the pieces weren't ready to
fit as yet, Shelley must be tied in with the trouble.
If only she had been Mannie's girl friend, if only
there were a jealous man or woman to have fired the
gun, if only the police had someone but Con on
whom to pin suspicion.

She thought she heard the hiss of a step behind
her and she half rose out of her chair, looked quickly.
There wasn't even a white-ducked figure slippering
away. She was quite alone on the deck. The others
had been gone too long. She came to her feet, moved
silently to the rail, but there was no small boat approaching. Hesitantly she walked to the door of the
salon, even more hesitantly stepped inside. She knew
Oriental authenticity and beauty. The room was
magnificent. And it was empty. Its silence was as for-

bidding as the ancient greening bronze Buddha hovering maliciously in the far shadowy corner. She stepped quickly to the stairs that led below; her black satin heels were reassuring staccato striking through the gemmed color of the rug.

She hesitated there at the top of the red-carpeted staircase. Her hand was colder than the cold brass balustrade. There was no sound from below. She moved silently now, step by step, waiting for sound at each small descent, hearing none. The corridor below was as soundless. It was as if she were alone on the ship. She didn't know which way to move; she went ahead, toward the dim light at the far end, past one narrow closed door, and another, and another. She might have been a wraith; there was as little motion and sound in her progress.

And then she heard voices and she moved eagerly, alive again, to the door from which they issued. She had been wrong. It was one voice and she backed away from its menace. Her hand faltered against the near door. She could hear too clearly those uncompromising words. If they had been spoken in anger, they would not have been so fearful. But they were as unaccented, as level in cadence, as if they issued from a mechanized transcription.

"You will stay out of this if you are wise. I do not wish any assistance. I prefer and intend to handle matters unaided."

She couldn't distinguish the murmuring response but the major's voice came again in dreadful clarity.

"This girl's death is nothing to me. I had no acquaintance with her."

Again the indistinguishable murmur and again audible words, more flintlike than before.

"I am slow to anger as you should realize. But there comes a time when any man's temper is strained.

I warn you again, stay out of my affairs. I will attend to all who interfere with me as soon as my business here is completed."

She heard movement and she pressed against the door where she stood, her fingers automatically fumbling the knob. It gave and she stepped backward, noiselessly, even as the other door was opened. She closed herself into the darkness and waited without breathing. She heard steps moving up the corridor; whether one or more, she didn't know. She waited, not daring to stir. It seemed as if she stood there for endless time waiting courage to venture out again, fearing lest she come face to face with that cold insensate voice.

She opened the door a lean, noiseless crack. The corridor was empty as before. She couldn't run up the stairs; she was so weak she clamped the handrail, lifted weighted slippers. There wasn't reason for this reaction; because a man's voice held the threat of death didn't mean she was in danger.

The salon was empty as before. She rushed to the doorway, stepped on deck. Each person was in place; she might have dreamed her vigil there, her journey into the dim world belowstairs. Each one looked at her with more than idle curiosity. And she heard at that moment the sputter of the returning boat.

She broke restraint. She ran to Con and he jumped to meet her. She heard the hysteria in her voice, "I want to go back to the hotel. I have to go back. I don't feel well. You've got to take me back."

His hands were strong, his voice steady, "My wife's evidently not feeling well, Major. Could you set us ashore?"

She couldn't see Pembrooke's face, only the color of the tip of his cigar. He said, "If you wish, certainly. Or Mrs. Satterlee is welcome to rest here. There are any number of guest cabins."

She whispered in horror, "No. No," and felt the reassuring pressure of Con's fingers.

"In fact, I was going to suggest after this late start that we continue our cruise through tomorrow. I can put everyone up."

Con said, "Awfully good of you, but I think we'd better shove off. Griselda's always been subject to seasickness." She welcomed the falsehood. "Even lying at anchor sometimes does this to her. So if we may—"

The brown sailor had come up the ladder. Griselda held tight to Con. But there was no captain or mate following. The major's face was cruel as he heard what was failure.

Descending after Con into the small boat below, Griselda didn't look at the black pit of the waters. She closed her eyes to the ruthless black swell as they sputtered toward St. Catherine's Landing. She didn't speak until they were in the hotel room again and Con staring down at her.

"For God's sake, what happened to you?"

She shook her head. She couldn't tell of the fear that had seized her there on the boat. She finally said lamely, "I didn't want to cruise on his yacht."

Con frowned. "I told you we wouldn't. I wouldn't have taken you on board if I hadn't known the captain was enjoying a night off."

"How could you know that?"

His mouth quirked. "I'm prescient. Did you ever hear of a Mickey Finn, mixed by a specialist?" He said, "It was safe enough anyway. Nothing's going to happen until those papers are found." He asked again firmly, "But what set you off?"

Her eyes were wide. "Con. You weren't the one
the major was talking to? In his cabin?"

He demanded softly, "What did you hear?"

Haltingly she told it. "You weren't the one? He
wasn't threatening you, was he, Con?" Was it Sergei?
Kew? A woman?

He reassured her. "Dare didn't let me out of her
sight. The sightseeing tour must have been on the
bridge when you went below. Just missed you. You
shouldn't prowl in strange places, baby." He kissed
her. "Might be dangerous sometimes."

She insisted frantically. "Was it you, Con?"

"I told you."

But he hadn't. Dare could have been in that room,
too.

She lay shivering later, alone again in bed, Con
gone, whether to yacht again or dance or spy, she
didn't know. All he'd said was, "I'm going out for a
little. Be back in one hour." She knew Con's one
hours and she went to bed. But she didn't woo sleep.
She didn't know of what dreams might be made.
They might be of the face of Major Albert George
Pembrooke.

3

They were wandering the bronzed street fronting
on the sea. She cried, "Con, look, there's the peanut
boy!"

Con mumbled, "Who?" without paying any attention. He was decorating himself with paper leis, rose
and white and purple, from one of the sidewalk
shops.

"Captain Thusby's son. The one who ate peanuts
in his hat." It was Vinnie Thusby. It looked as if he
were talking to Chang. Surely the queer Mr. Smithery

wasn't giving Con away again. He couldn't. There was nothing harmful to say.

Con turned then. "Where?"

But the gangly police officer had vanished, his companion with him. "He was there, right over there, by that hamburger stand."

"I don't see him." He replaced the leis in the open basket, took her arm. His question was unexpected, "Want to ride or walk back to the hotel?"

She looked searchingly at him but his face was without expression. "Walk." It wasn't far and the path followed the water. "Why do you suppose he'd be here?"

"Everyone comes here. Just like going to the circus." He was moving in great strides; she had to skip to keep up with him. "Let's have lunch in our room and take a nap before the boat sails."

Lovely. But she didn't say it. It only sounded lovely. It wouldn't work that way. She knew the formula. Wait until she was safely disrobed before saying, "I'm going out. Be back in one hour."

She didn't believe it when they did lunch together, alone, with laze on the bed after; no thrusting nose of outsiders, not even the flags of *The Falcon* decorating the sea view from their opened window. No interruptions, no excuses to get away. Con and she together at long last. She couldn't spoil it by demand for information that she knew he must hold. She even stilled the whisper that he might be avoiding young Thusby, might be afraid the boy had come for him. There was no earthly reason for the suggestion. Captain Thusby didn't want Con. He'd said not to leave Long Beach but that was merely for convenience if there was need of further questioning.

They took the hotel bus to Avalon Landing in the late afternoon. There was no familiar face among

the hundreds embarking for the mainland. Rob's
brass and woodwinds stood on the upper deck playing their farewell to Avalon. But no sweet sadness
welled in Griselda for the departure. No desire to
fling flower garlands to tie her to this island. Her
wish was that leaving it might mean leaving forever
the major's scarcely hidden brutality, Sergei's shrill
insistence. She didn't expect to be that fortunate.
For Kew and Kathie would return to Long Beach,
and Dare, and where these went, Pembrooke would
appear. Fatalistically she knew that.

She followed Con to the upper deck wishing there
were more than this small aisle of sea separating
Catalina from the coast. He was gulping the wind as
if it were one of his drinks, his face grinning from
eyes to chin.

"This is stuff!" he shouted. "This is what we
should have for a real honeymoon. Life on the ocean
wave, tra la."

All the near passengers also were shouting above
the wind; no one paid any attention to any one indi-
vidual. Yet again this was no place to ask questions
about the waning week end. Nor would he answer.
He was still believing that by not discussing this affair
with her, he might discourage danger from touching
her. She wouldn't think about it. He was right; this
was beauty, like being a little girl again, sailing to a
mythically serene England, a summer-gay France.
"Never no more."

He must have sensed her refrain for he said with
a scowl, "It isn't fair that the delusions of grandeur
of one small Austrian should have spoiled the whole
world for us."

She caught his hand tightly, shouted too, "Never
mind, darling. We've still the Hoboken ferry."

But she shivered. With the war so near, you didn't

know. She said no more; tried to be gay with him. If he didn't know it was sham, he wasn't very bright. As a matter of fact, she knew he wasn't bright. Had he been, he'd get out of this business now, before it was too late.

There was the usual gangplank crush as the boat was slurred to the Wilmington dock. And at the foot of the gangplank was Captain Thusby, easing his peg leg, happy as if he belonged to the ship. It was then Con said softly, "If I should have to take a little jaunt, darling, you'd hold the fort, wouldn't you?"

She turned her eyes up to him in sudden fear and caught his arm.

He laughed at her. "My God, angel, don't look as if the sky were about to bean you." But there was dead seriousness in his voice under the laugh as they approached the waiting captain. "You'll keep the candle burning in the window, won't you?"

She held his coatsleeve closely as if she might thus keep him with her. But she asked lightly, "You don't mean our little shack in Long Beach, do you, darling?"

"Right the first time."

They had reached the foot of the gangplank. Captain Thusby lifted his cap to her.

"Evening, ma'am. Evening, Satterlee. Heard you'd gone to Santa Catalina."

Con pretended surprise. He said, "How are you, Cap'n? Didn't expect to see you here. Yeah, we're regular tourists."

They were in a little huddle of three. She held on to Con's arm, too tightly, waiting, waiting for explanation, for movement, for something to still the unease of Thusby's presence and Thusby's pointed bluish eyes.

Con said, "What are you doing over here? Off your fishing ground, isn't it?"

"Not exactly, Satterlee." His head hung. "Fact is I was sort of waiting for you."

"You wanted to see me?" Con was still acting surprised.

The captain rubbed his neck. But his eyes were steady. "Fact is I'm here to place you under arrest." He spoke apologetically.

"Oh no!" Griselda whispered it, then she cried, "Oh, no!" Her body pressed close to Con's, clutching him.

His face was sober now. For once he had no answer.

Thusby said, "I'm sorry, ma'am." He fumbled at his coat. "I've got a warrant if you—"

Con said quickly, "That's all right. I know it's in order."

Griselda held more tightly. "But why—what—"

"It's that girl's murder," Thusby began.

"But Con didn't do it. He didn't even know her. He'd never seen her before."

Con loosed her gently but with a steady firmness. "Don't bother, Griselda. It'll be all right. Don't worry about me. It's all right." His eyes were steady on her. He turned to Thusby. "I suppose you want me to go over with you?"

"Uh-huh." He looked around. "You can drive me if you don't mind. Don't know how myself. Too old to learn."

"And Griselda?"

He continued looking around. "Vinnie's here somewheres. He can take your wife over." He raised a forefinger, shouted, "Vinnie!" The long, tall son came to them. He was as abashed as the chief.

"Vinnie, you'll see Mrs. Satterlee home, won't you?"

Griselda was angry, angry at the hopelessness of it, at Con standing like a sheep doing nothing, saying nothing, not even mentioning Garth. "I don't need anyone with me." Her scorn mounted. "I don't need a policeman."

Vinnie turned the color of a rambler rose. Thusby looked at the lining of his cap.

Con spoke quietly but there was command in his voice, "Griselda, Vinnie will help you back to Long Beach." He kissed her swiftly, said, "I'll get in touch with you. Here's the key," and was gone before she could do more than thrust out a helpless restraining hand.

She watched him disappear, tempering his long stride to the pegging Thusby. They were out of sight before she turned on Vinnie. He squirmed, finally stammered, "Want some gum?" thrusting out a package. It was Blackjack.

She said shortly, frostily, "I don't chew gum."

He put the package back as if hurt. He spoke with humility. "If you'll give me your checks, I'll get the bags."

She ignored him, walked to the stand, and passed the checks across. He was behind her. Without speaking to him she let him carry the bags through the arch into the terminal garage. The rickety car stood waiting as cockily as if it were a Daimler. Con must have chosen the car for its satisfied mutt air; he had that kind of humor. Con could do things like that, imbue a battered jalopy with spirit and pride; he could do anything he wanted to. But he'd gone off with Captain Thusby as if he were a criminal. Her fury rose. He'd gone off and left her in police custody as if she were a gangster's moll. Still wordless she climbed in, allowing Vinnie to take the wheel.

They had Con as often they had the wrong man.

But she wouldn't let them continue in their stupid blindness. She'd fight like an alley cat until they admitted their blunder. And although she knew this boy was but the smallest bolt in the machine, she struck her first blow at him. "What motive have you given Con for this? Has your father decided why he should kill a girl whose name he didn't even know? Or does he think perhaps that my husband is a homicidal maniac?"

Vinnie looked shocked. "Oh, no, Ma'am," he stressed. "He wouldn't think that of Mr. Satterlee. He likes Mr. Satterlee."

She held her lips tight-pressed to keep from laughing. If she laughed, she might cry. He likes Mr. Satterlee. Doubtless he would give him all the freedom of a cell, all the privileges a prison. She said, "He's making a ridiculous mistake. And it serves him right. He'll be the joke of the country arresting Con Satterlee in a murder case. Of course, he can't hold him a minute. As soon as Barjon Garth hears—"

Vinnie mumbled. He couldn't be saying what he seemed to be saying. Sharply she asked him to repeat and he did.

"It was Barjon Garth told my father to arrest Mr. Satterlee."

She smelled the acrid oil from the beach wells before she could see the lights of Long Beach. And she tried to understand. Vinnie had said it twice, haltingly, it was true, but unmistakably he had said it.

Now it was she who mumbled, "He couldn't have. He's away fishing. He couldn't know about the murder much less tell your father to arrest Con."

The boy said, "He sent a wireless. I saw it. Signed Barjon Garth."

Garth had sold Con out. That eliminated asking his assistance. There was only Kew left to help her. It wasn't that she trusted Kew implicitly; there was too much unexplained for that. But Kew was after a story; he would be curious, and he wasn't afraid to ask questions of Major Pembrooke. There could be others who wished Con removed from activity, but there could be none with less conscience than the major. And it seemed as if Dare were right when she said that Shelley's death was incidental, no more than a move to strike at Con.

She would call Kew in the morning. No matter what business of his own he was up to, he would want to help Con. They might be personal rivals but they had shared too much for one to default now.

They drove the bright way of Ocean Boulevard where vacationists moved toward the Pike or the movies in vacuous ignorance of what was happening before their eyes. Perhaps they discussed the Bixby Park murder as they would a story, not as something real. On up Ocean, past the dark menace of Bixby Park, winding through Belmont and beachwards to the cottage.

Vinnie opened the door for her. "I'll see you in." He took the bags in his big knuckly hands. She marched ahead up the steps to the narrow porch. She said, "You needn't," but actually she was grateful that he waited until she lighted the living room. Returning alone after a week end away to an empty cottage, one that anyone could open, was not reassuring.

He set down the bags and stood awkwardly; he seemed hesitant about leaving. At last he said, "G'night," moving slowly out the door. But he hesitated again. "If you should need us—night or day, ma'am—you just call. Any time at all. Don't you mind. Neither the Cap'n nor me is a sound sleeper."

Mechanically she locked the door after him. He wasn't a reassurance. She'd wager that he knew as little about things as she. She laughed, picturing the bewilderment on his scrawny face had she quizzed him on the ramifications of Pan-Pacific. But the sound was eerie in the empty room. She turned on the radio in futile reach for companionship. She didn't like the hollow of the cottage without voices in it, the creaking of the wind against the walls, the unending swish-unswish of the waves against the rocks. Fortunately it was music that sang from the tiny loudspeaker; she didn't want the news now. She took her own bag and opened the bedroom door.

She couldn't help the little scream that came from her throat. She couldn't act; she simply stood there terrified. She hadn't wondered why the door was closed; she hadn't consciously realized that it shouldn't be that way, that she and Con never closed connecting doors. Her hand ached on the handle of the grip but she didn't set it down.

Alexander Smithery, Chang or Buck, didn't speak either. He stood motionless facing her. Had he moved an inch the screaming she was holding in control would have been unleashed. But he was wise, or else he too didn't know what to do.

She finally whispered, "What are you doing here? What do you want?"

He relaxed then. He spoke just as normally as if he were in the Bamboo Bar waiting on tables, "Sorry I startled you, Mrs. Satterlee. Con asked me to pack some of his things and bring them down to him."

She didn't believe him. Con couldn't have seen him after the arrest. But she set down her bag. He did have one of Con's in the middle of the floor and he had been taking things from the bureau drawers.

He continued, "I had hoped to be away before you got home but I wasn't able. Some of the things he wants are in that bag there."

She said stupidly, "Not this one. The one in the other room." She stood aside like an automaton while he went past, brought Con's grip into the bedroom. She stood watching while he opened it, transferred razor, toothbrush, and daily necessities.

Although it was obvious that he knew for what he had been sent just as if the list were in his hands, she still wondered at the professed innocence of his presence. Suspicion heightened. And she asked, "Why didn't you come out when Vinnie Thusby was here?"

He said, "I didn't know who was coming in with you." He almost grinned, a simian grin. "But I wouldn't have wanted him to know. Con didn't want anyone to know I'd been here."

She didn't believe a word he said but she couldn't tell his lies as she could those of young Thusby. She started nervously at the sharp sound of the clasps made fast, and trembled just a little as he straightened up, lifted the bag. She stepped further aside.

He said, "You won't tell *anyone* I've been here."

She was afraid of him, even of his apparent respectful demeanor.

"Con wouldn't like it if you did."

She assured him with quick breath. "No, I wouldn't tell anyone."

She stood in the doorway while he walked across the living room. At the door he said, "Good night, Mrs. Satterlee. I'm sorry to have troubled you." His eyes met hers with no touch of servitude. "If there's anything at all I can do for you while Con is away, don't you hesitate to call on me. You can reach me through the Bamboo Bar any time."

She waited until he was gone before moving to lock the door. Her fingers remained on the cold of the key. She had been right in her previous assumption. A bent hairpin would open any door in the rickety cottage. She had neglected to ask Chang how he had entered. It wasn't by means of the house key; Con had given that to her; that was now moist against her fingers.

She hadn't removed her hat or her gloves as yet. She was undecided; she could go to a hotel. Why had Vinnie and Chang both thought it necessary to offer assistance to her? She pulled off one glove, then quickly the other. Con had told her to stay here; he had made a point of it before he was arrested. He wouldn't have asked it if it meant danger in any way. She proceeded into the bedroom, ignoring the creaking of the floor at every step, flung her hat on the bureau.

She stared at it where it lay, half-shrouding a revolver there on the yellow-white of the scarf. She touched the weapon gingerly, then grasped it. She wouldn't leave now, not even if fish-eyed Albert George Pembrooke came proffering assistance. There was not the slightest reason why she should. She could protect herself.

She wondered what mention of the network would have done to Chang's composure. Not a thing. He probably would have afforded an even more thorough and plausible explanation of its necessity than the British major.

The program changed before she could return to the radio. The inevitable news broadcast. And she heard with stark clarity the commentator announce, "Con Satterlee, well-known New York air reporter, was taken into custody tonight by Captain Charles Thusby, chief of the Long Beach police, for questioning in the Bixby Park murder—" She almost ran to silence the machine. Her uneasiness at being here alone was momentarily gone in her unmitigated fury at the stupidity of this business of thinking Con was involved. Con had never fired so much as a BB gun in his thirty-plus years. And she would prove it. She and Kew. Kew would obtain the information necessary to show up the Long Beach police for the utter fools they were, and Barjon Garth for the Judas into which he had degenerated.

The cottage resumed its rustling with the radio stilled. She switched the radio on again, found music, not words. She finished undressing with the revolver at hand, returned to the living room with the feel of comfortable metal on her palm. She blocked the front door with the one overstuffed chair, established herself in the comfortless cane-bottom rocker. Magazine and the dial, the pressure of steel in her hand, would keep her eyes open. She wouldn't sleep this night; not with the broadcasters announcing to the continent that she was alone, presumedly unguarded.

KEW said, "I don't understand it."

He was pacing. He certainly didn't understand. He behaved as if this were plainly a personal insult to his intelligence. He'd come rushing over breakfastless, although fully and well dressed, at her call. His eyebrows hadn't released that frown of puzzlement since he'd entered.

"If you only knew, Griselda, it doesn't make sense. It simply doesn't add."

She was almost amused. "Don't you think I know that?"

His eyes saw her then, her cinnamon flannel skirt, her brass-colored military coat. He didn't know about the crick in her back from sleeping all night in that rigid excuse for a chair. Her eyes must have closed before she'd read a paragraph.

"Of course, of course. Yes, of course," he said. But he wasn't thinking of what he said. His mind was miles away. He did know more than she, and knowing more, he was steeped in certainty that Con should not have been arrested. She saw that in the scowl, in the incessant pacing, in the preoccupation with his own knowledge.

She spread her fingers on the couch beside her. "Sit down, Kew. I want to say some things. And I want you to hear them."

He came out of his shock this time; he even tried to smile at her but his linked eyebrows defeated that. "I'm sorry, Griselda. But you don't know how impossible this is. You do, yes—but you don't know." He stressed it and then saw he had been afar again. This time he did smile at her. "I'll listen." He seated himself, carefully tending the creases of his olive-drab gabardine slacks.

"Really listen." She smiled back. "Please."

"I will," he apologized. "I'm lucid now. See?" He projected his hand, grinned. "Not a quiver. Except for slight coffee-nerves. Forge right ahead, Griselda. When did all this happen? We flew back about two this morning with no news."

"You and Kathie?" ·

"And Dare and Albert George. Special job. Major Pembrooke's gift to the laboring class." He stopped to light a cigarette. Something was awry in what he had said. "You can judge what a shock it was to have

you wake me to the fact that Con—Con of all people
—was arrested."

"That's just it." She seized upon it. "Con of all
people. You know he had nothing to do with it, and
I know it, but those disgusting Thusbys think he's
involved. And Garth."

"What about Garth?" he asked quickly.

"I didn't tell you that?" She was surprised that she
hadn't poured out the X head's perfidy. But Kew had
cut her off the minute, "Con's been arrested," was off
her tongue. She said now, "Thusby, the young one,
claims his father had a wireless from Garth authoriz-
ing it or something."

Kew said, "That's impossible." The lines about his
mouth betrayed bewilderment.

"That's just it. It is impossible. Garth is on a fishing trip. He couldn't possibly have heard."

"By radio?"

"But he couldn't know Con was involved. That
hadn't been broadcast. His name wasn't even mentioned in the papers."

He decided, "There's only one explanation. Thusby
wirelessed Garth."

"Kew, you can find out these things," she said.
"That's why I'm asking you to help me to get Con
out of this."

"You think he needs help?"

"But certainly he does." She was impatient to the
point of irritation. "What makes you think he doesn't
need help? He's in jail, isn't he?"

Kew said, "They can't keep him. Picked up for
questioning, the papers say." He'd brought them;
they lay on the table. "Con can talk his way out."

"He'd told them everything he knew about it."
That wasn't quite true but he had told them as much
as was needful. "Evidently they don't believe him or

why should they arrest him? Don't you see, Kew, it's worse than it seems, far worse. They've questioned him; they knew he was available here at any time, yet despite all that Thusby went to the effort of going to Wilmington to make the arrest."

"He did?"

"Arrested him as we came down the gangplank." Just as if he were a common criminal trying to escape. She was furious again.

Kew asked soberly, "What do they have on him?"

She made flat statement, "Nothing!"

He smiled with tolerance. "Darling, what do they think they have? Or do you know?"

She said, "I'm sorry. I'll try not to bite you. Yes, I asked Vinnie, young Thusby. He drove me home from Wilmington. Con went with the captain as if he were a Christian slave." She took a breath. "They have him with her that night. You know about that. And they have his fingerprints all over the gun."

Kew whistled and he looked grave.

She said angrily, "Of course, his fingerprints were on the gun. He took it away from her and unloaded it. He gave it back to her there on Junipero when he let her out. He was home with me hours before she was killed." But she broke off weakly. She couldn't mention that Con had gone out again. He had suppressed that in his version to Kew. It had been deliberate suppression. "He was home at midnight. I noticed the time because I'd been asleep and he woke me to tell me about it. Kew, how long would there be blood? It was one-thirty when she was found. He has an alibi, hasn't he?"

Kew said, "I don't know. The blood would be something to look into, I should think. That and the shells. If he unloaded the gun, she must have gone somewhere and reloaded it. She must have had more ammunition if the same gun killed her. She could hardly buy any at that hour."

"That's what Con thought," she admitted. She put her hand on his arm. "You will help me, won't you, Kew?" She had to know that before going on.

He took her hand firmly. "Yes. I'll do anything that it is possible for me to do."

They shook hands as if making a solemn pact. That much was gained. Now she could breathe again.

He too seemed relieved now that they were in covenant. "What do you have up your sleeve?"

She spoke eagerly, "You're a newspaperman. You can go places where I can't and ask questions that I can't. With your news sense you'll know if the answers are right or wrong."

"Any idea where to start?"

She was definite. "I certainly have."

He turned to her with new interest.

"Shelley Huffaker wasn't just going to kill herself that night. She was going to kill someone else too. She told Con that. She was going to 'blow' herself out but she wasn't 'going alone.' That someone else must be the murderer. We must find out who that someone was."

"But how?"

She faltered. Con had asked her to know nothing, to say nothing, to be beautiful and dumb. Yet his arrest had changed that status. She couldn't be the simple young thing he had suggested when he was being framed on a murder charge. And she wouldn't speculate to anyone else, but to Kew she must. Unless they talked it over from every standpoint they wouldn't know how to proceed. Her words came haltingly, "I don't know exactly, Kew. But we've hints to go on. We know she was the kind who'd step on plenty of toes getting where she was. That might be a motive. Or she may have been threatened. We have Dare who knew her in New York, and we have Hollywood which simply dotes on spilling the gore when it won't kick back. It should be that easy."

He stated what she was leading up to, "But maybe it's tied up with the Pan-Pacific deal."

Her eyes were wide and blurred on the white patch the newspapers made there on the scarred table. "That's what I'm afraid of."

He spoke slowly, "If that is it, there'll be no emotional aspect to the murder. It will be more difficult to trace down someone acting for an organization."

"But not impossible, Kew. Not if we could find out if she did evince any interest in the Pan-Pacific plan. We know she hung around the broadcasting studio. She might have heard rumors. Why stay with Dare? She hadn't seen her in years. Maybe she knew Dare was a friend of Major Pembrooke's." She didn't like saying that out loud. She shivered as she spoke, as if that man were listening or had sent some henchman to listen and report.

"Yes, she might have been a spy. We don't know these days who is in the Fifth Column; they don't sport badges." His face was squared with serious thought. "I've got to ask you a couple of things, Griselda. Off the record, of course. Things I should know before I start out."

She nodded gravely.

"Did Con come here to act for Barjon Garth?"

He had never said so actually; even to Kew she mustn't speculate on that. "I don't know."

"Truth?"

"Yes, Kew." She explained. "We came to California for our honeymoon. It wasn't my choice, or his, but I had a picture to finish." She realized suddenly what had bothered her about Kew's story of his chartered-plane trip. He hadn't included Sergei in the passenger list. "When I finished it we were going to Malibu. And then Con decided we'd do Long Beach instead. I didn't like the idea but you know Con when he makes up his mind. To Long Beach we came."

Kew said, "Garth was here."

She hadn't known he would be. She hadn't suspected that was why they came. "Yes. I didn't see him. Con was out with him a few times, doing the bars presumably."

Kew said, "Garth came out here for two purposes. One to look into the foreign agents who are digging in. He has to get something on them, even if it's only a misdemeanor, before he can step in and act. Times are too touchy to risk an incident. The other purpose, to find out why Mannie Martin disappeared. Con has worked with Garth before. As soon as I knew you two were here, that's what I thought his reason was for coming. If he's with Garth in trying to find Mannie, and if an unfriendly country is responsible for the disappearance, it might be possible that they have put the frame on him." Kew began to stride the worn carpet again. "But it doesn't add having Garth against him."

She knew one thing, knew it with cold terror stifling her heart. If he had been working with the X and had made a mistake, the organization could and would repudiate him. She almost cried out. But he couldn't, not in a billion light-years, be guilty of murder.

Kew stopped abruptly. "Do you think we should get a lawyer for Con?" He laughed then. "I'm going too far now. You're so deadly serious about this, Griselda, that I'm thinking in terms of a murder defense already. After all, Con isn't arrested for murder; he's just being questioned."

"Yes. That's all."

He frowned. "But I would like to know what was in that letter from Mannie. You didn't see it?"

She said truly, "I didn't know he'd had such a letter, Kew." There had been so much to think about, she'd forgotten to look for the letter. But she wouldn't mention Con's pocket-habits to Kew, not until she had first read what Mannie had to say. She didn't trust Kew that blindly. The message must have some import. Too many did not dismiss it as Con had.

His frown went deeper. "If he only hadn't thrown it away—" He erased the frown, coming to her. "I'll run along. We might make dinner tonight. And I'll get busy and have something to report."

She went with him to the door. "You don't know what a load off my mind it is to have your assistance. Kew."

He smiled down at her. "I'd always help you, Griselda." And then he grinned. "I might let that no-account husband of yours rot in jail but I'd never turn you down."

She laughed with him. And she remembered again the omission. "Kew, you didn't mention Vironova on your return trip. Wasn't he with you?"

"Thank God, no." He was hearty. "He wasn't hanging around Sunday. Is he included on your list of suspects?"

She shook her head, drew out the "N-n-n-o. Only I don't understand why he was clinging. Or just who he was trying to hang on to."

Kew said, "My own hunch is that he was just being himself, and trying to get in with the most important party."

She agreed, "Yes," but the explanation didn't satisfy her. After Kew was out of sight she stood looking at the sails winging on the bay, and wondering. Sergei

had used Kew and Kathie for a wedge at dinner but
after he was installed he hadn't been comfortable at
being in the group. He had been nervous; definitely
he'd been afraid of their host. His self-esteem had
oozed away so thoroughly that he was nothing but a
beret and a fluty voice. Still he had hung on. He had
turned down the invitation to the yacht, but without
urging had changed his mind and accompanied the
others. His purpose hadn't been to cruise the Avalon
coast. What had it been? Was he a spy; was he attempting to sabotage the proposed network? He
couldn't be. He was one of the truly high-priced directors of Hollywood, with an assured place, for there
was a touch of genius in the unpleasant little Russian.
There would be no reason for him to threaten what
he had by the crudities of spy-work. There must be
some other purpose for his leeching to the party.

Suddenly she saw it. Sergei Vironova. His cheap
blondes. Hollywood. Shelley Huffaker. What Dare
had told Con. The girl had looked for a golden bed.
She had found it. With Sergei it would be of solid
gold with minks thrown over it. Steady employment.
Sergei hadn't been trying to insert himself into a
radio circle. He was watching those definitely connected with the Huffaker girl. Dare, Con, Kathie,
herself by reason of being Con's wife. And Albert
George Pembrooke?

It explained Sergei's persistence. If he had killed
Shelley, he was trying to find out what they knew.
If he hadn't killed her, he was looking for the one
who had. Griselda was going on the assumption that
Shelley Huffaker had been installed as Sergei's latest
blonde; she had no information. That was what she
must acquire.

Oppy would know. He knew everything about his
staff. If he didn't know, he had ways to find out. She

went immediately to the phone but she didn't lift the receiver. This wire might be tapped; not that there was any reason for such police precaution, but she wouldn't take a chance. And others than the police might be listening in. She would go to a public phone booth, and quickly. She caught up her bag, locked the flimsy door.

A big house-dressed woman was standing on the porch of the cottage across, shaking out a rug. Griselda felt relief. Neighbors at last, a place she could flee for help if it became essential. She hurried to the street-front garage. She almost expected to be stopped before she could drive away. Her mission was that important, for if her hunch was right, she could gather intimate information about the girl. The murderer wouldn't like that.

2

The dead-fish voice of the Malibu butler patronized a Long Beach call. She couldn't speak to Oppy.

She demanded, "Why not?"

His voice managed to convey importance without any inflection, "He is in story conference, Miss."

It was fortunate for the man that she was not within striking distance. Oppy and his butler could cow most of the movie colony but not Griselda Cameron Satterlee. She spoke her name. "Tell him I'm holding the wire." She added, "I expect to speak to him at once."

The intermediary did not return. Oppy's sputter came almost as quickly as she wished it. "Griselda. It is Griselda. My poor Griselda. And I have heard on the radio your husband is arrested for murder."

"No, he isn't!" She almost screamed it. The error

would be multiplied a thousandfold if Oppy went around saying it and he would. He relished scandal just so long as it was not injurious to his box office.

"He is not? Good. It is a mistake. And now you will leave that corny Long Beach and come to Malibu where Oppy is and the most beautiful picture we have to do, such costumes—"

She interrupted firmly. There was no use trying to clarify things for him; he'd only be the more muddled. State her business simply, that was all. "Oppy, I want some information. I want it quickly. What is the name of Sergei Vironova's current mistress?"

"You ask me this?" He did scream, as if it were beneath the dignity of the great Oppensterner of O.C.H. studios to dabble in such earthy matters.

"Yes, I ask you this." She was stern. He had almost restored her good humor; he was always so Oppy.

He said mildly, "Let me think now. I have met her. A gorgeous blonde, yes. But her test! It stinks. Wait a minute now. Si Burke is here; he would know. Si always knows their name."

She heard him speak to the scenarist and Si's voice came over the wire, "What do you crave, Griselda?"

"The name of Sergei Vironova's latest."

He drawled, "My God, you ought to know. She was bumped off in your town a couple of nights ago."

Her heart contracted in cold surety. She was shaking so much that she leaned against the booth wall.

"Shelley Huffaker." He went on, "Sergei's supposed to be down there now. Haven't you run into him?"

She didn't answer that. But she asked quickly, "Did he come with her? I mean were they together?"

He said, "Sorry, honey. He has an alibi of about two thousand lugs. He was on the set when the heartbeat was meeting her sailor in the Park." His voice was kind. "Anything I can do, Griselda. Any of us. No one thinks Con Satterlee had any hand in it naturally. Case of mistaken identity."

She said, "Thanks eternally for this much, Si. I may want more. No, Con didn't do it. And you might pound into Oppy's ivory dome that there's a difference between being questioned, and being arrested for murder."

"What do you think I am? Superman?" His roar echoed after the connection was severed.

She stood there in the booth trying to regain momentum. She had been right. She had made the first step toward releasing Con. She dialed again. Sergei Vironova was registered but he was out. She left her name and number. "When he comes, ask him to call immediately." She drove again to the beach cottage.

There was a police car at the curb. It startled her and then there came quick surging hope. They'd brought Con home. They didn't keep a man in jail interminably for questioning.

Vinnie was at the wheel reading the funny paper. She called, "Good morning," and he saw her.

He said, "Morning, ma'am. Pa's up there looking for you." He didn't say anything about Con.

She climbed the steps to the porch. Captain Thusby was leaning against the railing, looking out at the sea. He said, "Morning, Mrs. Satterlee. I was looking for you."

She felt that he might have been looking for her indoors if she hadn't arrived when she did. She put her key in the door.

"You're out early this morning seems like."

She said, "Yes, I had business." She wouldn't tell him, not until she'd talked with Sergei, not until she told Con first. The captain was not her ally.

He followed her into the house. She made her voice carefree, "You didn't bring Con with you?"

"No'm, I didn't. Not this morning." He sounded ashamed of himself. "I sort of wanted to run through his things if you don't mind. There's something he told me—" His voice dwindled.

She motioned to the bedroom. "Go right ahead, Captain." She didn't mind what he did today. The information she was withholding gave her secret jubilance. She was on the right track; he couldn't hurt Con now. And he wouldn't run across her revolver and wonder. She'd hidden it under a seat cushion of the couch.

He pegged into the bedroom and she lighted a cigarette. She didn't have any doubt that Con would be released by nightfall. But the captain returned, his face sober-limned. He said, "I can't find them."

"Find what?"

His gnarled hands were empty. "Those shells, ma'am. From her gun. He says they're here."

She jumped from the couch. "They must be there!" From his look she knew it was essential they be. She ran into the bedroom, began tearing apart the drawer. He followed her, searching systematically after her upheaval.

The telephone rang. She cried, "Wait a minute," and hurried to answer. It was Sergei, now at the wrong moment. She hadn't time to be diplomatic, to make her voice other than worried. She demanded, "Meet me for lunch at twelve at the Hilton."

He tried to say, "But Griselda, I've promised—"

She cut him off. "I'm busy now. Can't talk. Be there." She rang off before he could say more.

Captain Thusby raised eyebrows at her but he didn't ask. Together they searched. They were with-

out success. It was in hopelessness that she sank on
the couch again. Another mark against Con, another
mistake.

She insisted stubbornly, "There were six of them.
That night there were. He showed me." She could
see them on the bureau scarf the next morning. She
said dully, "I'd like to see Con. Is that permitted?"

He thrust his still empty hands into his pockets.
"Any time you say. This afternoon?"

She kept her voice steady, "I don't want to see him
in a cage."

His face was red and shiny as a tomato. He mopped
the bald spot with his hand. He boomed, "You come
down, Mrs. Satterlee, and I'll fix things up for you.
Right in my private office. Fix you right up."

She tagged after him to the door.

"If you like Vinnie can come out and get you, drive
you down. He's not very busy."

She smiled. "Thank you very much but I'll be in
town anyway. I've a luncheon date." He knew that;
he didn't know with whom.

She watched him away, returned to the bureau for
another helplessly futile search. Six shells couldn't
just walk away—but her hands stilled. Chang had
been in this room; he had been in this, Con's drawer,
last night. He must have taken them. Her heart was
sick within her. They hadn't been mislaid; they had
been stolen deliberately to throw more seeming guilt
on Con. And with more sickness there came realization of another possibility. She hadn't gone into the
bedroom at first with Thusby. He could have taken
the missing shells himself to complete his frame. Had
there been more rattle than his wooden leg would
make when he pushed himself up from the chair?
There was only he or Chang to suspect. One of those
two had the shells. Con might have a hunch which

one; if it were Chang something could be done. If it
weren't—her mouth quivered. Other innocent men
had been railroaded, even without the encouragement
of the X chieftain.

She couldn't stay quiet. She straightened the
drawers, replaced them, and changed for luck. The
white knit Con liked, the swashbuckling white pi-
rate's hat. The reddest red for her mouth. She would
appear gay, not disturbed; no one would know it was
no more than a Hollywood makeup. She had as yet a
half hour to fritter; she drove to the hotel, parked,
and strolled on Ocean until twelve, buying for Con:
cigarettes, carton; pipe tobacco, pound; magazines,
pulps to slicks; newspapers, coast to coast; and what he
must be missing, a quart. She didn't know if the latter
would be allowed but she would attempt to give it to
him. Not that he wouldn't be better off without it but
it would help him pass the time. She put down ruthlessly the suggestion that her purchases seemed for a
man to be away longer than Con would be. A couple
of days in custody would seem long; he'd like a few
minor comforts.

Sergei wasn't in the lobby. Five and ten minutes
passed; he might have been stating fact not trying to
avoid her when he'd suggested he couldn't make it.
There could be a message for her at the desk. Before
she could move to ask, Kew and Kathie Travis saw
her. She wouldn't allow them to intrude on this
luncheon date.

Kew asked, "What are you doing here, Griselda?"
He didn't wait for answer. "Will you join us for
lunch?"

She said, "No," and saw the first tolerance of her
on Kathie's face. Kathie didn't want to share him.
"Sorry but I've a date."

Kathie wasn't deft. She put her hand on Kew's

beautifully tailored gray flannel coat sleeve. "We might as well go eat then." Her hand remained on the gray as if she believed it belonged there. Obviously she didn't know Kew well.

He didn't move. "Any more news of Con?"

She shook her head briefly. She wouldn't tell him of Thusby's discovery before an outsider. But her eyes tried to convey more than her words. "Nothing that won't keep."

Kathie edged closer to him. "I was sorry to learn of your husband's arrest." Her voice was too soft. "I know he had nothing to do with it. Not a man like Con." Something special in her great eyes always for a man.

"Technically it isn't an arrest, Mrs. Travis." Deliberately because she neither liked nor trusted this girl, she added, "I'll see you later, Kew."

He nodded, "I'll phone." Kathie's mouth was a rim.

Sergei must have been hiding behind a pillar waiting until the elevator closed on the others. He was taking a new part today, more Hollywood, more natural. "It's so good you should waste your time on poor Vironova. I have been lonesome, yes, for a friendly face in this Long Beach. No one I know here. No one to talk with." His hand waved like a wand. "We shall have lunch now. Yes?"

He jerked toward the exit but she stated, "We might as well eat in the Sky Room."

His lip quivered. "It is up too high. It upsets the stomach."

She looked into his eyes. "You needn't worry about Kew or Mrs. Travis bothering us. She'll see to that."

He agreed miserably, "All right. I go." He retained wariness.

She maneuvered the headwaiter to a table far from

the others, safe as possible from ears that might prick.
She didn't begin on Sergei until the order was taken.
He might have been lulled into security but he
clicked to alertness when she opened bluntly, "Why
did you come to Long Beach?"

"Why do I come to Long Beach? Why do I come
to Long Beach?" He was stammering for time to
evolve an acceptable answer. "It is for rest." He could
see that wasn't going well. "For research." He jabbed
his finger upward into the air. "For research, yes. To
do a grrreat picture on the Navy. Yes. On the Navy."

She let him elaborate before she spoke again with
knowledge and decision, "You came to Long Beach
because Shelley Huffaker was murdered."

His mouth was a static O.

She said, "I called Oppy this morning."

His eyes flicked with nervousness. He wet his lips.

"Why have you kept quiet? Why did you let my
husband be taken in by the police while you said
nothing?"

His voice was muted, "The police, they know this."

"The police know?" She was incredulous.

He bobbed his head. "Already I have talked with
the police. They have been seeking me in Hollywood.
But they do not want me. I was not here when she
is murdered."

She knew that his alibi was real. "She was your—
good friend?"

"Yes. For three years, yes. I have the good friends
more beautiful, perhaps, and more—" He tapped his
beret. "But none who knows so many people. She is
smart. Even if she do not have the right brain." His
breath expelled like wind. "She is dead now."

Griselda repeated, "Why did you come to Long
Beach?"

He waited until the waiter had placed the bouillon.

He looked cautiously over one shoulder and then the other before speaking. "I will tell you that. I come because I am curious." His face was peaked as a goblin's. "I am curious to know who killed Shelley and why did they do this." If he spoke truth, and she believed he did, their purpose seemed identical. He attacked the soup sibilantly. "She did not come to be killed," he announced without interest.

She leaned across the table quickly. "Why did she come?"

His head wagged sadly. "That I do not know, Griselda. She do not tell me that. She say she wish to drive down the coast. I am at the studio so perturbed over the big scene. The chauffeur come to me and say Miss Huffaker will stay in Long Beach a few days to see the good friend. She tell him to go home; she will telephone him when to come back to her. To me, she tell nothing." He souped. "But she knew she would stay. She had taken the bag with her."

"Did you know she had a gun with her?"

"No. It was my gun. She borrow it. That is how the police look for me. They trace the gun and then they look for me." His whole attitude was that of nothing to hide but he was nervous. Even as he ravished the food he was casting his eyes, scarcely restraining the urge to peer behind him.

If only he knew why Shelley had come. He could know even if the girl hadn't told him. He could have pieced it together from living with her. He was shrewd; he wouldn't tell Griselda anything important, anything that the police didn't know. He was cognizant of the fact that she was searching for any and all outlets for her husband's safety. She knew now that she wasn't going to find out much here.

But she asked, "Who was the good friend?"

He shrugged. "It must be Mrs. Crandall, yes? I do

not think Shelley go to Long Beach to see Mr. Brent. She could see him in Hollywood. He is much in Hollywood."

Kew hadn't said he'd known Shelley before. He had implicitly denied it. She couldn't believe. "Was she a friend of his?"

"Oh my, yes." He seemed well pleased. "I tell you she know the important people? When we meet him at the Hollywood party she say, 'Don't tell me, let me guess.'" He tittered. "Jokey always she was."

She pressed it. "Had she known him in New York?"

"But necessarily. Or when they meet in Hollywood—"

She wasn't certain. She knew the Shelley Huffakers, insinuating friendships; remembering faint occasions that others had long forgotten. She asked, "What about Major Pembrooke?"

His mouth snapped. "She did not know Major Pembrooke." His eyes were curtained. That subject was stamped *taboo*.

"Sergei, whom did she come here to kill?"

He spread his fingers. "She do not come to kill."

She said, "I suppose she carried a loaded revolver to do a little duck-hunting along the way."

He looked carefully all about again. "Maybe she was afraid somebody would kill her." He added simply, "And so they did."

Griselda hadn't thought of the gun as self-protection for Shelley. She might have been afraid of an old friend, or of a new one that Sergei didn't know or wasn't speaking about. She switched abruptly on him. "What about Mannie Martin?"

His lizard eyes were terrified.

"I know nothing of him. Nothing I beg of you."

"You seemed to Saturday."

"Nothing I tell you. I know nothing."

"Where did your information come from?"

He tried not to show fear but it was still staring out of his eyes. "I hear nothing. Maybe someone say. I do not know. Maybe I read in the newspaper—"

He hadn't been afraid this way at Catalina. Something had happened to him during the intervening hours.

He fluted hysterically, "I do not know. I do not know nothing."

It was unfair to pursue someone as weak as this. But it was necessary. It was for Con. She made her voice strong. "Why were you watching me at the Terminal Saturday? Why did you miss your boat and fly across? To get there first. You wanted to meet Con. Why?"

He was shaking as with palsy while she spoke. His eyes were almost popping out of his face. He kept cramming more and more of the torte in his mouth until crumbs were patterning his chin. When she halted he washed the mouthful down with a gulp of coffee and was on his feet. "I forget. I must take someone to lunch. It is a lady. You do not know her. We will meet again."

He was gone. She didn't try to stop his flight. When they met again she would do better with him. He could not hold out for long; no one as terror-weakened would have the ability to resist. Moreover, Kew, or Con when he was released, could put on the pressure better than she.

"Your companion rushed off in a surprising hurry."

She knew who it was without turning. The amusement in the words was cold as rain. And that cold was transferred into her veins as he came in front of her.

She attempted in her manner of answering to convey her will that this would complete their conversation, as well as her belief that it was none of his business. "He had a luncheon date."

The ludicrousness of the picture of Sergei rushing off for further lunch with his mouth practically full and the overflow on his chin must have touched some human strain in the major. He actually chuckled, a real not simulated sound. She didn't laugh; in his presence there could be no normal reaction save fear.

He said, "Mind if I sit down?" and took the empty chair. He hadn't been in the dining room when they arrived nor had she seen him enter during their luncheon. But Sergei might have watched his approach, that would be the cause of the director's fright. She couldn't rebuff him again; she didn't want him to know how much she feared him. She could retain some strength with which to fight him if he did not know.

He continued, "Perhaps it is a new Hollywood idea he is introducing, two luncheons a day. A reaction to the overdieting which has gone on there. But he didn't look hungry."

"He'd forgotten a previous luncheon engagement." She tried to speak normally; if she didn't think about him, it wasn't too difficult.

He asked, "May I order you a liqueur?"

"If you please. Cointreau."

He summoned the waiter, gave the order, and smiled at her. But the smile was false. After that momentary lapse, he had returned to his emotionless norm. "I am sorry that you and your husband left our party Saturday night. We had a pleasant cruise. Mr. Brent and his little friend were delightful companions."

She was casual. "Kew told me you had the party flown back. Do you keep a plane as well as a boat, Major?"

The softness of his voice was frightening. "One is available to me. I find Catalina extremely hospitable. But America is such an hospitable country."

"Sergei was not of your party?"

"No. Unfortunately he had pressing business on Sunday. We set him ashore shortly after you left."

Her eyes blurred. It must have been Sergei who had been receiving the brunt of that stateroom conversation. No wonder he feared.

He said, "We'll cruise again whenever you wish, Mrs. Satterlee. *The Falcon* is at your disposal."

She lied, wishing it were true, "I'm afraid it won't be possible for us to have that pleasure. We can't stay much longer. I have a job in Hollywood and my husband must go where he is assigned. His vacation is only for a month; almost three weeks of that have already slipped away."

His face was a mask now. "He has been released?"

The careful casualness went from both of them. He had joined her with a purpose in mind; he was moving toward it. He would move wisely but not slowly; he would crush.

She answered, "Not yet. But the charge is ridiculous." She added firmly, "I am seeing him this afternoon."

Con was not incommunicado; Major Pembrooke need not think she was unprotected.

He said, "Murder is a serious affair."

"He did not murder anyone. I told you the charge was ridiculous. He didn't know this girl."

"No?"

"No! He'd never even seen her until he offered to take her home that evening. She needed help."

"Quixotic." He made the word a blot.

"Or civilized." Albert George might be British but his viewpoint was something else. There was no doubting that. She hated him as much as she feared him. She wanted to get away. But he was not releasing her.

He said, "Yes," as if civilized ideas were as stupid as Con's picking up Shelley Huffaker that night had been.

She hated him and the hatred allowed her without trepidation to ask what she wanted to find out, "Did you know Shelley Huffaker?"

"I?"

"Did you?"

"My dear child, no!" He was amused as well as emphatic. "How could you think I would know her?"

She said, "You were in the Bamboo Bar that night."

He replied evenly, "I was anchored off Catalina long before the murder took place, having a drink with Mrs. Crandall and the Swales."

With a plane available. She hung on stubbornly. It would solve things if he had killed Shelley. And he was certainly capable of doing it. "You had heard of her. You knew she was Dare's guest."

He smiled. "Dare did not mention her guest until the police telephoned the evil news to her."

He was granite. But he had considered an alibi. It was presented without asking and had doubled its value by adding the witnesses' names. And he couldn't remove the available plane from the picture.

She posed another question, "Did you know Vironova before?"

"No." His lip curled. "I'm afraid I don't care for that sort. I don't quite understand how he became one of our party, particularly since both Mrs. Travis and Mr. Brent later disclaimed all responsibility for him."

She made her voice pertinent, "Do you understand *why* he joined the party, Major Pembrooke?"

His eyes held hers. "Perhaps he wished certain information. Russia is extremely interested in what your country and mine will do in the East."

Without reasoning she rose to the protection of Sergei. "But he's not a Russian. I mean not in that way. He's been over here for years. He's a movie director not a politician."

He asked coolly, "Are you certain, Mrs. Satterlee?"

She couldn't in all honesty answer yet. But she had to protect Sergei if possible from this man. He was too weak to be pitted against this adversary. She spoke with seeming conviction, "Certainly I know that. I've worked with him at the studio. I doubt if he's even sympathetic to the new Russian policy." He had been a supporter of Communism. The art in his propaganda films was what led Oppy to import him from Moscow. But she seemed to remember that he had publicly broken away when Russia invaded Finland. She repeated, "I doubt it very much. He's no spy." She had wanted to avoid that word in Pembrooke's presence but it came out. "He's an artist."

He seemed to be laughing at her. "The two are not incongruous. The business of spies does not interest you, does it, Mrs. Satterlee?" There was impact behind the laughter.

She said quickly, "No, of course not." She was ashamed of her nervousness.

"Nor interest your husband." His stone eyes belied his conversational tone.

"Why should it?" Her laugh was artificial. "That isn't his business. He's only a reporter, for the air not the press. All he ever wants is a story—" She broke off at the solidifying of menace in those eyes. She had said the wrong thing.

He didn't overlook it. He was quiet. "He does not go prying after stories. He would not employ infor-

mation which does not belong to him. He is not what
you call a crusading reporter, not in these dangerous
times?"

She wasn't allowed to speak, to deny that Con ever
had any interest in uncovering a story, to assure this
man that he spoke on the air only what was written
for him. Any and all lies to divert Major Pembrooke's
attention from Con.

His teeth were sharp. "I am certain that Mr. Satterlee is shrewd. He would not have attained the
unique position he has on the air waves if he were as
foolhardy as so many reporters." He spoke with grisly
quietness. "Some you hear of—they are like rockets,
one blaze and where are they? Perhaps cadging drinks
in some third-rate bar, perhaps in a sanatorium 'resting,' perhaps they are not seen again. I have known
many reporters. I respect the newspaper profession in
its proper place."

She had gathered her bag while he spoke; she
wasn't staying here longer. But her very fear gener-
ated a last flung banner of courage. Her hands pressed
flat on the table. "And what is your profession, Major
Pembrooke?" she demanded quietly.

His eyes met hers. He kept her waiting as if he were
considering what answer to extract from a well-filled
dossier. He lighted his cigar insolently. He was laughing at her. "I am—" His lips baited her. "I am a spy."

She was already half out of her chair and she didn't
hesitate longer. She didn't look back at him as she
crossed to the door, overpaid the headwaiter, hastened
to the elevator. If you called yourself an English officer
and were a spy—you couldn't be spying for Britain.
She pressed the button a second time without realization, stood there shivering as if winter had suddenly
come upon Long Beach.

CON didn't resemble in any respect a man locked in jail. He sat tilted back in Thusby's own chair, waving a cigarette, grinning all over his horsey face. He said, "This is a hell of a honeymoon."

"I've known that a long time."

"And you never told me! I always say the husband is the last to know."

She had moved to the desk as soon as the captain pegged out of his private office. She sat there above Con, as near as possible. She wasn't jittery now. Luncheon hour seemed long ago and utterly fantastic.

He was shaven, and cleaned and pressed better than usual. Chang must have packed well. There was so much she wanted to ask, so much she wanted to tell, but she didn't know how safe it might be. Thusby might be given to dictaphones or keyholes. She patted Con's lapel. "You look lovely, darling. Who's your valet? The same one who packed your bags?"

There was only the slightest shading crossed his face. He said, "You're a good little wife sending me all this stuff. Didn't fool me a bit. You wanted me to be dressed up when I was mugged, didn't you?"

"That's right." She accepted the warning. She'd let

142

him set the key of the conversation. "You so seldom do, you know. And I didn't want you looking like a passport in the postoffices all over the country. What would your friends think?"

"Unprintable epithets as usual. I can't repeat them. You're too young." He dropped ashes on the floor. "What you doing with yourself these days?"

. That was a keyed question, spoken unconcernedly but a look went with it.

She sounded casual, "Keeping amused. Kew came by this morning. He'd just heard the news of you and simply refused to believe it."

"Good old loyal Kew," he murmured, blowing smoke at the captain's ink-spattered penholder. "Probably out shopping now for the proper duds to wear at the arraignment. The I'd-rather-be-dressed-right-than-President boy."

She reprimanded. "You're never fair to him." She couldn't tell him Kew was helping her, not outright. She hoped he might guess. "We conferred a bit this morning, we're going to have another conference tonight."

"When the husband's away the Kews will play. He takes his cue—if I had time I'd think up a pun. That all?"

"No. I had lunch with Sergei Vironova." This she could say; the police knew. "Shelley Huffaker was his mistress."

"Yeah." He knew it then too. "What did he spill?"

"You want it all? Now?"

He nodded without hesitation.

But she kept her voice muted. "It occurred to me this morning. I don't know why I've been so obtuse. I suppose you knew it all along."

"Not quite. Matter of fact it didn't occur to me

until I was shaving at the St. Catherine before we left Sunday afternoon. Always get my best ideas shaving."

"You should shave more often, dear."

He put his teeth on her knuckle. "I was figuring how maybe this was a personal murder not political —and Vironova fits."

"He has a solid alibi. He was on the lot all that night. He says he's here to find out who and why. He seems more curious than heartbroken. I suppose he has a waiting list."

"Sounds like a good idea," he allowed absently.

She struck at him lightly and lowered her voice further, "He is scared green of something, Con. He ran out on me at lunch when I started popping questions. Said he had a date."

"Scared?" He was trying to figure it out. "Does he think the murderer is out for him too?"

"I don't believe so." Logically he should. The murderer wouldn't know how much Sergei knew about Shelley Huffaker's life, how much she had revealed to him of the reason why she was killed. She hadn't been murdered for her money or her jewels; it wasn't a discarded suitor if she'd been living with Sergei for three years; it must have been for some knowledge she possessed, something that threatened someone else. Anyone would suspect that Sergei wasn't entirely outside her confidence. And yet— "He seemed quite at ease in his rôle as sleuth. It was the mention of Mannie Martin that started the jitters, more than jitters, Con. He was terrified." Was it because he'd seen Major Pembrooke?

He scowled again.

She concluded with an ease she didn't feel. "After he ran out on me I finished lunch with Albert George Pembrooke."

Con came to life on that. "You what?" He shouted it. "Where did he pop from?"

"The bar, I think." Her voice was a blur, "I don't like him. He—he disturbs me."

"Then what the hell were you doing lunching with him?"

"He joined me. I couldn't help it. Finally I ran out on him." In as sheer funk as Sergei had run. She knew it now. Major Pembrooke had known it then; he had believed that he had frightened her into quiescence. He'd even been amused by his success. She set her chin. He didn't know her; he would learn.

Con said, "What are you deciding now, angel?" There was genuine concern underlying the words.

"Nothing. I was just thinking."

"Of Albert George." He laid his hand on her knee. "Lay off him, Griselda. He's poison."

"He's poison to me."

"You're not smart enough to play his game. You don't have enough blue chips. I'm telling you, lay off. Let someone his size sit in." His words were a definite order. "You—lay—off."

She leaned over and kissed his worried forehead. "All right, sweetheart." But if she had an opportunity to show him up she would do it. He couldn't make her scurry like a rabbit and then laugh at her. You didn't always have to be the same size as your adversary. Little David had done pretty well with a pebble.

"What did he want? Weakness for beautiful blondes?"

She spoke solemnly, "He wanted to tell me that reporters who meddle in business that doesn't concern them end up as bar-bums or seeking a cure or on the missing persons list."

She waited until he finished cursing and asked,

"Did he have any more tender messages for yours truly?"

"No. That was all." She added, "He told me he was a spy."

"My God!" He left his mouth open.

"I asked him what he did and he said he was a spy."

He repeated softly, "My God! He must have a sense of humor. Not that we didn't know it—but it can't be proved yet."

"Why didn't you tell me?" she asked.

"There are some things I can't tell even you," he said, and she thought to herself, "Some things! Practically everything!" but she didn't say it out loud. Con went on, "Wouldn't the higher-ups like to catch him admitting it!"

She was eager. "Could I do any good?"

"No. He'd deny saying it and prove he wasn't. You're to stay out of this."

"Con." How could he continue in his idiocy? "You keep saying that just as if I weren't in it to the teeth."

"What do you mean you're in it?"

"What do you think? You're in custody. I'm your wife, in case you've forgotten." Saying it made her realize her danger. The true murderer would be watching her, waiting to see if she uncovered information favorable to Con, unfavorable to himself. Major Pembrooke had already made it clear that his dealings with Con would be conducted through her. Doubtless there were others who would work through her. She controlled her voice, "I'm—I'm closed in tight on it."

He was solemn. "Not if you're a good girl and do as I say."

She was slightly irritated. "And what do you say now?"

"All I ask is that you play house and remain un-curious." He was pleading beneath jauntiness. "I told you before, if you don't know anything, no one can hurt you."

He was so wrong. It wasn't true. She could be in stark danger from what she would be presumed to know.

Her irritation flared. "You mean play house in that splendid mansion by the sea?"

"Exactly that. And remember what I asked you before. Be as dumb as you're not. Try to be dumb, baby."

She smiled suddenly at him. "I'm very dumb, darling. If I weren't, do you think I'd let you treat me like a case of mental deficiency?"

He kissed her without warning and with decision. "Be good, Griselda, and let who will be sleuths. Go easy on the conferences. Will you?"

She didn't answer. She patted his ears. "Do you know who killed Shelley Huffaker? And why?"

"No. I don't know where she fits at all."

"She wasn't spying on Mannie Martin for Sergei?"

His mouth was lean. "You're thinking too much. But if it will help you to take my advice, she wasn't so far as anyone knows conscious of the fact that Mannie Martin was anything but a rich exec who went for glamour girls. She wasn't a spy. And that's why it doesn't make sense. Now will you be good?"

She kissed him three times. "I will. If you'll come home in a day or two." She slid from the desk. "But if anyone—even your precious Garth—tries to pin this Huffaker thing anywhere near you, I'll find out the who and the why." She put her hand over his mouth. "You needn't waste your breath, my sweet. If that girl wasn't mixed up with Pan-Pacific, there'll be no danger for me." She went on without breath.

"I know your worry for me is some way concerned with that, with the information which was lost with Mannie. I don't know about it. I don't want to. I don't want to have anything to do with that." She shivered suddenly. She didn't want anything to do with anything that meant contact with Albert George Pembrooke. "But, my darling, if you think I'm going to let you be railroaded on the murder of a Hollywood bim, you're just not smart."

He held her by her elbows. "Griselda, I'm not going to be railroaded on anything. Will you kindly give up and stop worrying? I'm one-hundred-percent safe and sound and sane and I shall continue to be." He spoke in dead seriousness. "If you'll only promise to stay out no matter what ideas you may develop, then everything will be okay and we'll have that honeymoon and—"

The door opened to Captain Thusby's sheepish moon face.

Con said, "Well, Commodore?"

"Sorry to rush you but you've got another visitor getting sort of restless."

"Not at all." He gave Griselda a husbandly kiss. "Thanks for the hacksaw and the files, darling. I'll be home soon." Under his breath and with his eyes deep, he added, "Please do as I ask."

She nodded, her smile bright, but Con hadn't changed her decision. If Captain Thusby didn't send him home by tomorrow, she would continue her own investigations with redoubled effort.

Entering the dreary cottage, she remembered one investigation she had to make. Go through Con's pockets.

She had no doubt that the cottage had been entered to gain possession of that letter. Even now someone might be watching; she jerked her head quickly but there was no one on the porch. She needn't be afraid to search her own quarters. She raised the couch cushion and she stood staring, staring at little rolls of dust, broken peanut shells, a paper clip.

It had been Chang's gun; he must have returned for it. That was fair. But it had been hidden; he couldn't have found it easily; he would have had to search. Her heart thudded noisily. Her own search might be too late. She moved with rapidity now, made fast the front door, rumbled a heavy over-stuffed chair against it for greater security. She didn't want to be surprised by anyone at this. The kitchen door was secure, and, feeling a little foolish, she tilted a chair under the knob.

She went to the bedroom. What suit had he been attached to in Hollywood? The navy serge with the dim red pin-stripe, the one that made him look too thin. It had been her weariness with that wintry suit that had made her heckle him into buying the camel's-hair jacket in Beverly.

She found it. She went through the file of soiled scribbled-over envelopes and she found it. Tucked into the unpaid bill from the Madison and Fifty-fourth dispensary. He'd made that much effort to hide it.

It was important but it wasn't dangerous. It was dated Thursday, June fifth, four days before Mannie Martin disappeared. Sent air mail it would have reached Con in time, had he been in New York not Hollywood. She deciphered the scrawled handwriting with care.

DEAR CON:

I'm on the trail of something big, too big for me. Could you wire Garth to lend a hand? He's here but

*impossible to get to. Better yet grab a plane and join
me. It'll be a Pulitzer for you. I have all the dope.
I'll wait to hear from you.*

There was a postscript:

*The poor fish hasn't caught on but he's responsible
for a lot.*

The postscript she didn't understand. Who was the
poor fish? Not Garth. Pembrooke? Kew? Poor dis-
tressed Sergei? Or Mannie himself?

She read the letter again with relief. Obviously
Con did not have the documents that Pembrooke
wanted. Mannie hadn't heard from Con, and after
four days he hadn't waited longer to hear from him.
He'd gone ahead on the trail, ahead to oblivion.

She replaced the letter where it had been. It
couldn't endanger Con to have someone else find it;
it might help if Pembrooke could discover how little
Con knew of his affairs. She'd like to tell the major
herself how wrong his assumptions were. But even if
she had the courage to seek him out, would he believe her? And she couldn't be certain that Con
hadn't involved himself since their arrival here.

Kew telephoned at six. "I'll be delayed about an
hour. And what do you say we drive down to Laguna,
have dinner at Victor Hugo's?"

She was pleased at the idea of leaving Long Beach
behind for a few hours. It wasn't a sinister town; it
was a solid, law-abiding, friendly place where families lived and other families came with their children
for a summer vacation. But she was afraid of it now.
She wanted desperately to get away. Every creak of
the cottage in wind and tide quivered her nerves as

she dressed, wishing the smoky chiffon printed with pale golden poppies were for Con not Kew. Not that Kew would not appreciate it—and the black horsehair full moon of her hat—far more than Con. The only thing Con ever noticed on a woman was a bathing suit or a nightgown.

It was past seven-thirty before Kew arrived. He said, "I telephoned. We'll be served no matter the hour. I couldn't get here earlier. Washington had me on the wire." His face was set with anxiety but he erased it as he said, "You're exquisite, Griselda. I wish we were ten thousand miles from California."

"And I."

There was a moon but the mist was already rolling up an obscuring fog. They drove down the beach road.

"Tedious day?"

"Yes. Let's save shop talk until after we've had dinner. I could do with forgetting it a little. Couldn't you?"

"Rather." Yet she wasn't disheartened as she had been earlier. It might be leaving the Navy town behind; it might be the harmless letter; it might be in recalling Con's optimism. Con wasn't worried; why should she be? He hadn't even mentioned the missing shells. They couldn't be important as she had thought.

There was comfort in dining with no familiar faces identifying the landscape. After dinner they moved to the cliff garden overhanging the moon-veiled sea. There was peace here but it was necessary to shatter it, to find out what progress Kew had made.

He sighed. "Kathie is no help at all. I called it naïveté once, I recall, but it's nothing but sheer stupidity. Unbelievable, because you can't realize that anyone can be as unconscious and still function. She's like an animated doll."

She asked him then, "Did you know Shelley, Kew?"

"No. I told you that."

"Sergei said that you did." His look was swift. "She lived with him." She repeated the director's incident.

Kew was searching memory. "Perhaps I did run into her in Hollywood. I can't remember. You meet so many of the type. You know."

She agreed. "That's how I figured it. She might have met you in New York and considered it a friendship. That type again."

Kew said, "I can only just recall meeting Vironova. Although he greeted me at the St. Catherine as if we were old friends. How did you happen to lunch with him?"

"I figured he might be the man in Shelley's life and I checked. He has a perfect alibi for the murder. He's doing exactly what we are, Kew, trying to find out about it." She asked, "Do you think the whole thing is tied up with Mannie Martin?"

His mouth was firm. "I don't know. I do believe that Mannie found out something that meant curtains." He was suddenly not at ease and he spoke as softly as if there were listeners on the terrace, "I learned today that Pembrooke came here direct from Tokio. Vironova must be in it for Russia, if he's in. There's no division of purpose at this time. If Pembrooke and Vironova were on different sides, Shelley might well be some minor tool that fell by the wayside. But it doesn't make sense this way."

She demanded fiercely then, "Who is Pembrooke really representing, Kew?"

"I don't know."

Her heart sank. "You don't know?" Kew knew
everything.

"I'd like to know."

She saw his face in the moonlight. She accused
him, "You knew Pembrooke before."

"I met him in Washington."

"Before that." She was certain.

He spoke softly after a moment, "A lot of the boys
are back home, Griselda. Some have been kicked out
for filing too much; some have been hauled back before the kickoff. They're full of yarns. I heard of a
man, top of his field, one who always plays the highest bidder, and who is sure to be on hand whenever
there's a really delicate job to be handled. This man
was in Rumania before Carol's last abdication. He
commuted between Berlin and Moscow before the
pact was signed. He was in Spain before Franco
made a move, in London before Munich. He's no
secret. But he changes bosses too often to keep track
of who the current one is."

She didn't say anything.

"I don't even know his name. But I do know there
are important foreign agents on the coast. Garth
wouldn't have been here otherwise. And I do know
that some nations would prefer that the proposed
Pan-Pacific network not go through."

It gave the major a motive for the disappearance.
If England believed he was working for her, he could
sabotage, without suspicion falling on him. Martin
would not return. And if Con came too close to the
truth, he, too, would vanish. She clenched her hands.

Kew asked quietly, "When is Garth due back?"

"I don't know." If Garth hadn't sold Con out she'd
wish he would return. He could help if he were on
their side. She shook her head impatiently. Con
would be home in a day or two and she would insist

they leave Long Beach. He certainly wouldn't be helping Garth out any longer, not after what had been done to him.

Kew was tensed, chain-smoking from the white plastic case. Suddenly he spoke, "Has Con ever given you a hint as to what Mannie found out, Griselda?"

She opened her eyes wide at him. "He doesn't know, Kew. He didn't see Mannie."

Kew came over from his chair with suddenness. "He must know, Griselda. The letter. And Con hasn't forgotten what was in it. No one believes that."

She said then, "I've read the letter."

He didn't move.

"I found it. It didn't tell Con a thing."

He loomed above her. "What did it say?"

She repeated as she remembered. She flung out her hands. "There's nothing harmful in that, is there?"

He didn't answer and she didn't like his eyes. She asked a little frantically, "Is there?"

He said, "Nothing. Save that it links Con definitely with Mannie on this. And it states implicitly that Con is Number One with Garth."

She hadn't thought of it that way.

He caught her hands suddenly. "For God's sake, Griselda, for his sake and yours, make Con go back to New York as soon as Thusby sends him home. Will you do that?" Intensity solidified his face.

She was frightened. She whispered, "Kew! What do you mean? What do you know?"

He looked around slowly at the deserted terrace. If he hadn't been a big man she would have believed he was trembling. He said, "Let's start back to town. I want you to get rid of that letter tonight, before it's too late." He was visibly frightened, the way that Sergei had been. It wasn't by accident that he examined the rumble seat before starting on their way.

She had to ask again as they began the drive slowly through the thickness of the fog, "What do you know, Kew?"

"I know Con's life is in danger, Griselda, if he stays on here."

Maybe she had been wrong; maybe Garth had had him taken into custody to protect him until the secret-service chief could return from the high seas.

"How do you know that?"

He seemed reluctant to speak, as if he feared that even here on the highway his words might be overheard. "Major Pembrooke is a ruthless man, Griselda. He won't fail. He will never fail because he will never let anything or anyone stand in his way. Particularly he won't let one of Garth's men stand in his way. Forget what I'm saying. I'll deny it for self-protection if it is repeated."

She spoke in fear, "You do know Pembrooke, Kew."

"Too well. He's threatened Con. But he hasn't been sure Con was working for Garth; the arrest made him doubt. If he should have proof—Con had better get out."

She was chilled to the bone. "What happened on the yacht after we left, Kew?" Had he been the man in the stateroom; had there been further threats?

He said, "It was utterly normal."

"He put Sergei ashore."

"Sergei wanted to leave. Right after you did. He said he had pressing business. He told us that, with his face the color of moldy cheese and Pembrooke watching him like an eighteenth-century sadist." He added, "I wanted to shove off myself but I couldn't leave Kathie there unprotected. And Albert George wanted Kathie on board."

She asked quickly, "Why?"

"I've told you he isn't a man that misses. She's an important element. Walker could have those documents and furthermore could keep them till hell freezes over. You can't search a battleship. Moreover, Walker is one person who could know their contents without possessing them. He is an ever-present danger to Pembrooke."

"But Kathie knows nothing." That was obvious.

"She could find out." His hands were clenching the wheel. "She's stupid as hell and Pembrooke is smarter than Lucifer. He could maneuver her into a position where she would be forced to find out what Walker knows, and sell him out." He added too quietly, "Or to deliver her husband into the major's hands. That's why I'm keeping my eye on her."

She thought aloud with sudden horror, "Dare. Do you think he's using Dare that way?" Dare to get information from Con. To deliver Con. Because she could do what she would with him. She meant that much to him; he would never be able to see her as a potential enemy, even if he were warned.

He said slowly, "I don't think so. I don't know exactly what Dare's doing with him. Maybe she's looking for business. She's strapped—and stubborn as hell." There was a bitterness in his conclusion and she looked at him curiously.

He seemed to sense the turn of her head. He said, "It's no secret. I've been trying for years to get her to marry me. But I'm not her type evidently. I suppose she's—" He hesitated. "I suppose she's still torch-carrying for that rotten Crandall."

She wasn't. She'd never loved Crandall. She married him because she couldn't have Con. She was still holding out for Con. She'd never get him.

"I could help her out, at least I could give her a

comfortable life. And I'm not actually repulsive to her." He did break off now decisively, laughed, a short sound. "Kew Brent bares his heart. Forgive and forget. I'm shaky tonight."

He turned the car toward the ocean front and it occurred to her. She clutched his arm. "Kew!"

He swerved almost onto the curb. She was frightened at his lack of nerves, frightened and without understanding. She said, "I'm sorry if I startled you. I just wanted to ask you something."

He drove slowly. "Yes?"

"Kew, you said that Kathie was important because she could get information from Walker. If Con already has that information, isn't he more important?"

They were in sight of the cottage. He slowed the car to a crawl that his answer might be spoken before they were parked. "He is," he said. "Mannie told him in that letter where to go for it."

She faltered, "I don't understand."

He said, "The Navy in private refers to Travis as the poor fish. Knowing Kathie, you can understand why. There must have been previous correspondence between Mannie and Con."

Garth had introduced the lieutenant to Con, left Con to act for him while he went fishing. Kew wouldn't be the only one that knew Con had been dealing with Walker. Major Pembrooke was thorough.

"He can't have all the dope yet or the government would have acted. That's why I tell you to get him away from here the moment he is free. Take him away before he gets the whole story. Save his life."

Silently she climbed with him up the steps to the dark cottage. His words had given her a dreadful fatalism that couldn't be glossed over. It would be

there until she could get Con away. She took the letter from the blue suit again, passed it to him without
words. He read it before flaring his lighter, burning
it to ash. He took his handkerchief, touched his forehead, warned, "Don't ever let anyone else know you
read this. Don't let anyone know you even saw a
letter."

She stood at the door, heard his motor receding,
leaving her alone with fear. She wanted to call after
him, to beg him to stay. He couldn't hear her now if
she shouted at the top of her lungs. She set her teeth
hard. There were lights across the sand at the new
neighbors'. It wouldn't hurt to go over there, look
upon kindly faces, let them look upon her, know
that she was alone and—not frightened, alone. It was
early yet. She could make excuse, borrow a little
coffee for her breakfast. The impulse was necessity.
She took a chipped cup from the chipped cups in the
kitchen cupboard, left the lights glowing, ran down
the steps.

The wind billowed her sheer black cape, flung
back her hair, hatless now, as she made slow progress
through the sifting sand. The whole idea seemed absurd before she was half across the waste. But with
silly stubbornness she kept plowing on. She was out
of breath when she reached the opposite porch.
There was no answer to her knock. But someone was
there; lights were behind the drawn blinds. She
pounded now. The door opened an abrupt width.
The woman she had seen earlier blocked it. She was
big and square and her face was as rigid as soap.

Griselda began brightly, "I saw your light—" but
she faltered. It wasn't that there was no answering
response in that face; it was that there was no response at all. And at that moment, the lighted blind
was made dark.

She tried to make her voice normal, to explain the reason she had evolved for intruding. But she was speaking to a void. And without warning the door was shut in her face.

Her halting words gaped to silence. The cup fell into ghost shards at her feet. She turned to go but, incredulous, swerved back again. She must be certain: it could have been a whim of inhospitable wind.

The door was a block of wood. The blind had moved. Who or what was peering at her from behind it? She stumbled to the warped steps. She couldn't run across the sand; it wasn't sand; it was evil spongy hands pressing her heels backward into the creeping shadow of that strange cottage. The wind too was evil, twisting her golden hair across her eyes. Her breath came in whimpers as she struggled on to her own lights, a haven now.

She shut the night outside, shut and locked it out with an insufficient key. She muted the radio, dance music was an anachronistic dream. She wanted Con. She wanted to feel the strength under his blue shirt, to listen to the strength under his flippancies. She had known that he was involved more deeply than he had told, in a matter far more dangerous than a girl's murder. He had been ordered to obtain the information Pembrooke wanted to suppress. When he had it complete, he would be killed even as Mannie must have been killed. Garth was safe, vacationing on the sea. Travis was safe, guarded by the Navy, possessing but part of the knowledge; the postscript implied that. It was reckless Con on whom the major would converge.

Weakly, she wanted to cry; if he didn't come soon she would cry. She couldn't go on alone. She could be brave about Albert George Pembrooke in Thusby's office with Con near but not in this unprotected beach house.

She heard the rattling but the wind had given false alarm too often. She ignored it until it became staccato insistence. She went shivering to the door. No outer light to turn on, no hook on the screen to ascertain what menace was without. She called before opening, "Who is there?"

"It's I."

Dare edging in, holding the door closed as if pursuers were after her. Too many in this with shattered nerves, Dare, Kew shying at shadows, Sergei, even Con prowling and jittering until they locked him up. The incongruity was that none of them should have this reaction. It didn't fit any of them. It didn't match their customary range from cocksureness to arrogance.

Dare's tweed Burberry was buttoned under her chin, the collar upturned to her cheeks. Her brown riding hat shaded her face. She kept on her driving gloves. "Where's Con? I've got to see Con immediately." Her green eyes were bright as baubles.

Griselda said, "He's in jail." She laughed after she said it. What was the proper way to announce a husband's incarceration? But she didn't want to laugh.

Dare looked at her as if she were lying. "What for?"

"For being seen with Shelley Huffaker." She asked Dare's shocked face, "You mean you didn't know it?"

"I've been away. Just came from the airport now." She sat down. "Tell me about it quickly."

Telling, it seemed invented incident: the Wilmington Terminal, an author's set.

"Who's responsible?"

She started to answer, "Thusby," but she went deeper into truth. "Barjon Garth."

Dare said, "I don't believe it. Rot." She stood up again. "I've got to see him no matter where he is. Do you suppose they'll let me in?"

Griselda answered, "I don't know at this hour." It was nearing midnight.

Dare repeated, "I have to see him tonight." She went to the door. "If I don't have any luck I'll come back and get you. You'll have a better chance."

She banged out, Griselda standing there with hands clenched. She wished she had but one gram of Dare's insolent assurance. She'd walk right up to Pembrooke and tell him to get out of her honeymoon, and the same to Captain Thusby and all the rest of them. She couldn't go to bed yet; Dare might return. She walked the room and she heard the news-flash warning, ran to turn up the radio.

The announcer's voice was so certain and so impersonally disinterested. "Captain Thusby announced tonight a sensational development in the Bixby Park murder case. Con Satterlee, well-known news commentator, who has been held since Sunday for questioning, has been charged with the murder of Shelley Huffaker. He is held without bail. Recent developments which have come to light—"

The voice went on and on in dreadful clarity, rehashing the known facts and the conjectures. It was the missing shells added to the fingerprints and the time element, ruling out all human intuition. It didn't enter into a murder charge that it was not in Con's character to have done such a thing. All the police wanted was the unimportant circumstances, the things that didn't count.

She didn't know she was sitting on the floor there

before the croaking box, until the air touched her
ankles and she looked up at Dare again in the open
doorway.

"Griselda, Con's been—" She stopped, realizing, it
was known. "You've heard. They wouldn't let me see
him. Said he didn't want to talk to anyone until he'd
seen his lawyer in the morning." She dug her hands
in her coat pockets.

Griselda saw her through a blur.

"You don't want to stay here now. Come to my
apartment. I have an extra bed." She must have remembered who'd last been her guest for she added
quickly, "Or I'll drive you to the hotel. You can't
stay here alone."

Griselda spoke with decision, "Con asked me to
stay until he returned. I will." With battered dignity she rose from the floor. "I'm tired. I'd like to
go to bed. If you don't mind."

She could sleep now. When you are purged of all
feeling, you can't be afraid.

2

The Long Beach morning papers had it in scare-
heads. So did the Los Angeles papers. The New
Yorkers would have it served the same style with
their breakfast coffee. Griselda sat in the ugly room
waiting for word from someone. There wasn't any.
Not even Captain Thusby. You would think that
the police would inform the wife when they made
such a move, not let her learn it from the radio and
press. She wondered why the reporters hadn't descended; probably haunting the hotel lists; they
wouldn't expect the Satterlees to be in a ramshackle
beach cottage.

When the phone did ring near noon, it startled

her. She didn't know the voice. Captain Thusby's
compliments and would she come down to headquarters immediately?

The old car crept. She would get to see Con, confer with him. She must get a lawyer, a good lawyer,
who would know what next should be done.

Her eyes were puzzled when she entered the office.
There was Dare in the same tweed and brown felt,
her gauntlets still dug into her pockets. There was
Kew biting at his mustache. There was Major Pembrooke's stony face; Kathie Travis turning her great
gaze from one man to the other. There was a type
officer acting as doorman. All of them looked at
Griselda when she entered and all looked too quickly
away.

She crossed to Kew, spoke under her breath, "Why
this? What's it about?"

He shrugged, then touched her arm. The door
was being opened again by the officer. She began to
tremble, wanting, not wanting, to see him here in
front of everyone. But Con didn't enter. A grimly
silent Captain Thusby marched in to his own swivel
chair and sat down hard. Vinnie came through another door with a yellow pencil in his mouth and a
notebook in his bony hand. He sidled to a place near
his father.

Thusby barked, "Nestor, get some more chairs.
Everybody sit down." The officer brought them to
Kew and Griselda. "I'll tell all of you right now, you
don't have to answer my questions. But you'd better
unless you want to look suspicious."

Vinnie took the pencil out of his mouth, licked the
sharp point and regarded it with a faint surprise, as
if it had disappointed him by not being flavored. The
captain drew on his pipe, his face reddening with
each puff, and he spoke on top of the stem.

"You start in, Mrs. Satterlee. What did you do last night?"

The question was so unexpected to all that they looked at Griselda, and she said nothing. She simply didn't understand.

Captain Thusby barked more sharply. "Go on. What did you do last night? Where'd you go? Who'd you see? Don't try to think up any fancy way to say it. Vinnie's going to write it down and he don't spell very fast."

It was simply absurd to sit there, holding her bag damply in her hands, unable to say one word. Save for burning the letter, she hadn't done anything that couldn't be repeated to the police chief and the entire roomful. It was nothing but a bad case of stage fright, looking into eyes whichever way she turned.

Thusby spoke to his pipe in exasperation. "Mrs. Satterlee, don't you know what you did last night?"

"Of course, I do," she answered back. "What time?"

"Start with dinner. Go on from there."

She began, "I had dinner with Kew Brent in Laguna," and watched Kathie's eyes darken. She didn't have to tell what they talked of; what they did was simple and innocent. But when she reached the homecoming, she faltered. She hadn't meant to; she hadn't intended to think of the letter, to remember that obscene cottage that could be another of Pembrooke's shore quarters. Nor did she wish to mention Dare. It might hurt Con. How, she didn't know because she, all of them, were steeped in ignorance, only Thusby had the right book open. She had to go on. Better Dare than those other items.

"What time was this?" Thusby nudged Vinnie and the son used his new pencil as if it were a more useful stub. He wasn't transcribing every word, only what the captain wanted.

"I don't know. Yes, I do. It was before midnight." Before that news broadcast. "Between eleven and midnight."

. "What did she want that time of night?"

She said, "She wanted to see Con."

The a-ha! look on his round face was as strange as anything else in this strange gathering.

She looked about bitterly, "Why isn't Smithery here?" He had everyone else connected with Con, everyone but Chang and Vironova.

Vinnie said as if delighted, "We couldn't find him."

His father scowled. "His name was on the list but we were unable to locate him this morning. Mrs. Crandall, you next."

Dare was at ease. "A friend of mine flew me in from Hollywood at eleven o'clock. You may check that without any trouble at the airport. I went directly from there to Satterlee's, then down here as you jolly well know, and after you turned me down flat I went back to Griselda. She told me to go home and I did."

"Any visitors?"

"No one. None." She was lying but she knew how to do it, answer promptly, fish out a cigarette and light it as you spoke. Dare anyone to question you further.

Thusby coughed and put away the gaseous pipe. He was as dictatorial as an old-fashioned school-master.

"Mr. Brent, start telling about after you left Mrs. Satterlee. You turned up at the Hilton."

"Yes. I went up to the bar for a drink. Pembrooke and Vironova were there and I joined them."

Griselda was cold. He'd gone from her to meet the major.

She couldn't be certain that Kew wasn't in this on the major's side. His oblique suspicions of Pembrooke

could have been to divert her and to terrorize her.
Had all that he'd told her, frightened her with, been
pre-arranged, to make her force Con to give up his investigation of Mannie's disappearance? Had that letter he destroyed incriminated Pembrooke in some
way, or Kew himself?

He continued, "Mrs. Travis joined us when her
party broke up. I escorted her to her room later and
I went to my hotel. And so to bed."

"What time?"

"I don't know exactly. About one."

Captain Thusby said, "It was exactly one-forty
when you reached the Villa Riviera."

He'd stayed longer with Kathie than he knew. Still
there seemed no reason for his hand to waver as he
lit a cigarette.

Kathie answered Thusby's inquiring eyes, "Walker
and I had dinner with Admiral Swales. It was so early
when they left that my husband suggested that I stay
with Kew a while. He took me to my room just like
he said." She smiled sweetly at him. She knew she'd
done nothing wrong.

Thusby had turned to Major Pembrooke. "You left
the roof a bit after midnight with Mr. Vironova?"

Major Pembrooke said, "Yes, Mr. Vironova and I
were discussing a sea spectacle he was planning to
produce. We went to my room to continue discussion
in peace, without the night-club accouterments, as it
were. He left at one-fifteen. I know the time con-
cretely because he kept surreptitiously consulting the
watch on his wrist as he talked. At that hour he
leaped up as if surprised, remarked at the lateness,
and rushed away. I presumed, rightly no doubt, that
he had an amorous rendezvous."

Captain Thusby crumbled the paper slowly in his

fingers. "He had a rendezvous, like you call it, but it wasn't what you thought it was. It was like in that poem Vinnie recites. What's it called, Vinnie?"

The son's face was magenta. He choked, " 'I have a rendezvous with Death.' "

No one said anything, not even—Vironova dead? No one did anything. No faint gasp disturbed that still. The shocked silence on each face was as unbecoming as it was unrehearsed. Yet one of these, unless it were Chang, must have known the reason for the police chief's peremptory morning summons. And there was no one who did not take murder for granted.

Thusby put on spectacles, started reading from a paper as if he hadn't mentioned anything of import. "Mrs. Travis, Major Pembrooke, Mr. Vironova staying at the Hilton." He looked over the old square lenses. "Not a stone's throw between the two hotels. Mighty easy to step from one to the other without nobody saying a word, don't need to take out a car or anything. Mighty near the Village."

"What are you trying to say?" Pembrooke demanded. No one else breathed.

"Other hand nobody to check you in and out when you're not in a hotel. Not too easy in an apartment; somebody might hear you taking your car out. Could be done. Park the car on the street; who's to notice if you go in or out?" Dare's lips emitted smoke. Griselda waited. "Easier in a house of your own. Nobody to check."

Kathie cried it softly, "What are you trying to say? What happened? You must tell us what happened!"

"I'm going to tell you what happened." He took his time, putting his fingertips neatly together, clearing his throat, as if he didn't have the right words.

"Fellow that sweeps out the Village found Mr. Vironova in there this morning. Shot and killed. Know about the Village?"

Visit the Village. Signs everywhere. Under the ground. Subway walk beneath Ocean Boulevard. Curio booths, fortune tellers, street artists, gawkers, hodgepodge.

Kathie whispered, "I've always been nervous about the Village. I don't like it. I've always been afraid of it."

Captain Thusby waited. "Not much of a walk from either hotel to the Village, is it? Is kind of scary when it's deserted. I went through it once that way. Heard every step I took twice as loud as it should be. Echoes." His eyes hardened. "There wasn't any gun there. Any of you keep guns?" The chairs rustled faintly. "Never mind getting anxious. Your rooms are all being searched while you're here."

Albert George's eyes gave his fury away. But he was silent.

"Search warrants all signed," Thusby snapped. "Not that I expect to find the gun that killed Vironova to be setting out in the open marked with finger-prints. Not unless somebody planted it. Too easy to get rid of a gun. Kick it under the board walk. We're scavenging. But not so easy to dreen the ocean. The tide'll bring it in some day." His voice roared as he brought his fist down with a startling thump on the paper-ridden desk. "But we aren't going to wait that long to find who did it. Because it's going to be easy now. The man or woman who's running around killing people in Long Beach"—he spoke as if it were treason to pick his town—"made a big mistake when he killed Mr. Vironova. I'll tell you why." He became confidential. "Mostly when murders happen in a little place it's hard to get to the bottom of them. It's not like New York where there's all kinds of big experts, laboratories, and money." He stressed the latter. "And that's where the murderer made a mistake." He chortled. "Because I got the money now. I got 'unlimited funds.' That's it. 'Unlimited funds.'"

Major Pembrooke consulted his watch. "This is all very interesting, Captain Thusby, but I—"

He was ignored. Thusby said, "Mr. Oppensterner —Jacob Oppensterner himself—told me on the telephone this morning that he'd foot the bills to crack this case, just so long as I cracked it and cracked it fast."

Griselda began to titter deep within her. She could just hear Oppy offering everything, sun, moon, and stars. Any finger laid on a member of his staff was personal to him. He'd be certain that he was next on the list. Poor Oppy, always with the jumps. He'd be frog-green with fear now.

Thusby demanded, "What's so funny, Mrs. Satterlee?"

She hadn't realized her mirth was visible but at his question she let it ripple aloud. "I was just thinking about Oppy, how scared he must be." She laughed and then choked it quickly. The eyes were turned in suspicion on her. She angered. "Never mind. It isn't funny to anyone but me. One thing certain. You can't blame Con for this. He's out of it now." She glowed with triumph as she flung the challenge in all of their stupid faces.

The chief's eyebrows moved up into white bushy points. His voice was gentle but beneath the gentleness was rock-hardness, "Con Satterlee escaped last night."

She'd never had the breath knocked out of her but she knew this was how it must feel. She caught her

lip tight with her teeth and then all at once she began
to shiver as if it were she being hunted. She turned
pathetically to Kew. He was unreadable. She looked
around the room. None of them had known of this.

Dare was sitting upright, her pretensions gone. And
she cried it, "He couldn't have escaped!"

"That's what I thought." Thusby was complacent.

"It's absurd." She was certain of herself. "That
doesn't happen today. It isn't necessary. All you need
is a lawyer."

"Maybe," the chief allowed. "He's gone. He was
gone by midnight."

"You didn't tell me." Her green eyes slitted.

"Didn't tell nobody. Thought maybe I'd made a
mistake and he'd be around somewhere. But he was
gone all right. I'm telling you now because it'll be in
the papers by the time you leave here. I gave it to
the reporters after you folks arrived."

Griselda shook her head. "There's some mistake."
Piteously she asked him, all of them, to believe her,
"He'll be back. I know he will."

Dare said briskly, "He's probably gone to get someone to help him out of this mess. He has influential
friends, Captain Thusby."

"That so?" He tweaked his nose.

"Yes, that's so."

She mustn't mention Barjon Garth. Garth had betrayed Con. She didn't. She said, "The broadcasting
company isn't without influence."

Captain Thusby complained, "He could have told
me what he had in mind. Doesn't look well to have a
prisoner escaping from you."

Griselda pushed back her hair. The room was suf-
focating. Why didn't Thusby say what he must be
thinking? Con's flip line about hacksaws and files.
The police would be certain she had effected the es-

cape. She had to get out before the room began to
swirl; it was already teetering. Thusby and Dare went
on talking like end-men in a minstrel show.

She felt Kew's hand on her arm and she steadied.
He interrupted the dialogue. "I have a Washington
call coming at two, Captain Thusby. And I presume
the women must be feeling rather faint without
lunch. Do you need us longer?"

Thusby looked to Kew, then Griselda. She probably appeared as moon-yellow as she felt. "You can
go, I guess," he said. "Leave your fingerprints in the
outer office." He scotched the major's borning protest. "If you're innocent as you all make out, you
won't mind doing that. And don't any of you leave
town."

Major Pembrooke did protest now. "I must return."

Griselda didn't wait. She was first in line to press
her fingers on the pad, and she was brusque in refusal
of Kew's offer to drive her home. She didn't want to
see or hear of him or any of them again.

3

Con would come. She was certain of it. He would
come and explain all this pother about escape and
murder. The headlines—MURDER SUSPECT ESCAPES
FROM LONG BEACH JAIL—wouldn't scare him away.
The actual story of the break was scant as if Captain
Thusby weren't quite certain as yet that his prisoner
wasn't still playing hide-and-seek about the building.
The box with description didn't sound much like
Con. Any tall, thin, youngish man in a nondescript
dark suit would fit. You couldn't describe Con with
much accuracy. He didn't have a black beard or cauliflower ear or wart on the nose. He was remarkably
average unless you knew him.

The trouble was that other persons would come here too. All of them wanted to reach Con. In particular, Major Pembrooke would come. If he didn't find Con, he might try to make her tell him what Con had learned. She shunted that thought quickly. She'd read too much of Axis methods of persuasion.

She should really put up a sign with her hours on it. The line would form outside the door. But she wasn't prepared for the first entry. Not for Kathie. Yet there she was in her sleazy red dress. "I thought Kew would be here," she said. She looked around as if he might be hiding.

Griselda said coldly, "I came home alone. Did you try his hotel?" She wished there were some way to tell this girl that she was welcome to Kew, that his heart didn't repose here.

Kathie shrank into the big chair. She didn't answer. She was pulling on her handkerchief as if it were made of elastic. She whispered suddenly, "I'm afraid, Mrs. Satterlee. I'm afraid."

"What are you afraid of?"

"Somebody killed Mr. Vironova." Her eyes were startled. "Why was he killed? Who's going to be next?"

Griselda herself had no strength; she couldn't reassure another. She'd be hard put to it to protect herself until Con came. But there might be some infinitesimal piece of information to garner from the frightened girl. "Did Shelley say anything to you about who—she might fear? Why she was carrying a gun?"

Kathie's eyes widened. "Did she have a gun? I didn't know that. I went back to the apartment with her after lunch. She didn't say anything about being afraid." Her nose wrinkled. "I didn't like her really.

I didn't stay long. She was awfully common, wasn't she?"

Griselda repeated as before, "I didn't know her."

"Well, she was. Bleached hair and lying around with not a stitch under her negligee and swearing into the phone." .

"Swearing?" Griselda feigned polite interest, hiding her avidity. "To whom was she talking?"

"Some man. He called her up. At least I suppose it was a man. I don't think she would have talked that way to a woman. Cursing and swearing like a streetwalker."

Griselda had greater interest. "Why was she so annoyed?"

"Well, it sounded as if some man were trying to break an engagement. She was saying if he didn't take her out to dinner that night he'd never have another date in his life."

Griselda's eyes widened. This was important although Kathie didn't know. "How did it come out?"

"Well, I really don't know. She finally said with a lot of swear words that she'd wait for him at the Bamboo Bar and if he didn't come she'd go gunning for him."

"She said that?" Griselda stared. It was so plain now; find the man who had called Shelley, the man who didn't keep his appointment at the Bamboo Bar. There was the murderer delivered unto you.

"Yes, she did. I heard her say it. But I didn't know she really had a gun."

"You didn't tell the police?"

She shook her head. "I told them about lunch. They didn't ask about anything else. You don't think that phone call was important, do you?"

Griselda stated clearly, "I think Shelley Huffaker

was talking then to her murderer. I think if we could find out who made that call—"

It was essential. It couldn't be traced, not this late, but it would be possible to find out where each man had been during the afternoon. All that was needed was investigators and Captain Thusby could afford as many as he liked with Oppy supplying the unlimited resources. She'd telephone to him after she'd rid herself of her guest.

But Kathie lingered. She was talkative now. "Do you think she might have been talking to Mannie? She was always chasing after him. He couldn't stand her. He didn't like blondes." On and on nervously. She seemed frightened to leave, as if there were safety here of all places. Wearily, Griselda manipulated her eventual departure.

Why was Kathie suddenly afraid? She hadn't seemed to be before. It must be because of Vironova. Did she believe that the murderer would think she knew something about Shelley's death, because she'd had a drink with the little Russian the night before?

Griselda's laughter was hysterical, there alone in the creaking cottage. Kathie need not fear. It wasn't Kathie who was endangered. It was she. She was next in line. She had been doing what Sergei had done, seeking the killer. She put her hands together about her throat to stop that dreadful sound. She didn't even know from whom to run. She was without defense, but it was better to go on. There was always the outside chance she could discover the killer in time to tell the police, before he killed her too.

She locked the door. Shelley Huffaker. Sergei Vironova. They were linked as tightly in death as in life. In one of their histories was motive. She couldn't sit idly; she had to further the action. And Si Burke knew everything about everyone. She put in another call to Malibu. He'd still be there. He had a gift for prolonging story conferences when a guest house and cabaña and Oppy's slice of the Pacific were thrown in.

Kew came before the call was completed. Worry ate in his face but she hushed him, spoke into the phone, "Ask Mr. Burke to call back when he comes in."

Kew didn't wait for the receiver to be cradled. He began, "I must see Con. It's of the greatest importance."

She looked at him. She didn't trust him now. He had burned the letter that would have protected Con.

"It's important." Kew was pacing again. She wondered how many furlongs he'd walked since the case was begun. "Griselda, why would he be such a fool as to run out this way?"

She said furiously, "Doubtless he saw he was being framed. He got out before it was too late to prove someone else did it. That's what I'd do. You'd do it. You wouldn't sit there waiting for them to sentence you for something you didn't do."

"But it won't work. My God, Griselda, he can't make it work. Everyone will be tracking him, the police, the murderer, and all the honest citizenry of Southern California. He can't stay escaped. This makes him sign his guilt to everyone but the few of us who know him. If I could only talk to him."

Her eyes narrowed in suspicion. "Why is it important you talk to him? Does the major want you to?" Without caution, she demanded, "What did you report to Pembrooke last night?"

"I? Report to Pembrooke?" The amazement on his face couldn't be simulated. She'd made a bad guess in her weary fear. Relief flooded her, weakened her, and she caught at the chair before she fell.

Kew came to her. "What is the matter, Griselda?"

She touched his hand. "I'm sorry, Kew." Her voice was hysterical. "I'm sorry—"

He said, "Take it easy, darling."

She was babbling, trying to explain, "But you went from me to the Hilton and joined him and—"

He said, "I went to the Hilton to make sure that Kathie was safe. I knew he was stopping there last night and I was afraid that he might have thought up some plausible scheme to get her back on *The Falcon*—alone. I needn't have worried. Walker was there with the Admiral. And Pembrooke was immersed in Vironova."

She was controlled now. "Do you think the major killed him, Kew?"

"I don't know what to think," he said slowly.

"Sergei told me at lunch he was going to meet a woman," Griselda said. "That I didn't know her. Maybe it was true. Maybe he was meeting her last night again. But why the Village?"

"I think he was passing through." He began to walk up and down again. "The killer was following and let him háve it because it was safer there than on the Pike." He was scowling. "If I could only see Con." He went to the door. "Dinner tonight?"

"I'm not going out." She didn't add to it; he understood.

He said, "I'll drop by and help amuse you, if you'd like."

She preferred to be alone if Con came. But if anyone else came, she would welcome his assistance.

He asked, "You do believe he'll come?"

"Yes," she answered almost hopelessly. "He'll come." It was a part of the blueprint. Nothing in this whole affair, save the actual killings, had been a surprise to Con. He had even known he would be arrested, would escape. That was why they came to Long Beach, why she had to promise to remain in this cottage. It had been planned this way. She still didn't know why.

$$\{ 7 \}$$

S H E was restless; she knew how Con must have felt the night that Barjon Garth left, the night that things were scheduled to begin. She couldn't sit quietly, although every step creaking the floor stretched her already tight nerves. She drank a glass of milk; the thought of food was leaden. Slow gray covered the nervous sea. The knock came. Her mouth was dusty as she hurried through the unlighted room.

It wasn't Con in the dusk outside. She wasn't quite certain who it was until he entered, closed the door after him. And then she saw with wonderment the uniform, the tired face of Walker Travis above it.

"Is Con here yet?" he asked.

She said, "No," and the weariness changed to anxiety.

"He isn't?" Surely he knew. "He told me to come here."

"When did he tell you that? When did you see him?"

He seemed sorry to disappoint her eagerness. "He didn't actually tell me. He sent a message."

"When?"

"Yesterday. Yesterday afternoon. I was to come here at seven-fifteen exactly and bring him this." He fumbled the thick brown envelope from an inner pocket.

"Did he say he'd be here?" She couldn't believe it.

"He said, 'Bring it to me,' but—" Again he seemed sorry to disappoint her. "I was to leave it if he wasn't here."

"Oh." There was no assurance then that he would come.

Lieutenant Travis said, "I guess I'd better leave it." He laid it uncertainly on the table. "I'd hoped to see him. Tell him I'd like to see him, will you?" He stood fingering his cap. He said without expression, "I suppose he knows they've found Mannie."

"No!"

"They called me to identify him last night." He swallowed. "It was hard to do."

Her voice was hoarse. "What happened to him?"

"They think he was caught in a riptide." He swallowed again as if there was an obstruction in his throat.

Her hand pointed to the shape of the envelope. "These are—his papers?"

"No. These are just some notes Con wanted."

She withdrew her hand as from a licking flame. The information the major was after, the knowledge of the poor fish. She didn't want it threatening here.

He said awkwardly, "I guess I'd better go. I haven't seen my wife yet. She doesn't even know I'm ashore. I came straight here from the landing. You tell Con I'll be in town all day tomorrow and I'd like to see him. He can reach me at the hotel. Any time tomorrow."

He managed to open the door. "Good night and thank you, Mrs. Satterlee."

She watched him across the tracks, rolling up the street past the bay toward where the trolleys and busses ran, hurrying to Kathie, to Kathie whose eyes hungered for Kew. She heard the creak that meant

footfalls and swung around. Chang was across the
room watching her. She pushed back closer to the
door; she could get away if she could open it quickly.
But she had no breath; her heart was racing noisily,
her whole body weighted.

And then her eyes jumped to the table. Even in the
deepening dusk, the outline of the envelope was not
there. She moved and lighted the floor lamp in one
rapid motion. The envelope was not there.

She forgot fear. "You took Con's envelope. Put it
back."

He was polite as always. "I didn't take anything,
Mrs. Satterlee. Is this what you mean?" He stooped
behind the table, raised up with the envelope in his
hands.

She crossed and snatched it from him. And then
fear returned and again she backed from him toward
the door. "How did you get in?"

He nodded his head toward the bay window opening on the sea wall. "I climbed up. Used to be a 'cat'
once when I was younger."

"Why did you break in here?" If he'd come to steal
the envelope, why had he given it up to her?

"I wasn't breaking in, Mrs. Satterlee. I haven't done
anything like that for years. Con can tell you. I'm
honest."

"Why are you here?" Ignorance and suspicion made
her panicky.

"I came to see Con."

"He isn't here. I don't know where he is." She
frowned. "That's no excuse for coming through a
window." She must remember to keep them locked.

"Yes it is. I wanted to see him private, not with the
coppers."

She looked at him under her lashes. "The coppers
will be checking who comes in or out. And you don't

want to be checked?"

"No'm, I don't. I've got a criminal record, Mrs. Satterlee. I wouldn't want them to fingerprint me. They might find out and think I had a hand in these murders."

She was suspicious. "I suppose you know nothing of them?"

"Not a thing except what I've read in the papers."

"Is that why you hid out this morning when Captain Thusby was looking for you?"

He asked in mild surprise, "Was he looking for me? I didn't know. I had to get some groceries for my niece. She and her husband have come to pay me a visit. What did Captain Thusby want, if you'd be so good to tell me?"

"He wanted to ask questions about Sergei Vironova's murder."

He shook his head. "I wouldn't have been any help. I never met that Mr. Vironova, so far as I know. Why would he want to ask me about it?"

She told him, "Because he knows you're mixed up in this some way. You're always somewhere around when these people are together—even at Catalina." And she asked with sudden idea, "Did you help Con escape? Were you the one waiting to see him yesterday?"

"I saw him yesterday, Mrs. Satterlee. I dropped in to find out if I could do anything for him. But I didn't help him escape. I was working last night." His face suddenly listened. He said, "You're about to have company. I'd better go."

Before she could speak he was at the windows, had flung himself over the sill and vanished. She restrained the desire to run over and watch the descent. He must be experienced to negotiate the sheer drop. And what was Con doing with a second-story man?

She faced the door with resignation, wondering who this one was to be. She saw his bulk through the pane, momentarily held the knob fast. He knew she was there; he could see through into the lighted room better than she could out into the dark. She was terrified. But she could not refuse to admit him; if he wanted to enter, the rickety catch would not restrain him. Appeasement might be a weak game but it was better to play at it, try to keep him neutral, until she had the defense of Con in back of her again.

She opened the door. "Major Pembrooke?" she queried. "I couldn't be certain. We've no porch light and without my glasses I don't see well." She led him into the living room, went on talking, making her voice natural as if she were calm, "I didn't expect you." She realized then that she still held Lieutenant Travis's brown envelope. There was no way to hide it; she was not a sleight-of-hand artist. "Won't you sit down?"

But he stood there, his mouth curved up at the corners, no smile on it. "You did expect someone? Con?"

"No indeed." If she could be seated her trembling wouldn't be so noticeable. But she could move with more rapidity standing. "No. Con certainly won't come here with the police watching the house." Warn him.

"Are they watching the house?" The curve widened. "Captain Thusby is on his way to visit the *Antarctica* with Admiral Swales. The boy is being amused in Mrs. Crandall's apartment. To be sure they may have delegated a watcher, with their 'unlimited funds,' one who doesn't know one of us from the other." He was amused. There was no use keeping up pretense; he wasn't disguising himself as a lamb tonight. She waited warily, holding the envelope against her.

"Just whom were you expecting, may I ask?"

"Kew." She repeated with emphatic truth, "Kew is coming."

"Then I must be quick. I want no trouble. Mr. Brent is not busy tonight. Lieutenant Travis is in town." His hands were in the pockets of his tweed topcoat. His hands and a gun?

She stood without moving. If he had come to kill her too, she could do nothing.

"Give me that package."

She didn't know what to do. If only the police, or Kew, or someone would come now. She asked brokenly, "You mean this envelope?"

"Yes." He put out one hand to take it but she pressed it closer to her. His eyes burned at her but otherwise he controlled his anger at her refusal. He kept his hand outstretched. "I. came for that. I have been waiting for the authorities to make just such a stupid mistake. Give it to me."

She couldn't defy him but she did, brazenly. "You can't have it. It's for Con."

Their eyes held and she didn't falter at the cold decision she read in his. Then he spoke, softly, between his teeth, "I said I wanted no trouble." Without warning he took one-long step to her and slapped her across the face. The sound was a thunderclap. He picked up the envelope from the floor, put it in his pocket. Her glazed eyes watched him, one empty hand held to a throbbing bruise.

He spoke without inflection, "I do not expect you to mention my visit or its purpose to anyone. I have ways of dealing with those who make trouble for me. You do not wish to be hurt. Nor do you wish your foolish husband to be hurt. And just in case you or he should consider offering yourselves as sacrifice, let me say it will be of no value. I am safe from such irritations. Do you understand?"

He waited for her response and she whispered, "Yes." He was safe; powerful, mechanized governments were protecting him with false papers and a fast ship and an available plane. He could move more swiftly than she. Kew and Con had both warned her that he was out of her class; he was. Nails were pounding into her head. She closed her eyes for a moment. If he would only go.

He said, "I believe you do," and then both heard the voices and footsteps. It mustn't be Con; dear God, not at this moment.

Major Pembrooke spoke quickly, stonily, "There has been no trouble."

She let him open the door; when she saw Dare and Kew she sank weakly to the couch. They had been in high spirits; the major only slightly dampened them.

Dare greeted, "What are you doing here, Albert George? Looking for Con like everyone else?" She and Kew were stowing paper sacks and paper cartons on the table. "Griselda wouldn't dine with us so we've come to dine with her."

The major said, "I'm sorry I can't join you. But I've been delayed as it is." His eyes warned Griselda again while hers tried to convey her frantic promise. "Good-night, Mrs. Satterlee. Don't bother to get up."

She watched him go, watched Dare close the door after him. Then together the two looked at her; they had noticed; it was too much to hope that they would not.

Dare's voice was tense, "Griselda, what happened to your face?"

She put her hand up and away, looking at the palm as if there would be blood on it. She tried hard to smile, to say, "A wave knocked—"

Kew came toward her, his deep voice sick with shock, "Griselda, my dear."

She ran into his arms, hiding her face against his coat, sobbing without sound. He meant nothing to her but he was comfort and strength at this moment. His hand smoothed her hair.

Dare's words were flippant, "Am I necessary?" But there was tension underlying them.

Griselda fought for control. She must stop the terrible silent tremors that were tearing her apart.

Kew asked quietly, "What happened, Griselda?"

The fear that froze her made her steady. She mustn't point any hint at Major Pembrooke, nothing that Dare could carry back to him. She stepped away uncertainly. "I'm sorry. My nerves just went all at once, I guess. The strain's been too much." She pushed back her hair, tried for natural words. "Let me wash my face and I'll join you. I didn't know I was hungry but it smells good. You're angels to remember me. I didn't have a chance to market." She went into the bedroom. She didn't care what they'd say of her behind her back. She wouldn't change her explanation.

One side of her face was mottled red; it must fade before Con came. He wouldn't accept any explanatory lie about a wave knocking her down.

She didn't expect to find food edible but it was more than that. It was worth increasing the ache in her jaw. With the coffee courage returned. She could ask, "What's the latest? I haven't had the radio on nor seen a paper."

"No news," Kew replied. "No sign of Con. The papers are saying unofficially that he's left this neighborhood, maybe gone into Mexico."

"The papers are silly." Dare was blunt. "He's not leaving till he sweeps up. Con wouldn't."

That was true. He hadn't run away. Not when he'd told Griselda to keep a candle burning here. He

would come at his first opportunity. She didn't know
how much was safe to say; she didn't know where
Dare fitted in. Dare was seldom the wholesome, well-
fed, and relaxed young woman she appeared now.
The real Dare was thin as a snake with a sharp face
and wise emerald eyes. She knew Major Pembrooke
too well.

She asked, "Was Vinnie Thusby at your apartment
this evening, Dare?"

"Yes." Dare wondered. "Why and how? Oh, Albert
George, of course. He dropped in to talk about doing
over his salon but as soon as Vinnie appeared, he
skipped."

Talk about decorating, her eye! "What did Vinnie
want?"

"The nearest I could judge," Dare laughed beautifully, "it was to share a sack of peanut brittle. He
worked in some questions about Shelley. When I told
him I did not know she was Vironova's mistress, he
almost choked."

Her eyebrows met. "I'd like to know why she
descended on me to get herself done in. I wish I'd
murdered her myself long ago. I'd have done a neat
job, one of those careful poisonings that no one suspects until after you've served up a baker's dozen.
Of course, Shelley wouldn't have cared for that, no
publicity. But there'd be no involving everyone who
happened to be in town that night."

"You weren't in town," Griselda reminded.

"No." Dare fitted a cigarette into the elongated
scarlet tube. "I'd be clear of the mess if she hadn't
descended on me."

"Major Pembrooke wasn't in town."

Dare looked under her brows. "He has nothing to
do with this. What about Walker Travis, Griselda?
The *Antarctica* isn't as far as Avalon, and he has spe-

cial privileges, you know. You can't cross him off just because he is Walker Travis. I don't believe Thusby has. He and the Admiral weren't going out to the *Antarctica* today for the choppy ride."

"You mean they were going out to question the lieutenant?"

Dare laughed. "What else?"

Griselda said, "They won't see him. He's on shore."

Dare cut her laugh as with a knife. "How do you know?"

"He came here." She couldn't say why. "Looking for Con."

Dare was stamping out her cigarette in the tray.

Kew said, "There goes our theory. I thought Thusby might be searching for Con on the *Antarctica,* that Walker Travis could have been hiding him out. But if he doesn't know where Con is—" He rammed his hands in his pockets.

Griselda spoke softly then. "Mannie Martin has been found." Both of them looked at her and her heart stopped beating. This wasn't news.

Dare turned away. "I'm going. Griselda, I don't think you should stay here alone. I don't think it's safe. I'll offer you a bed again—if you're superstitious, I'll take it and you can have mine. Won't you?" She seemed sincere, almost likable.

But Griselda refused. "I can't leave here, Dare. Thank you."

Dare knew why but she was certain it wasn't safe. She stood hesitant.

Kew said to her, "Don't worry. I'll stay with Griselda."

"You're being absurd," Griselda told them. "I'm not afraid." But she was. Her eyes saw the bay window, the thin door. They saw the neighboring cottage, too near now.

Kew continued, "I'm used to night shifts. I'll do my sleeping daytimes. Griselda mustn't be left alone."

She was helpless between them. He and Dare were saying something secret to each other. She didn't know exactly but she knew they were determined she was not to be left alone.

Dare smiled. "I knew I wasn't essential. I'll see you tomorrow. Happy dreams."

Griselda locked the door at once. Even if Kew were present, there should be no unannounced intruders this time. She said, "I really don't think you need stay. I'm not worried. I've been here alone before and safe."

"You weren't safe tonight before we came."

She didn't answer him.

"Two are stronger than one, Griselda. I've plenty of work to keep me busy. I'll park out here." He came to her, spoke seriously. "Mannie has been found. That means this thing will tighten up. I'm sure if Con could let us know, he'd want us to watch out for you. You don't mind, do you?"

"I don't mind." It didn't do any good to mind. She smiled. "And I'm going to bed right now. I'm frazzled."

"Good night. Will it bother you if I use Con's typewriter? Keep you awake?"

She answered, "Will it keep me awake? With Con my husband?"

She closed the bedroom door.

If she could tell Kew about the envelope! But she was afraid to speak; she had been warned. She didn't know what to do. Maybe it was better this way, better that Con didn't receive the information. Maybe Pembrooke would go away now that he had what he wanted. For the first time since Con's abrupt desertion she prepared for bed comfortably, not hearken-

ing to rasps and rustles. Kew was outside the door.
Nevertheless, she wished him miles away. If Con did
appear, she didn't want an audience.

2

Waking brought knowledge. She had been foggy
thinking Con would come here. He'd figure by staying away she would be safe, not realizing that she was
more menaced than he at the moment. All along he'd
stressed keeping her out of it. She could go out without fear of missing him. And she must go. The lieutenant must be told that it was undelivered, the envelope containing the information which he didn't
know he had. Not who had stolen it, no suggestion of
that, merely that it was gone. She dressed rapidly.
The navy-blue reefer—mornings were cool—would
hide the bruised look of her cheek.

Kew said, "You're up early."

"I'm going into action." She had no nerves now.
Daylight was reassuring.

"Take my car if you'd like."

"I'd like." Anything but that shattering wreck.
"Shall I drop you at the hotel?"

He looked at her. "I don't think we should leave
this place empty. If you have an extra blanket I can
throw over me, I'll take a snooze on the bed. When
you return, I'll go back to the hotel and change."

She didn't tell him Con wouldn't come. Even reasoning didn't make that absolutely certain. Con had
unexplainable vagaries. She didn't think he would
come but if he did, it would be well for Kew to be
there.

It was no more than nine but surely Walker Travis
would be up; reveille made early habits. She used the
house phone. Kathie's voice answered, even half

asleep it wasn't irritable, it held that unbelievable
sweetness. "No. He went back to the ship this morning." He'd changed his plans then because he couldn't
reach Con.

She asked, "When will he return?"

"I really don't know, Mrs. Satterlee. He never tells
me."

Griselda hesitated. "If he comes in today, tell him
I want to see him, will you?"

"Yes, I will." The voice asked softly, sleepily, "Is
Kew with you?"

"No. He's at the house."

There was no response to that as if sleep had
claimed the voice upstairs again. Griselda left Kathie
to her slumbers. She went again into the open.

She didn't want to stop at Dare's but she must find
out if Dare had seen Walker Travis. She'd certainly
rushed off at his name. His change of plan could have
resulted from that meeting.

The apartment faced Bixby Park but on the Junipero side. Shelley would have had to walk the entire
square of the park to meet death.

There was a slight wait before Dare's voice said
through the speaker, "Second floor front. Come up."
She opened the door herself to Griselda. "I'm not
dressed. I was getting ready for the beach." She didn't
look messy before dressing as Kathie did; her dark
hair was sleek against her shoulders, the gray slipper
satin robe was pulled tight about the figure men always mentioned, the color of her lips and nails was a
bright foil to her perfect tan. "Come on in while I
step into a suit. I've a day off. The admiral took the
major to San Diego early—to view Mannie's effects."

The bedroom was sleek, clean, too. Dare caught up
the flag-red suit and went beyond into the bathroom.
She called back, "No trouble last night?"

"No." Griselda was staring at the ashtray on the bed table. Some of the stubs wore the red circlet of a woman's. More of them didn't. That was the way Con put out cigarettes, crumpled them up on their sides, all the same length. One was still sending up smoke. And the closet door, ajar, showed a paisley heap on the floor. Dare didn't throw her clothes on the floor. Con's aim at a closet hook had never yet been successful. She felt a little sick inside. Chang had packed those orange pajamas, bought special for the honeymoon. The blue paisleys Con had bought for the first honeymoon had done a one-horse chaise just before the second wedding. Con didn't believe in being overstocked with night clothes; he didn't believe in night clothes.

Dare returned quickly. The red on the golden brown was a flaunt. She said, "I asked, any trouble?" She went to the closet, opened the door wide, hung up her robe, stooped and hung the pajamas. She brought out white clogs and a white beach reefer. But Griselda wasn't watching this. She was looking out of the window at the fire escape. Dare went on talking, "I tried to reach you this morning but no answer."

"Kew went to bed when I left." Why couldn't they choose up sides again? Kew wanted Dare; she wanted Con. But Con and Dare wouldn't trade. "Nothing happened." Why had Con married her again? Did he have to be married to her to have any fun with Dare? It wasn't her idea of fun. She came back to sit on the bed. The closet door was closed now; the ashtray was emptied into the wastebasket. "Have you any news?"

"Nothing at all. I tried to see Walker but the Travises were out. That's her kind. I knew it when I met her. Coldblooded, selfish little beast with all that icing on top of her face. Walker comes in worn out, sick, to spend a quiet evening, and she drags him out.

Her first husband was a suicide, did you know? Shot himself. Couldn't take it any longer I presume. And this second doesn't have any sense where she's concerned, follows where she beckons. I could spit on her."

She reddened her lips again, perfumed them, brushed down the shining hair. No wonder Con went for her. She flaunted sex like a new hat. But it wasn't fair. He should come home.

She went on, "She hustles anything in pants. Regular small-town Kansas belle. She trailed Mannie until he practically had to tell her to lay off. He needed Walker too much to risk trouble. Then Kew came along and she moved over on his side, lock, stock, and barrel." If Dare hadn't known Mannie, she certainly had known where to go for information.

But Griselda couldn't stay here trying to meet Dare's gossip, trying to ignore that sickness licking over her. No wonder Dare was pleased with the world. She wasn't. She had to get away quickly. She made some sort of excuse; she would never remember what, and she ran.

If she wanted to reach Con, she knew now who could make arrangements. Her eyes stung. She had too much stubborn pride ever to ask Dare. She needed him the worst way but she'd do without him forever before that. She braked the car the way she would like to brake all roving husbands, particularly her own.

Kew met her at the door. "I was about to borrow your car. I have to run into town and file some stuff."

She'd meant to ask him before. "Did I have any calls last night or this morning?"

"Not last night. I wouldn't have heard a fire alarm this morning." He was ready to leave. "I'll run in again after lunch. Anything you want to do?"

"No." She would stay right here and mull over the perfidy of the genus male species husband. She was a fool to let it matter. That's what had made trouble before. If she had any sense she'd take Con as he was. For better and for worse, usually worse. Her sickness was leaving as her anger increased. Some day she'd serve him the same way, see how he liked it! He wouldn't. All males (species husband) believed in the double standard. And she wouldn't anyway; no man in the world save Con meant any whit to her. Con had spoiled other men simply by being Con.

She didn't understand why Si hadn't called back unless he were on a really good one. Just in case it happened to be actual work delaying him, she'd wait the day before checking. Apparently that was her rôle in the affair, to sit and wait. If only the omniscient Burke would call.

A watched phone never rang. She changed to her bathing suit, descended to the beach below. Flat on her back she looked up at the sea wall, the rocks smoothed by endless planing of the waters, seemingly no possible foothold. Maybe Chang was a pixie, really hidden in the cottage, creeping out when best to upset her.

It was late afternoon when Kew returned. He halloed from the cat walk and she ran to join him. He'd brought a grip. "You don't mind? I'm not moving in on you but it's rather hard not to have a few things handy."

She didn't think his pajamas would be orange cotton or that he would wad them on the floor. They weren't and he hung their monogrammed ice-blue perfection as carefully as a suit. He said, "I had lunch at the Hilton. Garth's back from the fishing trip."

She didn't believe it. It was to last two weeks. "Are you certain it was he?"

"Saw him face to face."

"Do you think—" She couldn't ask it. Garth wouldn't turncoat so entirely to return to track Con in person. "Did you see Kathie?"

"Talked to her by phone. She was spending the day in bed resting up from last night. Said she and Walker got in pretty late."

"She didn't say why he went back to the ship?" She explained, "He planned to be in town all day."

"Maybe he went to rest up." Kew mixed a drink.

The telephone rang. Si at last. But it wasn't. It was Dare. "Griselda, can you hop over here at once? I need help." She didn't sound worried; she sounded efficiently decisive.

Griselda didn't ever want to go near Dare's again. This might be an invitation to see Con. She wouldn't go. Another woman had no business inviting her to see her own husband. She began excuses but Dare cut her off.

"I can't handle this alone."

Griselda suggested, "Kew is here."

"Good. Bring him along. But get over quickly." She rang off.

"What's that about?"

Griselda shrugged. "The queen commands, darling. Dare."

"Why?"

"She says she needs help." She didn't believe it. "I'll dress."

Kew said, "I wouldn't take the time." He was serious. She looked questioningly at him but he added no more, stood there with worried scowl.

"I won't then. Let me take off this suit." She hurried; Dare might be in trouble.

Kew was waiting anxiously. They ran down the steps and into the car. She conjured Albert George and a full Oriental army standing guard but the apartment looked normal and Dare opened the door. She said, "She's been like that ever since the police came."

They saw Kathie then, weeping hysterically, her crumpled white rayon quivering face-down on the magenta couch.

Griselda was sharp. "The police?"

Kew had gone to the girl, knelt beside her, touching her hair and shoulder, speaking in undertone.

"Yes, the police." Dare sighed. She raised an eyebrow privately and sardonically. "He's good at that."

Griselda sank into a chair and Dare perched across.

"I got myself into it. I'll admit that. I'd gone down to the hotel to see if Walker were coming in tonight by any chance. Captain Thusby was behind me at the desk and insisted I go up to Kathie's room with him."

"But what did he want with her?"

Dare answered quietly but distinctly, and Kew turned in amazement. "Walker Travis is missing."

Kathie was shrill. "He's dead! I know he's dead! He's been murdered!"

"She won't talk," Dare drawled.

Kew ordered, "Quiet, Dare!" He spoke to the girl as if she were a hurt child. "Kathie's going to tell me, aren't you, Kathie?"

Dare's lip curled like a scimitar. She told Griselda but she knew Kew was listening, "Captain Thusby asked her where her husband was and she went like that. He couldn't get anything out of her. I finally . brought her here thinking she'd calm down but she's damnably persistent. That was at four o'clock and she's never stopped since."

"Why did you call me?"

"You saw Travis. I thought maybe he might have

said something that would give a hint of his plans."

"He said he'd be in town today. That's all." The envelope for Con had something to do with it. Had Major Pembrooke done away with Walker Travis? But how could he? The lieutenant had been with Kathie last night. Pembrooke and the Admiral were together today.

She cried, "But of course. He's gone to San Diego with Admiral Swales."

Kathie turned off the sobs. Her tear-starred eyes were hopeful. "Are you sure?"

"Naturally, I'm not sure," she returned in irritation. "But it seems logical, doesn't it? He planned to stay in town; he isn't in town; obviously he isn't on the *Antarctica*, that would be checked first. Who but the admiral would change all his plans?"

Watching the reaction of Dare and Kew she wasn't so certain. Kathie believed it, was eager to believe it; the other two were pretending.

Kew said, "That's it, Kathie," and Dare went to the phone. "I don't know why that didn't occur to me. I'll call Cap'n Thusby and tell him."

Kathie smiled tremulously at Kew. "I must look a sight." She went into the bedroom.

Dare had finished the conversation. She spoke quietly. "He's coming up here. For God's sake, Kew, don't let her go screwball again."

"Me?"

She half-glared. "Yes, you. You can handle the little fiend. You have the right touch with bitches." They stared evenly at each other.

Griselda was certain. There was something between them, something secret, and it was a part of this business. She would go. Kathie was weak, could be handled, but they weren't going to handle her further. More important at the moment, she didn't want to answer Thusby's questions.

She said, hoping it sounded casual, "I forgot a call I put in. Hollywood business. I'll have to get back."

"You can switch it here," Kew suggested.

"It's private." She didn't apologize for bluntness.

Dare too was blunt. "You'd better stick around. Thusby wants to see you too." She softened it. "He said for us to stay together until he—that's probably he now." She answered the buzzer.

Kathie returned, her crumpled dress smoothed a little. "Is that the police?"

Kew took her to the couch beside him. "Don't be nervous about Thusby, Kathie. Griselda probably has the answer, but if Walker is missing, you can help out by giving full information."

She smiled at him. "I'll be good."

The captain eased down as if the low white-leather chair were a bear trap. "What's this important information you have, ma'am?"

Dare spoke. "Admiral Swales took Major Pembrooke to San Diego today. Mrs. Satterlee thought Walker Travis might be with them."

"What made you allow that, if you don't mind saying?"

Griselda explained her reasoning, realizing too well that she was wrong. All of them were telling her so, all but Kathie who didn't seem to care now that Kew was here.

Thusby nodded, raised his voice, "Mrs. Travis, your husband say anything about San Diego?"

"No, he didn't." She wasn't interested in this old man. "But he never tells me what he's doing."

"Mrs. Travis." He was determined to have her serious attention, although fearful of her turning on the hysteria again. He tried for a medium between cajoling and commanding. "Did he say anything at all about his plans for the day?"

Wide-eyed she said, "No, he never tells me."

He was helpless, shaking his white fuzz.

Kew took over. "Kathie, you were going to tell me all about it. From the time Walker surprised you yesterday. Why don't you? It might help Captain Thusby out." He nodded aside to the subsiding officer, urged, "Start in, Kathie."

She told it with that dreadful sweet naïveté that made Dare's nostrils quiver. "It was about dinnertime when he came. I didn't expect him but he said he had some business on shore. We had dinner in our room because he wanted to. That's when I called you that we wouldn't join you, Kew. He didn't want to go out. And then after dinner—we had such a nice dinner, everything he liked, steak and cabbage and chocolate ice cream—" She didn't even notice the resistant faces. "Then he wanted to run down to our house, see if everything was all right."

"Your house?" Thusby asked.

"Yes. We have a cottage at Huntington Beach. But I've had to stay on at the hotel because you said not to leave town—after Shelley's death, you know—"

It hadn't occurred to Griselda to be curious before about the lieutenant's wife living at a major hotel. She was certain that Thusby's order, however, hadn't been a hardship on Kathie; she would have made another excuse to stay in town with Kew if this one had not arisen.

"We don't have a car but a friend of ours keeps his in a garage on Pine. He lets us use it. He's away with the fleet. I went for the car."

"You took it out?"

"Yes. Walker wanted to telephone. I don't know

who. He stopped in the drugstore. I went for the car and I picked him up and we drove to Huntington Beach." She looked at Kew. "We stayed there all evening. It was such a beautiful night. We just did about everything the way we used to—" She swallowed hard.

"Used to before what?" Captain Thusby's eyes had leaped.

Kew took her hand. Her eyes were misty. "Before Mannie disappeared. It's changed Walker so dreadfully. We used to have fun but now—" Her voice quavered. "You don't think anything's happened to him, do you? He hasn't been himself at all lately." She pleaded for the right answer.

"Probably in San Diego," Thusby grunted without assurance. "You took the car back to the garage?"

"Yes. Walker still wanted to reach whoever it was. I let him off at a drugstore; it was just before midnight. I parked the car and walked back to the hotel."

"Alone?" Dare asked.

"I'm used to it." She was as sweet as Dare wasn't. "I knew he was anxious about something. I was in bed when he came in. He hadn't had any luck, he said. This morning he was gone when I woke. I thought he'd gone back to the ship just the way he always did. Then when he"—she just glanced at Thusby—"came this afternoon, I was frightened, Kew. I was afraid something awful had happened to Walker. So many dreadful things have happened lately."

Kew said, "You needn't worry. Nothing's happened."

"No, nothing's happened," Thusby agreed. "Nothing we know about. Maybe I've been worried for nothing. Like as not he'll turn up with the admiral tonight. It's like Mrs. Travis says, so many things happening, you get to seeing shadows." He took his cap, struggled up from the chair.

Griselda let out her breath and then she caught it tightly again. He hadn't forgotten her.

"Now, Mrs. Satterlee, what's this about Lieutenant Travis calling on you?"

"Not on me," she rejected. "He came to see Con. He'd had a message telling him, he said. But Con wasn't there."

"He leave any word with you?"

"Only that he'd be in town today if I could tell Con." She looked stonily at him. "But I don't know where Con is or how to reach him." Deliberately she asked Dare, "You haven't heard from him, have you?"

Dare lied flatly, "No."

Thusby grunted. "If you hear from either of them, call me." He stumped away.

Griselda didn't hate him any more, now that he didn't have Con locked up where he could railroad him for murder. She felt safe in fact only in his reassuring presence. He was the one person in the whole set that she could be certain represented just what he appeared to be, an old dog with no new tricks.

Dare said, "We'll have a drink all around before you go."

Kathie was doleful, her fingers itching at Kew's coat sleeve. "I just can't bear to be alone. I hate hotels; you're so alone in them. And now not knowing where Walker is. I'm so worried. I don't know what to do." She looked helplessly at Kew. "If Walker is missing, I haven't hardly any money. He never gives me any. He makes enough but he takes care of his mother and sister and all his relatives besides. I can't stay on at the hotel running up bills—"

Kew did not rise to the bait.

Kathie's eyes saw every luxury of Dare's apartment. "If there were only somewhere in Long Beach that I could stay."

It was an obvious bid and surprisingly Dare accepted it. "I have an extra room. You can stay here for a few days."

Kathie demurred; Kathie protested, but she would stay.

Kew said, "If it's settled, I'll run you down to the Hilton, Kathie, and we'll gather up your things. After that what about dinner for all of us?"

Kathie was delighted. "Let's dress up, go to the Sky Room."

"Forget our woes," Dare said in disgust.

Griselda refused. "I've that business call. I'd rather be home under the circumstances."

Kew told her, "I won't stay late. You won't be afraid until I get there?"

Kathie looked from him to Griselda. The icing was scraped away showing almost animal hate beneath.

Griselda said quickly, "You needn't come, Kew."

He told her definitely, "I'll be out."

She didn't look at Kathie again. She refused his offer for a lift, waited until they had left before calling a cab. She stated, "Three's proverbial."

Dare was watching from the front window. She turned. "I don't wonder you're dodging tonight. I would if I could. But we both can't desert Kew in his hour of need." To herself she added, "That woman is determined to have him."

Griselda agreed. "You might tip her off that I'm not a rival." She laughed. "I don't like the way she claws at me."

Dare was frowning. "You mean she thinks you want Kew?"

"Didn't you notice?"

"No." She held the frown. "Wouldn't you think Kew would explain to her?"

The cab sounded below.

"I will tell her, Griselda. I don't want her thinking that. If you can stand it, join us later. Four is less a crowd."

Griselda shook her head. "Sorry. Doesn't interest me."

She went down, directed the driver. But she changed directions on the main street of Belmont, paid him off. She must have the papers, see what they were saying about Travis and Con. It was but a few blocks to the cottage and still twilight. The major wasn't in town. She crossed to a sandwich shop, and while she waited for the steaks to broil, sat on the twirling counter stool, watching the green and gold neon sign of the Bamboo Bar cater-corner across. It would be so nice if she could go over and pick up Con from his accustomed haunt inside.

Her newspapers under arm, the paper sack of sandwiches in hand, she walked on past the firehouse, crossed again to stroll along the bay front toward the cottage. She didn't want to get there. This early evening peace was better if only she had Con, and no one else, to share it. The yellow light coming slowly out of the sea might be truly a honey moon.

Imagination. Banal imagination. But it wasn't imagination, peering ahead, that her garage doors were open and the wrecky motor gone. Con had been here! She ran then, stumbling across the tracks by instinct, not looking for the trolley, stopped there in front of the empty garage.

There had been no need for haste; if the car was gone, so was he. And then she heard it, no other motor sounded that much like an amateur on the trap drums. She swirled, began waving high her arm, there on the curb. The wreck was scrambling slowly down the street as if it had been parked above waiting for her to appear.

"Con, Con—" She forgot his defections in her greed to see him. "Oh, Con—" But peering out as she peered in was no Con. Chang's face was ugly as well as blank and she drew up stiffly, clutching the news and the brown-paper sack.

He croaked, "Con sent me after you, Mrs. Satterlee."

"Kind of him." He wouldn't come himself; he'd go to Dare's but he'd send his second-story man for her. She wondered if this were the truth as Chang's other incredible lies had been. She didn't want to disappear. She didn't want to fall into Albert George's hands. If she could only leave word for Kew, but the car was waiting impatiently, the engine coughing.

She stepped back warily as Chang leaned across to fumble with the door. He stated, "Con don't have much time, Mrs. Satterlee. We'll have to hurry if you're going to see him."

She decided. With even the faintest possibility offered of seeing Con, she would risk it. Without words, she climbed in beside him. The car continued east toward Seal Beach. It had been ridiculous to suspect Chang; he was driving their own car; Con must have had another set of keys to give him.

She asked no questions. But night was closing in rapidly. When he drew off the road at a lonely, fog-ridden curve, her jumpiness impelled speech. "What's the matter?"

He didn't look at her. "I wonder, Mrs. Satterlee, would you mind being blindfolded the rest of the way?"

She drew away. "I most certainly would," she stated.

He said, "Con don't want anyone to knew where he's hiding out at. He told me to ask you."

She had her hand on the door catch. She knew how it had to be wrestled with but she hoped she could bluff him; certainly he couldn't remember all the vagaries of the chassis. She said, "I don't believe a word of it. Con wouldn't ask me to go in for such hocus-pocus."

His face had expression enough now. His jaw was set. He declared, "Con said to bring you to him and not let you know the way." He took her arms, pulled them behind her.

She heard the clink of steel before she realized that the sound meant the fastening of handcuffs. She opened her mouth for a futile scream. There were no cars in sight; those that would pass would speed up, not hesitate, at screaming; only the thousand-to-one chance that a radio patrol would be cruising near would bring help. While she hesitated, he was grousing, "When Con says something to me it's orders." She did let out a faint sound as the sleep mask covered her eyes. The car had started again with Chang muttering furiously, "It's orders, that's what it is." They were going at rapid speed; they curved and turned and curved again. When they stopped she would run for it; she wouldn't let herself be delivered helpless into Albert George's hands. At least she would try to save herself.

But the car didn't stop in the open. She sensed the move under cover, probably a garage, and she heard the doors clang behind them before he cut the motor.

He told her, "Slide out, Mrs. Satterlee, and up this way." His voice wasn't obsequious now.

With her feet on the floor, she balked. "I'm not going any further. Let me out of here."

He made no pretense of courtesy. "Mrs. Satterlee, you're walking up them steps if I have to drag you. Now get going."

He propelled her, up, up, up. She was more angry than frightened, feeling her way step by step, his heavy breathing beside her. He opened a door and she saw light under the mask.

"Sit there," he said.

Her head was swirling as his footsteps receded. She sat there, feeling the overstuffed chair under her; sat there trembling now, waiting for door sounds, for more footsteps, for that voice.

THE voice wasn't stone; it was almost gurgling. "Why don't you take off those fool things?"

A hand lifted the mask, Con's hand, Con standing there, laughing down at her. Con. Fury shook her. Con having the nerve after all this to leave her handcuffed while he draped himself over the opposite chair and began eating one of her steak sandwiches. She had no words.

He said, "All you have to do is press that little jigger by the wrist and off they come. They're Junior G-man's. Bought them for a dime at Woolworth's."

She felt the scarcely hidden clasp with her thumb. In unbroken silence she dropped them indignantly. They clinked.

"Hungry? How about a sandwich?" He held out her own sack.

She was starving but not nearly enough to accept her food from him.

"No?" He unwrapped the other one. "They're pretty good."

She encased her words in ice as she uttered them. "Will you kindly tell me the meaning of this childish mumbo-jumbo?"

"Didn't Chang explain?"

She hadn't heard him come in. "I tried to, Con, honest, but she wasn't buying any. I'm afraid I lost my temper, Mrs. Satterlee, but when Con gives orders, they're my orders."

Con said, "That's all right, Chang. Keep an eye on the street, will you?"

He nodded. "Sure, Con." He went out.

Con asked, "Smoke?" He held out his usual disreputable package. She refused.

"Who slugged you?"

She touched her cheek. "I fell—"

"Yeah. I know that one. You charged a doorknob." He scowled. "Did Chang—"

"No, not Chang," she reassured him.

"Kew?"

She laughed out loud. "No."

"Who was it?" He advanced on her.

She said quickly, "It was Major Pembrooke." She hadn't meant to speak but anyone's sudden motion at her, even Con's, had power to startle now. Her nerves were that shaky.

Con said almost with deadly calmness, "I'll take care of Albert George for that."

She cried in sudden terror. "You mustn't! You mustn't! He's dangerous, terribly so. You mustn't do anything to him!"

He set his chin. "He's not as tough as he thinks."

"You mustn't!" she reiterated. She repeated Kew's warning. "He's after you, Con. He will kill you."

"Why did he sock you?"

"Because I wouldn't give him the envelope Walker Travis brought for you."

"My God, didn't you see Chang take that one?"

She stared at him. A ruse. Chang picking up the envelope. Sleight-of-hand. And she'd been taken in as she was supposed to be.

"Did you think I was risking that falling into Albert George's hands? Chang trailed Walker from the time he left Navy Landing until he passed over that envelope to you."

"Chang is working for you."

"Didn't you ever catch on to that?"

Why didn't he put his arms around her instead of sitting over there asking foolish questions? He pretended to love her; she'd married him again because she'd believed he was as crazy about her as she about him. Yet after this tense separation he could loll around chewing on a steak sandwich as if it were the most important thing on earth.

She reminded him frigidly, "You forget. You haven't been particularly garrulous about what's crashing all around me."

"That's out now," he cut in. "You didn't stay clear. And I need some help."

"That Dare and Chang can't give?" She spoke with scorn.

"That's right. But why drag her in?"

She retorted, "Perhaps because she has the privilege of seeing you without being bound and gagged in the process."

"Now what are you referring to?"

"I haven't seen your pajamas in my closet recently."

He had the grace to look embarrassed. "You weren't supposed to snoop around her place."

"Snoop!" She'd like to Albert George him. "They were in plain sight. Where you usually hang them. Where were you? Under the bed? Or sneaking down the fire escape?"

He didn't like "sneak" any better than she did "snoop." "I used the fire escape, yes, when you barged in unexpectedly. I didn't know it was you."

"I'm certain it was unexpected. I don't see how you dressed so quickly. She hadn't time to do more than wrap a negligee and pretend she was going to the beach."

He was beginning to answer her anger in kind. His eyes were kindling. "You can't talk. You certainly moved your boy friend in fast enough."

"You're making a mistake," she stated.

"Yeah? He goes in before dinner and comes out the next noon. Not to stay. No indeed. Just to go pack a bag and come in again. While you're making yourself swell all over town in his Lahdedoosenberg."

He couldn't really believe his insinuations. "You must have efficient spies. I can only tell you they aren't efficient enough. If they were they'd get facts, not suggestion of facts. Kew believes I need protection."

He shut his teeth together. "Does he think I'd be fool enough to leave you unprotected? Chang's been on you since I left." He scowled at her. "He wasn't gone five minutes with that envelope and if I'd known Albert George was in the neighborhood I'd have come for it myself."

"I'm glad you didn't," she said under her breath.

The major might strike her; he wouldn't use such gentle persuasion on Con. She didn't want to think about that. She asked, "What do you want me to do?"

"Get Walker Travis to the cottage tonight—alone."

Her eyes lifted quickly. "That's not as simple as it sounds. Don't you know that he's disappeared?"

"What?" He was so startled that his question was bullet-hard and Chang poked his rolling eyes in at once. Con walked over to her. "He couldn't disappear." He seemed so certain of it she hated to insist.

"He has. Captain Thusby is investigating."

"He couldn't disappear. Chang, get Thusby for me."

"Be right back." He pounced for the garage door.

"Now tell me." Con sank down again.

She told him what she knew. He was up walking the room before she'd finished.

"It couldn't happen. My God, Garth's had him guarded like the crown jewels."

She said, "Garth's in Long Beach." She couldn't bear the sick look over his face. She forgot all fancied rancor, going swiftly to him. "Con, what's happened? What is it?"

He asked harshly, "Where's Pembrooke?"

"He went to San Diego today with Admiral Swales to—" She broke off. "They've found Mannie Martin."

He said, "Mannie was found the night Shelley was murdered." That was where he had been that night, all night. Called to identify a friend. He knew all along that Mannie had been murdered.

He said, "Garth suppressed it to give us more time. A fishing smack found the body, what was left of it. Off San Diego. It wasn't a convenient riptide. Riptides don't return a speed boat to Navy Landing when the pilot's gone overboard. And riptides don't leave bullet holes."

He still didn't move to touch her; without touching him she sat on the floor in front of his chair.

"That letter I had from Mannie—"

She interrupted, "I've read it."

"What did you do with it?"

She didn't meet his eyes. "Kew burned it."

He said after a moment, "It doesn't matter anyway. You know then. Some way or other Mannie caught on that Pembrooke's scheme was a lot of hot air."

"You mean there isn't a plan for a Pan-Pacific network?"

"That was a blind. We know that much. Mannie told Walker Travis that the night before he disappeared. But he didn't spill the whole story. Trivial as it may seem, he didn't have time. He had to get back to the studio for a big movie broadcast. He told Walker he'd meet him at Navy Landing the next evening, Monday, and give him the rest of the dope. Before he went to *The Falcon*. He realized something might happen to him there. But he also told him, as if it were a joke, Walker says, that he, Walker, was already in possession of all the facts."

He lit two cigarettes, handed one down to her.

"And then, as you know, he didn't meet Walker. He called that he'd make it later after his appointment with the major, not before."

"But he didn't meet the major either."

"No, he didn't. The major's alibi is unbreakable. He sat there at the St. Catherine in view of the staff and guests from nine until after one. Just as he says." His mouth was hard. "But Mannie might have met one of the major's men."

She breathed, "Oh." Only, "Oh."

He spoke loudly, "Maybe that did happen. I wouldn't know. One thing doesn't fit. Mannie's papers weren't taken from him. They were safe in the waterproof glove compartment of his launch. Garth's had them from the first. Nothing but contract and plans. Nothing incriminating to anyone." He looked at the tip of his cigarette. "We know that Mannie had the real dope on Pembrooke. He wrote that to me. We figure that in one of his last confabs with the major, possibly by mistake, he picked up the wrong notes. That's what the major has been after. If he had Mannie killed, he didn't get what he wanted. That's what we're after. A document that tells what Pembrooke's actual purpose is here."

"But without that—if Lieutenant Travis has the facts—"

"Garth's fishing trip was a blind," he broke in. "He's been shut up on that battleship with Travis since last Wednesday trying to work it out, trying to get Walker to remember. They've gone over Mannie's papers and Walker's notes until they've worn out the script, and they still haven't solved it. Codes and chemicals—everything known to the department— nothing works." He said, "Garth left me to take charge of things on shore."

She stated simply, "That's why we came here."

"That's why." He admitted harshly, "When I had Mannie's letter, I got in touch with Garth. He asked me to take over while he concentrated on Walker. Not that I'm any big shot but he can trust me, and he can't trust many, even those closest to him." He spoke without hope, "We've failed."

She tried to comfort. "You can't be certain it's failure."

"Can't I?" he demanded. "Garth's coming ashore doesn't mean success. Not with the major running loose. And if Walker's gone, it is failure. We'll never know. Pembrooke will go scot-free, free to carry out whatever his plan is."

She cried out, "Well, what did you expect? Letting the lieutenant run around by himself at all hours."

"There's always the Achilles heel," he admitted. He was staring into space. "We had it. The human element of Walker Travis. But he simply couldn't function under the supervision Garth wanted. He went all to pieces when it was tried. The job they were doing is worse than any mental third degree, and added to it, to a Navy man, was the element that failure meant danger to the country. We had to give in on one thing; Walker had to see that woman of his or he couldn't go on. He's been too near a complete breakdown since Mannie's disappearance not to coddle him to some extent. Don't think he wasn't guarded. An X chief and two of his closest Navy pals were always on the tender that brought him in to Navy Landing. The Naval Intelligence and the X picked him up there, without his knowledge. The only time he wasn't under their eye when on shore was when he was in his own room with his wife. We couldn't do anything about that." He lit a cigarette. "Where the devil is Thusby?"

She said, "Chang will bring him in. Even if he has to slip him a Mickey Finn or a blackjack, he'll bring him in." Ten-cent-store handcuffs! "But you haven't explained why Garth would let Lieutenant Travis run around loose carrying an envelope of dangerous documents if the whole Navy was guarding him. Or why it had to be brought to our cottage."

"It wasn't what Pembrooke wanted, Griselda." But it was just as bad; the major thought it was. "I tell you we don't have that information. It was a report to me on what they'd been doing and some instruc-

tions from Garth. The envelope had to go to the
shack for Chang to get it. That was the safest place
with me in hiding. Neutral ground. Innocent ground.
The major wasn't expected to join the party. He
must have a stooge we don't know about. And it's
still incredible that he'd force the issue instead of
sending an underling with some plausible lie and
forged credentials from me." He scowled horribly.
"Maybe he has a weakness for bullying women."

"Never mind that. Why have a duplicate envelope?"

"In case someone tried to take that one from Chang
before he could get it to me."

She breathed, "You've been in cahoots with the
police all along? On the murder charge and the
escape?"

He snorted, "You don't think that old shark
Thusby would let a real prisoner escape? And it was
essential to stage one when we heard of Sergei's murder. Otherwise I wouldn't be suspected."

"Why let me worry about it? Why couldn't I
know?"

He said, "Pembrooke would spot a phoney. That's
why. I wouldn't be telling you this now only that it
looks as if I'm about to come out of retirement. It
looks as if it's over the wrong way. Unless Garth's on
shore to make a move, with or without evidence. I'll
have to help."

"Two—three—persons have bullet holes in them
already." She wasn't certain that she kept her voice
from quavering but she tried.

"I duck well if that's any comfort to you." He put
out his hand to touch her hair but he didn't. Sounds
below thwarted the move, the creaking door, the peg
tapping the stairs. He said gently, "Take care of
yourself. Don't trust anyone."

Chang was announcing, "Did you think we wasn't going to get here, Con? I never thought of looking for Captain Thusby in the social dives. That's where I went wrong."

Thusby in dress suit looked embarrassed. "Had to go. Big celebration. Admiral Swales's farewell party for Major Pembrooke."

"Farewell?" Con was sharp.

"It's all right." Thusby looked suspiciously at Griselda but Con signaled go ahead. Evidently no one was trusted without credentials. "Garth was there too." He sat down. "Pembrooke thinks he's sailing in the morning. Maybe he ain't. Maybe he is."

Con was rubbing his forehead. "I don't get it."

"Looks as if he's aiming not to stick around now that Garth's back from fishing."

There was a more sinister explanation to offer. It was in Con's eyes. Pembrooke had learned that Mannie was found. He was no longer in danger from that source. If he had also silenced the only other person who might betray him, he was safe. He could go and come as he pleased; he could continue his secret plan.

Con asked, "Travis?"

Thusby was disheartened. He eased his peg leg. "Not a trace."

"Could he be on *The Falcon?*"

"Impossible. Government fishing boats watching it night and day. There's not been a person on or off it since Tuesday morning, and nothing delivered either."

Con said, "Great God, don't be so close-mouthed. What's the dope? Who saw Travis last? Who was on him?"

"Now don't you get het up." Thusby was soothing. "Don't know who saw him last. The fellows trailed him to the cottage he owned down at Huntington

Beach. They parked near as they could, thought it was an all-night job. Then about midnight didn't he start hell-bent back to the city. Outrun them in the fog. They didn't pick the car up again till it was back in town going in the garridge. And Mrs. Travis was alone in it."

"Imbeciles."

"She says she let him off at a drugstore to phone and she doesn't know which. We've checked the whole neighborhood but one sailor or another coming in didn't mean nothing to any of them."

"Absolute imbeciles!" Con shouted. Chang's growl agreed.

Con was trying to think, his face so haggard Griselda ached to touch him. But she sat quietly, daring not breathe lest she be run off.

"What does Mrs. Travis have to suggest?"

"Nothing." Captain Thusby breathed sarcasm. "She don't know nothing except how to go in hysterics. All she says is he was trying to get somebody on the phone and that's why he wanted to come back to town quick."

Con was walking again, his hands dug in his pockets, his eyebrows together as if they could scowl out the answer. "He couldn't have sold out. It can't be that. I'd sooner believe it of Garth or myself." He pounded a fist on his head. "He can't be murdered. Not yet. Pembrooke wouldn't give up so easily. Not until he made an effort to wake Travis's memory. He knows we don't have the information yet or he'd be in Garth's custody, not dining with him. Just as we know he hasn't it or he'd have made a move."

She said to the look on his face, "And now he's making a move."

"Yes." The monosyllable was hopeless.

He held out his hand suddenly, pulled her to her feet. "You want to help?"

"Yes." She didn't. Her throat was closed by the lie. But she would, anything Con said.

"I want you to relieve Dare on Kathie so she can take on the major long enough for Garth to come to me. Chang will see that they get the word."

She said, "I don't understand. What am I to do with Kathie?"

"Just stick by her side until Barjon gets back in the party. That's Dare's job now but I want Dare to stay with Albert George while Garth's away."

She told him, "Kew's the one taking care of Kathie."

He looked steadily at her. "Kew isn't one of us. No matter where his amatory instincts lead him, he doesn't belong. You might remember that."

She denied it flatly, harshly, "He isn't a spy!"

"I didn't say that. Get it straight. I only said he isn't one of us. For God's sake, don't tell him anything tonight." He put his hands on her shoulders, pleaded, "Just this once do it my way, will you? Don't think for yourself at all. Things are bad enough without any more upsets."

Without reservations she said it, "Anything you say."

He moved away from her, not answering what was in her eyes. "Chang, take Mrs. Satterlee to dress and wait for her. You go home masked, Griselda, by cherce or ferce." His mouth touched a half-hearted smile at that. "Wait and drive her to the hotel. Get Garth." He took a key from his pocket. "Then go to Dare's and search through Kathie Travis' things. See if Walker left any message at all for me, no matter how hidden."

Griselda saw him pass Dare's doorkey to Chang. Dare and Chang belonged. Kew didn't. She didn't.

She asked, "After Garth returns what do I do?"

His look was quizzical. "After that you're on your own. I doubt that you'll be lonely."

Even if he didn't know that you could be surrounded by Kews and still lonely, this was no time to argue. Not with Thusby in a dour fog and Chang worrying Dare's key. She had promised to be good like any minor cog. She followed Chang into the garage below, placed the mask over her eyes without a word.

She dressed with quivering fingers listening to Chang's restless dissonantal humming in the living room, wondering where Walker Travis was. Poor ineffectual little man; he'd been of no more value to the secret service than to his wife. There was nothing now to interfere with Kathie having what she wanted through Kew. Nothing except Kew himself, and he'd have a harder time escaping her than he'd had with less determined women. Poor rabbit. The poor fish. If Mannie Martin hadn't been so smart with his jokes, he wouldn't have brewed this caldron of fear and destruction. The poor fish. The pink fish. Her eyes met her startled mirror eyes. Her lipstick posed in the air. Feverishly she applied it, crammed it into her organdie evening bag. It hadn't been easy deciphering Mannie's scrawl. It was possible. Walker had given Kathie the fish. When? Where did he get it? Chang had the key to Dare's. Kathie wouldn't be wearing it tonight; she wore it only with Walker.

Griselda returned to the living room. Chang stopped his discord, looked at her as if unable to believe that anyone could take so long to don so little. She said with urgency, "I'll have to stop by

Dare's. You can loan me the key. I left something there this afternoon." To his hesitation she insisted, "It won't take a moment."

She left him in the car, ran up the flight of stairs, without caution let herself into the blackness of the apartment. She found the unfamiliar light switch, made her way into the guest room. Kathie's belongings littered the bed, the bureau, the chairs. There was no pink fish. Frantically she pawed through the few things again, ran her hands over the cheap dresses in the closet. It was gone.

Kathie might be wearing it tonight. But someone else might have thought of it first. It would account for Dare's surprising invitation to someone she despised, for the major's success. Con hadn't taken the mote of Dare out of his eye. It wasn't until that moment that nervousness overtook her at this search. Suppose the apartment hadn't been empty.

She turned out lights behind her, locked the door, fled back to the grimly impatient Chang. She spoke above the dispirited cough of the starting motor, "Tell Con the pink fish wasn't there."

2

The difficulty in remaining by Kathie's side was that Kew too remained there. The lieutenant's wife was certain that Griselda was trying to take him from her and she didn't like it. She assumed possession of Kew's arm the moment Griselda entered the room. But Griselda stuck. Minor jobs were seldom pleasant. Grimly she tagged them.

The preliminaries had been smooth. She had crashed the party, even as Kew and Dare and Kathie must have crashed it, to a welcome of her with implication that she was overdue in her starched white organdie. She stated, hoping her face had that eager party look which Kathie's wore, "I was bored sitting alone in that dismal shack. I wish someone would find Con."

The major didn't believe her. He was a realist. He believed it less when Garth excused himself to answer the phone. His eyes were glacial, not leaving her face even when Dare moved beside him with animated trivialities. And a new fear struck. He would have read the false contents of the envelope, known their falsity. It was beyond hope that he would believe her innocent of the exchange. She was Con's wife. Her hands clenched. Garth and Con and Thusby were in conference at this very moment. They could move swiftly against him before he could do her more harm. Con wouldn't let him kill her. But without the information of the fish, what could they pin on him to keep his brutality away from her? He continued to enjoy the diplomatic immunity of the British. Unless he were apprehended tonight, he would come to her. She must not be alone; this one night she must make certain that Kew would be with her, not Kathie.

She'd been thinking too hard, watching the wrong person. Kathie and Kew had left the table. She trailed quickly after them. Kathie sat on the low parapet, gardenia tulle, doubtless borrowed from Dare's wardrobe, in ballet moonburst about her. No pink fish ruined the ensemble. She was exquisite, leaning over to watch the panorama of the Pike below. Her eyes resented the intrusion; Kathie's suspicion couldn't help but seem rational; Griselda had no valid excuse for intruding on a tête-à-tête. And she didn't have the courage to speak before the girl. She asked instead, "Cigarette, Kew?"

He put his hand into his pocket. "Left my case on the table."

She said, "Don't bother," but he'd already gone for it. Before she could step back from the ledge, Kathie had reached out and caught her hand, caught it and pulled.

"Look!" she whispered. Her eyes were malicious with no man to observe, as if she recalled Griselda's once spoken fear of high places. And then a sudden terror paralyzed Griselda. There was more than malice on Kathie's face; there was evil. A quick jerk and release could send her catapulting over that low unguarded rail, down to smash into the vacation crowds below. That soft-looking hand was tightening on hers with menace and purpose. She didn't dare turn to call for help of the others half across the sky terrace. Moreover, her throat could make no sound. She could only stand there desperately trying to thwart the steel, to draw back from that almost maniacal force.

From behind her, hands touched her shoulder and she was limp. Albert George. He and Kathie together in this?

She spoke huskily "No. No."

But Kathie's hand had relinquished hers in that moment and it was Dare speaking coolly over Griselda's shoulder. "The party's going to break up, early as it is. Major Pembrooke sails from Avalon tonight."

She might have nightmared the momentary incident. Kathie's wide-eyed innocence was lifted to an approaching Kew and to Dare. "I was just showing Mrs. Satterlee how beautiful the Pike looks from here. Have you noticed, Dare?"

Dare said nothing. But Dare must have known. She'd broken her orders, left Albert George's side, to aid her. She must have noticed Griselda's terror, whether real or imaginary, from across the terrace.

Even now Griselda didn't know how much her shaken nerves had imagined, how much was fact.

Dare held Griselda back by her blue-velvet sash, allowing the other two to precede. She said, "Get hold of yourself. You look as if you're about to keel over. Garth isn't back yet but the major is determined to leave and I can't stop him. Chang'll be around somewhere and pass on the word, I hope. I certainly can't follow Albert George to the yacht, and God knows I can't afford a trip to Kobe this year. I'll have to trust him to Admiral Swale's tender mercies. I'll have Kew take Kathie and me home, then he will go on and stay the night with you. Don't veto it. You need someone at hand."

She wouldn't veto it. It was inconceivable that the major would sail without another attempt to secure what Garth had sent to Con. Even if he had regained his own missing document, he would make certain that the others hadn't seen it first. And even if he knew that it would not now be in her possession, he would come in reprisal for her thwarting him. She was trembling so that she could scarcely reach the table; her lips merely simulated drinking of the toast, and she elbowed Kathie aside with no apology to cling to Kew's arm as they left the hotel.

Kathie was reluctant to go with Dare into the apartment. She stood there on the sidewalk prolonging farewell to Kew, the wind lifting her night-black hair, her beauty as it should be, as it would be if she always had access to luxury. But Kew bespoke no reluctance as Dare led her away.

He drove on to the cottage, opened the door, and went ahead to the lights. She was grateful; she couldn't have entered the darkness alone.

He said, "Thank God everyone folded early. I'm way behind on some commitments but I think I'll nap on the couch first. This business has me about licked."

Fear of unknown bestiality had keyed her to franticness equivalent to that of the waves clutching desperately at the sea wall. She suggested, "Why don't you take the bedroom? I'd go crazy if I had to try to sleep now." That was fact. "I'll do some work myself and wake you when I'm ready to call it a day." It was safe. He'd be in the next room subject to call.

He accepted. "An hour or two will fix me up."

She had her sketchbook out before the door closed, her pastels opened. But she laid the crayons aside. It was pretense that she could concentrate on costumes with her heart pounding to every whisper, even to sound of her own breath. She sat very quietly there, not daring look toward that non-protective door. Further terror made her rigid. The major would not come only to her. He would be seeking Con even while Con was stalking him. Con wouldn't be the hunter because Walter Travis had disappeared; Garth and his aides would handle that. It would be because he was what the major had sneered, Quixotic. Inevitably they would meet. Pembrooke would kill him. Pembrooke wasn't civilized; he scorned civilization. She covered her face. Con would die never knowing that her love for him was great enough to permit without question ever again his vagaries. He would never know that Dare's doorkey wasn't important if she herself might only have a small share of him.

The suddenness of the phone jolted her. She hastened to answer; she realized she had been expecting it. A person clung desperately to hope even when hope was gone. She was waiting a call from Con that all was serene. Of course, Garth wouldn't let Major Pembrooke get to Con.

It wasn't he; it was that long-awaited Malibu call.

Important once when Con had been held for murder, now it was necessary to search memory for what information she had sought from the scenarist.

Si was saying, "I've been calling on the hour, Griselda, ever since I sobered up and got the message." He didn't sound very sober yet; party sounds were a noisome background. "What did you want? More dope on Shelley Huffaker? Can't see why you don't get it at the source. Kew Brent is there, isn't he?"

She hardly realized his words and then she did. She cried, "What are you saying, Si?"

He repeated, "Kew Brent was her latest boy friend in Hollywood. Took her away from Mannie Martin. They were being seen together at some out-of-the-way spots. He could tell you more than any of us."

She listened, her eyes motionless on that closed bedroom door as if the man beyond were listening too to the voice in her ear.

"Are you certain?" she pleaded.

"Sure I am." He was talking too loudly. "Everybody was gabbing about her giving Mannie the air. And no one was surprised when she followed Brent to Long Beach."

She cut in, "Why didn't you tell me this before?"

"You didn't give me a chance," he complained gayly. "You weren't gossipy. All you wanted to know was if she was Sergei's bum and she was. Then you hung up on me. And say, Oppy wants to know when you sleuths are going to catch that murderer for him. Here he is spending plenty of dough and he still has to sleep with bodyguards under his bed."

His imitation of the producer wasn't funny; nothing was now. Kew Brent. An outsider; that was Kew, no connection with Axis activities but connection with Mannie and Shelley and Sergei. He'd lied about knowing them. Of course, the Hollywood papers

hadn't suggested his name. Newspapermen had loy-
alty to one another. Even if they thought him guilty,
and they wouldn't, they would never offer him without black and white proof.

Motive? That self-centeredness, egoism. Rid himself
of the encumbrance of a cheap blonde who had taken
him seriously, who could spoil his chances with a
beauty whose husband could give him the scoop of
his career, the secret that only three men knew. It
wasn't Albert George to whom Kathie was selling out;
it was to Kew. Sergei's death? The man who had reason to suspect. Alibi? Griselda realized that she was
his only alibi for the night of Shelley's death, but he'd
left her, and a big hotel wouldn't check on the time
he had returned. Sergei's death. Thusby had caught
him on misstatement of time there but evidently had
no way to place him near the Village. Or Thusby was
waiting for the more important business of Mannie's
death to be cleared up. But why had Kew killed
Mannie?

She watched that motionless door. If only she knew
where Con was, she'd fly now to him, not remain here
under protection of a murderer. Con had tried to
warn her of Kew; he'd told her that first night the
attraction wasn't her beautiful eyes. Kew had taken
her into custody with Machiavellian wisdom. From
her he would learn when suspicion of murder was
diverted from her husband. No wonder he had found
it impossible to believe Con's arrest.

How could the whole of the Long Beach police
and the government X division have been so blind?
How could she herself be so blind? Shelley made a
date with a man. She waited at the Bamboo Bar. But
Con had spoiled his meeting with Shelley by going
over to her himself. And Shelley had gone away after
Kew joined Griselda. Was there provision for a later

meeting at Saam's Seafood Place if the Bamboo Bar plan was interrupted?

Kew couldn't be responsible for Walker Travis's disappearance or as yet undiscovered murder. Her eyes ached with staring at that noncommittal door. Or could he? With Kathie as accomplice, yes. But there was no reason to kill Walker. Unless— The palms of her hands were wet. Kew himself had warned her of fifth columnists. A man who lied well of one thing could lie as well of another. Kew working with or for the renegade Britisher. That also explained Mannie's murder.

She raised up softly from the chair and moved to the bay window above the sea wall. The floor didn't creak any more than was customary. She leaned far out into mist and spray. The tide was high and Chang didn't materialize now that she needed him. She dared not call, wake Kew, rightfully cause him to wonder. The floor creaked again as she returned to stand indecisive in the middle of the room.

A light in the window. Con had told her to keep a candle in her window. Maybe it was his oblique way of telling her to signal. Surely he'd have a man watching her tonight even if Chang were playing guardian to the X head, letting a scared wife fend for herself. Whoever was watching might understand. She lifted the floor lamp, set it squarely behind the frame. Even as she did, Kew spoke from the doorway.

"What on earth are you doing, Griselda? Furniture moving at this hour?"

She didn't turn at once; she stood there clutching the standard with both hands. She spoke, "I thought you were asleep." She turned, fearful of what she might behold, but Kew hadn't been transformed into her mental picture. He was handsome as ever in his heavy silk pajamas and fine wool robe; his face was still keen and sane.

He said, "No, I found I couldn't. Too tired perhaps. Besides no reporter sleeps when he has a hunch things are going to break. I have. With Albert George's departure scheduled, the X will move." Curiously he asked, "Who called?"

"Malibu."

"Oppy. What did he want?"

She tried to be casual, careless. "He wants the—her tongue tripped on the word—"murderer found so he won't have bodyguards under his bed." She laughed a little, a little more; laughed to keep fear from climbing up on her shoulder for him to see.

"Don't we all?" He leaned on the arm of the couch.

She edged gingerly into the chair. "Maybe the police aren't looking in the right direction. Maybe the murders have nothing to do with Major Pembrooke. Maybe it was an outsider."

He raised his head. "You've returned to that theory?"

She would go on pretending they were allies, pretending to be the blundering idiot she had been up until that phone call. "Yes. Ever since Kathie told me she heard Shelley talking to some man on the phone that afternoon." She was garrulous in reckless courage. "Making a date to meet him at the Bamboo Bar. But he didn't come, did he? Con spoiled it taking her away. We'd have seen him if he'd come, wouldn't we? We'd have seen the murderer."

"Yes."

She had to keep words spattering. Con had told her not to talk with Kew but he hadn't guessed that Kew was the murderer. You couldn't be closed within a lonesome beach cottage with someone who took a gun and shot people. You had to try to make things seem normal.

Then she heard the hand on the doorknob. Kew heard it too, came to his feet listening.

Maybe at last this would be Con. But someone had pushed the key from the inner lock, another key turned from the outside.

Major Pembrooke entered, stood there, looking from one to the other. He said, "I didn't know it was this way, Brent. Sorry to interrupt."

Kew ignored his insinuation. He asked harshly, "What do you want?"

"I'm leaving tonight. I haven't finished my business with Mrs. Satterlee. Unfortunately I haven't time to finish at the moment. I'm taking her with me."

Griselda shook her head, "You can't do that." She spoke as a child who believed in Santa Claus. "That's kidnaping."

Kew said, "Are you mad? You can't get away with that, Pembrooke."

"I believe I can. I am not under your laws. I care nothing for them."

Her voice came as from far away. "Why do you want me? I don't know anything."

"I believe you can enable me to have a personal interview with your husband—in friendly territory."

He was right. Con would come for her no matter what the danger. She heard herself pleading, "Why do you want him? You don't need him. You have the fish."

He didn't know what she was talking about; he didn't have the fish. Dare must have taken it to Con, too late. But Con would never reveal anything to Major Pembrooke. He would kill Con trying to find out. She closed her eyes.

He was continuing in that ugly voice. "If you wish to get a wrap, perhaps pack a small bag, but quickly . . ." He looked at his watch. "At the most I can allow you fifteen minutes. After that time the conference will break up that they are now having with the Admiral at Villa Riviera." He smiled coldly. "Being assured by him that he saw me enter the plane and watched it take off for Catalina. He didn't wait for it to land again. It hadn't entered their stupid heads that the yacht might sail without me, pick me up at a Mexican port. My car is waiting outside. The engine is running. It will take us no time to cross the border. If you wish to pack, Mrs. Satterlee—"

He glanced at his watch again. She couldn't move; she was too weak.

And Kew spoke. There was an electric sureness in him that hadn't been there before. "You don't think you're going to get away with this, do you, Pembrooke? You don't think I'll let you do it, do you?"

"I think you will." There was amusement as well as superb confidence in Pembrooke's voice, as if Kew were a straw man waggling at him.

"I don't intend to. I won't. I'm through."

The major's face was ugly. "You don't dare."

"I do." Kew's voice rang. "You'll take Griselda over my dead body as we say in my country. While you're killing me, she can get out of here. She'll scream loud enough to wake those new neighbors before your Jap soldiery grabs her. Someone will call the police. And before your high-powered car is across the bridge, radio will have all roads blocked."

He was telling her what to do and strength was returning to her as he spoke. She could do it. She didn't understand why he would go so far to save her. But no matter what he had done, she couldn't let him be killed defending her. There must be some other way. The lamp in the window must work.

Major Pembrooke's mouth was cruel. "There are penalties for informers in these times."

"I'm not an informer!" Kew was proud. "I've never been that."

"I could tell a different tale."

"Tell it. I made a mistake, yes. I was so puffed up with myself in that small town of Washington that I thought I was Brent the invincible. I wanted a scoop on your Pan-Pacific network. You promised it for my help. I was fool-enough to think you'd gone national in Britain's peril and were working for your own government this time. That's why I was willing to get you some dope on our monitory stations. You got your hooks on me. I'd been supplying secret stuff to an enemy agent; that made me a fifth columnist if it came out. But I don't care now. I don't even care if Garth and Con don't believe I'm innocent. I'd rather be stood up against a wall by my own people than ever trade with you again. And I'd rather have you shoot me down than let Griselda fall into your bloody hands."

Pembrooke was shaken with anger. "You are not armed, I see. I am. If I were to kill her—"

Kew interrupted, "You would have to kill both of us. After that perhaps you would get across the border. But you can do it more safely without gunplay which might be discovered too soon. I won't give any alarm if you leave. You know that. Because there's nothing to pin on you now—"

Again he broke off, listening. All three of them heard the rapid steps to the door. Not Con. Woman's steps. She didn't knock. She opened the unlocked door, confronted Kew and Griselda. She didn't see Major Pembrooke at first. When she did, she didn't say what she had been about to say.

She turned her great lashes upward. "I didn't know you were here, Major. I was so lonesome at Dare's apartment. I thought maybe—"

Pembrooke's lips moved. Kathie didn't know the evil in his smile. "Perhaps then I can persuade you to join me for the evening. These two were reluctant."

Griselda whispered it. "No!" No matter how silly and selfish Kathie was, she didn't deserve this. She was an innocent bystander.

The whisper choked in her throat. For Kathie's eyes swept to Kew's pajamas; she accepted the implication Pembrooke had proffered. Back to Griselda and a fury of hatred burned in them.

Kathie spoke softly, "No, I don't believe I will go. Not unless Kew goes too."

Kew said even more softly, "Kew isn't going." He made a mistake then; he lunged at Pembrooke. The scream in Griselda's throat was stifled as the major's fist crumpled him to the floor.

The major had removed his mask. There was a gun in his hand. "I have no time for further discussion. You two will precede me. I am an excellent shot." Kathie's face was unbelieving. She opened her mouth, closed it when he ordered, "Come."

Griselda began, "But Kew—"

"You need not worry about him." The gun pointed. It was Pembrooke's face then that turned stark with amazement. The sharp crack, the clatter of his weapon from his fingers, the red stuff spurting from his limp hand—it happened too quickly for understanding. Only Griselda turned her head unsurprised to the source of the bullet. The pixie was in the bedroom doorway.

He was croaking, "I'm an excellent shot myself, see? I don't mind shooting to kill neither. But Garth don't want you killed yet, Major Pembrooke. He wants to question you. And Con would like to beat you to a pulp." He was wet to the knees but his gun hand was steady. "You girls can take it easy but don't move. I don't want nobody in my way. Mrs. Satterlee, maybe you ought to hand me that gun of the major's. Just in case his Jap army heard the shooting and figures on investigating. Probably won't. Probably just think he's had a little trouble like always."

Kathie said, "May I sit down?" She did in the nearest chair. She looked as if she had never been so near reality.

Griselda heard the crunch in the kitchen. Her voice shook. "Someone's coming—there—"

"Probably Vinnie," Chang said. But he protected himself behind the bedroom door. "That you, Vinnie?"

"Yeah." He slouched into the doorway. "Looks like you had a little trouble."

"No trouble at all. Can you get some assistance up here?"

"I already called them. When I saw that car out front. That's why I'm late getting here."

Griselda asked, "Chang, have you been here all the time?" He hadn't been. She'd looked. But he'd been a second-story man; swinging from bay window to bedroom window would be nothing to him.

"Ever since you moved the lamp, Mrs. Satterlee. When Con saw that he figured you wanted help so he sent me over. I couldn't understand why till the major came. You knew he was coming."

She shook her head. It seemed long ago that she had assumed Kew a murderer. She knew better now. Circumstances alone couldn't point guilt. Character had to be counted and he had proved himself tonight. And then she looked at Chang wondering. "Con saw me put the light in the window? But—"

Vinnie pointed. "The Cap'n owns these cottages, ma'am. He's kind of in the real-estate business on the side. Barjon Garth rented the both of them early this summer."

Chang made it plain. "Con's been hiding out over there, Mrs. Satterlee. My niece came down to do for him. She was scared the night you went over; she didn't know who you were; that's why she wouldn't talk to you. It was before me and Con moved in." He cleared his throat. "Nobody'd ever suspect Lucinda and that husband of hers of harboring. That way Con could keep an eye on you."

He was that near all along. She needn't have feared. He himself had seen Kew move in. And all that ridiculous drive around just to confuse her, but, she admitted, rightly so. If she'd known he was near, despite all good intentions, she couldn't have helped but seek his aid prematurely, lead the major directly to him before he was ready.

"Garth thought they'd make good headquarters," Vinnie said. "Thought it might mix some folks up having one of them open, with Con setting in it; and the other one closed, for emergencies. They've got the sweetest little shortwave set over there that you ever saw." His gum cracked. "But Garth should of told Pa sooner who Con was."

It was Con at last, Captain Thusby peglegging along in the rear. Now she could relax. Now nothing could go wrong.

Con said, "Major Pembrooke, there are a few questions Barjon Garth wants to ask you in the name of the United States government. There's a car waiting." In the doorway stood an officer.

Albert George moved without words. His mouth was clenched. His bloody hand dripped at his side.

Griselda took a deep breath but she didn't move.

She was too weak. "Con, you're home at last—" and then she stopped. It wasn't over. That was in Con's eyes. Vinnie was still standing there and Captain Thusby was sitting down in the chair Major Pembrooke had vacated. Chang was attempting to revive Kew but he hadn't laid aside his gun.

She realized sharply. Major Pembrooke was a spy but he wasn't the murderer. No one had said anything yet about who was the murderer.

KEW had come to. Con was asking, "Where is Dare?" His voice was careless. He stood by the music cabinet. He was setting out bottles and glasses but he hadn't mixed drinks yet.

Kew spoke anxiously, "Hasn't she been with you?" and then he turned to Kathie, "When did you see her?"

"Not for hours." She raised her face as a flower would. "That's why I came over here, Kew. She hasn't been at the apartment for hours. She left almost as soon as we got there. She said she'd send you to keep me company but you didn't come." She was reproachful. She took the best chair.

Kew turned on Con then. "What were her orders? What did you tell her to do?"

"You knew she was working for me?" The two men measured each other.

"She didn't have to tell me. You've had her on Pembrooke." He took two glasses from Con. "I know

Dare and I know how you two work together. But where is she? Where should she be?"

Con said, "Vinnie and Chang don't drink. Cap'n, what about you?"

He held out three horizontal fingers. "And none of that fizz water spoiling the taste."

Con poured one straight, passed it across. He moved to the couch but he didn't sit by Griselda. He said, "I don't know where Dare is. She was supposed to be guarding Kathie tonight"—Kathie jumped—"so Albert George wouldn't nab her. She must have thought of something more urgent." He turned directly to Kew. "You knew Shelley Huffaker. You lied about that."

He admitted it. "Yes, I lied about that."

"Why?"

"To save my own skin." He didn't glance at anyone. "I knew her, Con. I knew everyone who could get information for me on Pan-Pacific. I came to California to break that yarn. I came here blown up on my tuppenny Washington importance. That's gone, Con."

Kathie's face was wide open.

"I was the man Shelley was to meet at the Bamboo Bar. We did meet. But Pembrooke interrupted. She told me aside to join her at Saam's Seafood later, when I got rid of him. Then you stepped in. After I took Griselda home I went out to this Saam's. I waited until after one o'clock but she didn't come."

Kathie whispered, "I knew you were the one she was looking for that night."

Captain Thusby asked, "Why not tell anyone, Brent? You had an alibi."

"No. I didn't wait inside. When I saw she wasn't there I went out and sat in the car. I didn't like the fish."

Con lit a cigarette. "You might as well spill it all, Kew."

"Yes." He looked at his hands. "Yes. I don't know if you'll believe me." He looked directly at Con. "You must believe me."

Griselda put her hand on his arm, leaned across him. "Yes, Con," she said. "You must believe him. It's true." A man who'd offered himself as sacrifice for her, and for his country as he had tonight, had spoken truth.

Kew said, "Thanks, darling. She knows part of it, Con. I tried to tell her so she could relay it, when I thought you'd find me on a slab. I wanted you to know."

"He saved my life, Con."

Con's face wasn't legible. He repeated without inflection, "Spill it."

Griselda relaxed and then she stiffened. Kathie was facing them as an audience watching a rehearsal. There were jealous eyes and a thinned mouth. She was still guessing wrong about Kew and Griselda.

Kew began, "I met Shelley Huffaker in Hollywood."

He was interrupted. The door was flung open and all of them came to their feet with sick horror wincing their faces. It couldn't be Walker Travis swaying there, his pajamas ribboned, his bare feet grinding dirt and blood into the carpet. The deviled eyes in his drawn face were not human. He saw Kathie, only Kathie. His voice was rickety, "So you're here."

Con asked, "What happened, old man?" and Kathie cried brokenly, "Walker."

She started to him and then she faded back in terror. He spoke hoarsely, "Stay where you are. Don't come any nearer. I might kill you. The way you tried to kill me. The way you—" Con was at his side as he slumped.

Kathie wept, "He's delirious." Vinnie stood behind her patting her shoulder.

Kew helped Con lead the lieutenant to the couch. Captain Thusby was pouring a good-sized straight one. Only Griselda was watching Kathie, watching her out of thoughtful eyes, listening to her words, "He doesn't know what he's saying. He isn't himself. Oh, Walker, Walker." Her grief wasn't real. She was spacing it and she was peering behind her fingers. And then she noticed Griselda. When their eyes met, Griselda knew.

She clutched Kew's arm. "Dare!" She shook him. "Why isn't Dare here? Kathie did try to kill Walker. She tried to kill me tonight."

She had been right in her fear on the roof! Had Kathie come here tonight not to find Kew but to kill Griselda? To try again? She shuddered. "She's killed Dare!"

Con and Kew heard. They turned to look at Kathie. She couldn't get out of the chair because Vinnie's hand was on her shoulder. She shrank back further and her beautiful face wasn't beautiful.

Griselda wasn't sane herself at that moment. She wanted to claw those murderous eyes. She had to hurt someone. Dare had saved her but she hadn't saved Dare. She cried it again, "Dare! What did you do to Dare?"

Travis said, "She'll be here. She went to get Kathie. Dare found me. I couldn't walk any further. She helped me." His voice wavered. Kathie was sobbing. He said, "Give me another drink, Con." He looked like a rabbit but he wasn't one. His voice was firm as he fixed it on his wife. "You killed Mannie. You told me he'd postponed our appointment. You kept it. I suppose you told him I'd meet him later. Why did you kill Mannie?"

She sobbed. "I didn't—I couldn't—"

"You could handle his boat. You've had plenty of experience with them at the beach. No one would suspect anything seeing you on the Landing. Mannie was packing a gun. He was going after Pembrooke but he wasn't taking chances." He held out his glass. His mouth wore wry scorn. "You'd be close enough to him to know about the gun, to get it. Why did you kill him?"

The sounds she was making were indistinguishable.

"Last night you meant to kill me. You thought I was asleep when you slipped back to the living room. I saw you through the door. I saw you making sure my revolver was loaded. I didn't wait for you to use it. I went out the window."

She cried in frenzy, "You're lying! You're lying about me!"

He started to her but he fell back. His eyes closed. Con said, "Can't drink on an empty stomach. Probably hasn't eaten in twenty-four hours. And he was exhausted to start with. Chang, give me the gat and you and Vinnie get him to the hospital where he can be cared for." He took the gun and slid it into his jacket pocket just as if he were as accustomed to handling them as was the too widely experienced Mr. Smithery.

Kathie wept, "Oh, Walker, Walker." But she saw Thusby scrape his chair between her and the door. She saw Con's hand casual in his pocket. She didn't move while Travis was carried out.

You could read about such women in the tabs and the pulps, women who wouldn't stop at anything to get the man they wanted. She'd tried to kill Walker because he stood in her way; Griselda, thinking she was after Kew. Dare had been safe because Kathie didn't know.

Con said, "Well, Kathie."

She lifted tear-blurred eyes. "I don't know what he was talking about. He must be crazy."

Con spoke carelessly, "You pitched Mannie overboard before there was any blood in the boat, didn't you? You didn't expect him to be washed up but you thought you'd be safe even if he were. Drowning— or a riptide— The gun was at the bottom of the Pacific. It couldn't tell tales." He hardened. "You weren't very careful about leaving your fingerprints on the wheel, were you? Maybe you thought the spray would take care of them."

She turned a frightened appeal to Kew.

And Kew said slowly, "How did you know that Shelley was looking for a man that night?"

She was trapped between them. She twisted her head one way and the other but there was no escape. It was hard for her to breathe. She flung at Kew, "I suppose you knew it all along. I might have known. Playing me along and living with her." Her eyes scorched Griselda. "If I'd known that sooner . . ."

Kew asked as if he were interviewing her, "You don't mind killing people, do you?"

"No, I don't." She tossed her head. "I don't mind at all. Then they're out of my way."

Dare's voice was fresh. "May I intrude?" She was gay in scarlet, only faint circles under her emerald eyes gave hint of ordeal. Griselda had never thought she could feel a surge of joy at seeing Dare, an alive and arrogant Dare.

Kew met her, held her. "You're all right?"

"But, of course." She extricated herself. "Travis?"

"Taken care of," Con said.

Kathie was looking with bewilderment from Griselda to Dare, from Dare to Griselda.

Con put out a long arm, drew Griselda over close to him, "You made a mistake, Kathie. It's always been this way."

Dare drawled, "Don't play it heavy, darling," but she held to Kew's arm and now it was she looking at him as if he were wonderful.

Captain Thusby scratched an embarrassed fuzz. "Ought I take Mrs. Travis in, do you think?"

Con said, "Maybe she'd like to tell us first why she killed Mannie."

She was sullen. "I won't tell you anything."

"I will." Dare was a crimson streak brightening the worn chair. Kew sat on the arm of it, his hand enclosing hers. "She killed Mannie because he gave her the run-around."

Kathie's face was a snarl as she sprang up. "I'm not going to stay here and listen to lies about me! They've been against me all along. Just because I don't have diamond bracelets and a big car and lots of money."

It was Captain Thusby who pushed her back now. "Reckon you'll have to stay till Vinnie gets back. I'd forgotten he wasn't here to drive the car. Glad I never learned. I want to hear this." He sat down again. "Go on, Mrs. Crandall."

"Kathie killed Mannie Martin because she found out he was using her in an attempt to bring Shelley to heel. She'd had experience in getting away with murder. I mean that literally." She flicked a glance toward the girl. "This isn't all intuition. I'll admit I've pieced some of it out of pretty small bits but I've done my checking. When I got suspicious I took the plane back to Kansas to go into her past life."

Kathie didn't look at her.

"Parsons doesn't talk much about home-town products that have gone wrong but obliquely they give you the picture. Rufus Treat wasn't happy with his wife, and her always wanting to live above herself, but he wasn't the fellow to kill himself. The two were alone in the house. It looked like suicide. Nobody wanted to make a fuss with Kathie's folks nice as the next, old friends of the Treats. Most everyone suspected his wife did it and laid it to her but there wasn't any way of proving it." She dropped vernacular. "She got away with it once. She might have again if she hadn't gone hog-wild and kept adding to her notches."

Captain Thusby blinked.

"Shelley was Mannie's woman. Vironova was only board and occasionally bed. When she fell for Kew, Mannie wasn't going to take it lying down."

Kew said, "She didn't fall for me. Maybe Mannie thought so. Shelley was doing a bit of work for me. But when she saw Mannie making a play for Kathie Travis, she was mad as hell and did try to make him jealous to get him back."

"They were both wrong," Dare admitted. "Mannie made his play for Kathie to make Shelley jealous. But Kathie didn't know it. She thought it was on the up and up. She came down with delusions of grandeur about moving into that palace of Martin's. She wasn't smooth about it, however; she'd never had experience in big time. He wasn't interested in her; it was Walker he needed, Walker was his friend, and he didn't want any trouble. Kathie was in his hair. I figure it was that night he told her straight out."

Griselda said, "But you don't kill someone for that."

Dare spoke coolly, "Haven't there been times you've been furious enough to kill? And with the means, and that extra madness that makes a killer, you'd do it."

Kathie whispered, "I've never had anything. I've never had what you've had and you—all of you. I'm beautiful. I like nice things. I have a right to have them." Her voice broke.

Dare said, "Shelley must have found out something. So Shelley had to die."

"No," Kathie spoke up now. She looked at Kew for exoneration. "I killed Shelley because she was going to kill you." She was pathetic at the moment, huddled there alone, her eyes eating Kew.

He said, "She wasn't after me. It was Mannie she was gunning for. She thought he'd run out on her for good because of you. She came to me because she hoped I'd know where he was, or could find out from you. I didn't get to tell her he'd disappeared. Pembrooke came in before we had a chance to talk."

Kathie repeated with conviction, "No. She was going to kill you, Kew."

Dare said, "Shelley wouldn't have killed anyone. She might have tossed the gun around for dramatic effect but she wouldn't have shot Mannie if she'd found him in bed with you."

Kathie repeated stubbornly. "She was going to kill Kew. She told me that afternoon she had come to Long Beach to take care of a man. She showed me the gun. I knew you were the one, Kew, because you'd said she was here and had broken a date with me for that night. After I left her I kept thinking about it. I went back to her apartment that night to stop her but she'd gone. I waited across in the Park." She was crying a little. "I saw her come back. I followed her upstairs. She had a box of shells and she was reloading her gun. I asked her where she was going and she told me to meet you and find Mannie. I said—" She sucked in her breath.

Dare smiled, "You said Mannie was dead."

She cried, "That didn't make any difference to her. She went right on loading her gun. She was kind of tipsy but she was still going to kill Kew."

It would have made a difference when Shelley sobered up, discovered that Kathie alone knew Mannie was dead. Kathie's rationalizing was a flimsy cover for her real purpose. "I knew then I had to kill her." She looked at Kew. "She didn't have a car. I offered to take her to Saam's Seafood place. I'd parked over on Cherry because I didn't want anyone in the apartment to tell about a car driving off."

"How did you get her to give you the gun?" Thusby asked.

Vinnie had come in. A sack of candy bulged his pocket, his mouth crunched, but he held it stationary, his cheeks askew, to catch Kathie's words.

"I told her that her lipstick was messed. I said I'd hold the gun while she fixed it. She was so conceited she wouldn't let a man see her unless she looked right, not even a man she was going to kill."

The blonde girl opening her bag, taking out mirror and Kleenex. Turning to the street lamp. And Kathie shot her in the back.

"I had worn gloves." She stood up shakily. "Vinnie's here. We can go." Her eyes were sick on Kew. "I'm not bad. I wouldn't have killed her only she was going to kill you."

2

Con and Griselda, Kew and Dare. The way it should be. Con mixed fresh ones. They could speak out loud after a while.

Kew began as before, "I met Shelley in Hollywood. I asked her to get the Pan-Pacific dope from Mannie that he wouldn't give me." He was bitter. "Kew Brent could do no wrong if it meant a story and I was determined to break that one. So far as I was concerned the Navy had been damned offensive to me on it, practically kicked me out of their office. I was going to show them. Didn't they know who I was? I was Kew Brent." Savage shame mottled his face. Dare touched his hand.

"Shelley Huffaker was a rotten little tramp. She was nuts about Mannie but she'd do anything for money, even steal from her lover. I paid her high; she came high. I was on the inside, I thought. Mannie didn't tell her his suspicions of the major."

Con said, "He didn't tell anyone. He couldn't reach Garth, he only hinted to Walker and to me. But he wanted to have it straight before he started tackling a man whose credentials were beyond suspicion."

Kew drank. "Yes, Pembrooke stood O.K. I had met him in Washington. No one was suspicious of him. I traded some dope with him. It didn't seem strange to me that he could get information on the new network which I couldn't; if he were a part of Britain's high command, that was logical enough. I didn't trust him but I didn't doubt his connections. Until some of the foreign correspondents began throwing hints, and he was missing. I wanted the yarn more than ever then and decided to tackle Mannie. I didn't run into the major out here until the night I went to the Bamboo Bar to meet Shelley. When I returned to my hotel after leaving Saam's, he was waiting for me. He didn't try to hide his real purposes then; he cracked the whip. Things were so tight he needed me. Incriminating documents had been stolen from him by Mannie Martin. He wanted them back. Either Man-

nie still had them or he'd passed them on to Walker
Travis. Pembrooke knew they hadn't been turned
over to Garth or Garth wouldn't have gone off fish-
ing, leaving the major to carry on with his work.
Pembrooke thought Mannie was hiding out but that
I could get in touch with him.

"Pembrooke told me flat, either I'd help him out or
he'd inform on me furnishing secret information to
an enemy agent. I knew what that meant. Even if I
could clear myself, there would always be suspicion of
me. I wouldn't be of any value in Washington again;
no one would trust me." His mouth was dry. "I gave
him the impression that I'd play ball." He begged
Con to see it.

"I was almost crazy. But I'd made up my mind.
You were in town. You could arrange for me to see
Garth. I'd tell him the whole yarn whatever it did to
me. At least I'd be clear; I could hold up my head
again."

Con said, "Take it easy."

"You can imagine what a slap it was when you
said Garth had left town, inaccessible for two weeks.
I didn't know that you were working with him again.
Even if I had, I doubt if I'd have told you." His face
was shadowed. "There's some things you can tell to
an outsider that you can't to your friends. And too,
I wanted to clear with the top." He drank again.
"The safest way I could figure it was to keep Albert
George believing I was standing with him. He
wanted to meet Kathie Travis, to work through her
on Walker. That was easy enough. She'd been playing up to me after Mannie's disappearance. And I
wasn't averse—I wanted to reach Walker myself
through her. Pembrooke ordered me to bring her to
Catalina that week end. I knew I could show him
he'd better let me act as the go-between. Her feelings

by then were obvious to anyone. That way I could protect her too until Garth returned."

"What about 'Sergei?" Con inquired.

Kew said, "He was looking for you, Con. Not because you were Garth's man but because he thought you'd killed Shelley."

"He couldn't have!" Griselda was indignant.

"He did. That's what the papers were insinuating. He asked if I knew Con Satterlee. I said I'd put him in touch with you when I returned from Catalina, hoping to avoid him. I was leaving then. He must have had a hunch you were there too. Maybe Thusby hinted. Vironova was closeted with the police Friday evening."

Griselda said, "And he checked on it through me. Thusby saw me packing. And he knew I couldn't get away until next morning." She asked then, "Maybe you can tell me now, Con, why Chang was at Catalina."

"He gets worried about me," he admitted sheepishly. "But he came in handy. When I decided to break away where I could do my work uncluttered—"

"By a honeymoon," she said quickly.

"By too many parties and too many people, angel. Plus a damn suspicious major. I wasn't going fast enough. Sergei's rumors made it obvious that we couldn't suppress the finding of Mannie much longer. I had Chang call Vinnie to come over, gave him a faked message from Garth to the captain. Too much danger in using the phone. Vinnie flew the message back to old Thusby just in time for him to meet us at the dock."

"Thusby was in on it?"

"Not until after Sergei was murdered. He was so determined to release me then that I had to tell him. He hadn't liked taking me in the first place, Garth or no. I had to think fast all along to keep him amused so he wouldn't kick me out."

"Like having Chang steal the shells?" she suggested.

"Sure. I sent him to pack so he could get rid of them before Thusby could find them." He said, "Let's freshen these, Kew."

Griselda's voice was tight. "Why did Kathie kill Sergei?"

"She thought he suspected her," Dare said quietly. "She told me he kept asking questions and asking questions every time he saw her at the hotel. It made her nervous."

Kew said, "He didn't dream she had anything to do with it. He was just trying to find out all he could to pin it on Con."

"I'd like to know how she lured him into the Village where the shot wouldn't be heard," Con said. "If I suspected someone of murderous intent, that's the last place in the world I'd go willingly with them."

Dare's lips curled. "Con, if I were Kathie Travis I could do it with a knife in my teeth." She mocked, " 'Oh, there's someone coming. I mustn't be seen. Let's slip in here a moment.' But he didn't suspect her. To him doubtless it was, as Albert George thought, an amorous rendezvous."

Griselda asked, "Why was he so afraid of Pembrooke?"

Kew said, "They'd crossed paths in Europe. I had to insist he go in to dinner with us that night. Just seeing the major had thrown him into a panic. Sergei must have done some governmental work on the continent at some time. Albert George was certain he'd come to muscle in on the deal. He warned him off that night we were all on *The Falcon*."

It had been Sergei in the Major's stateroom, too

frightened to be shrill. Griselda's voice was small. "Just what was the deal? Was the information in the fish?"

"Yeah. A wad of paper inside had notation where the key was to Mannie's new strong box. The dope was in that. A complete report on all of our important radio stations, including monitory and field ones, with the names of the men to take care of sabotaging them. Even the names of men who would jam our Naval sending stations when orders came. The Pan-Pacific was a blind to get full information on our radio." He grinned. "Dare had the hunch about the fish tonight before you did. She filched it and passed it on to Garth."

Dare took no credit. "It wasn't a hunch, Con. While I was doing the great friend act tonight, trying to see if I couldn't get Kathie to let something slip, she told me Walker had given it to her on his return from Hollywood that Sunday night. Add it to Mannie's statement that Walker had possession of the facts, add the postscript to your letter; I was sure it counted. I asked Walker about it later. Mannie handed him the fish that night, told him to give it to Kathie to square himself. She was mad as hell because he wouldn't let her go with him to meet Mannie. He never thought of the fish as being important. But Mannie was smart. He knew Kathie would never give up any possession no matter how trivial. And he must have been certain that if anything happened to him, eventually Walker would catch on."

Kew's eyes were dark, his voice curiously shaken, "Dare, you knew she was the murderer? You knew it when you asked her to stay with you?"

She laughed patiently. "But of course, darling. That's why I invited her. You didn't think I wanted her company, did you?" Her face was sober. "I wanted her where I could keep an eye on her."

"She might have killed you."

"I was careful not to have lethal weapons lying about. And I was going to bolt my doors and windows tonight."

Con said, "My God, Dare, why didn't you tell me she was the one? I had everyone from Griselda to the Fuehrer on my list, particularly Kew."

"I gave you plenty of hints."

"You thought you did."

"All right." She tossed her seal brown head. "I didn't want to worry you with a minor matter. I could handle Kathie. You had enough on your mind with Mannie and the major, and worrying that something might happen to Griselda."

Griselda said to Con, "Kew was taking care of me. But you didn't like that."

"I thought Kew was on the wrong side. He'd seen too much of Pembrooke in Washington. I was sure of it when he was throwing Kathie to the lion at Catalina."

Kew said, "I pointed Kathie up that night so you'd know she was in danger. I tried to tell Griselda all along what I was up to—without putting myself in a spot—but I don't know if I got it across." He admitted, "I didn't trust you at first, Con. You lied to me the first day about taking Shelley to Saam's. I'd have seen you if you had. I didn't even trust Dare."

Dare said, "Nor I you. That's why I forced the issue after Sergei's death. If you had made a mistake, I wasn't going to let you continue in it." She tried to laugh. "I was going to save you in spite of yourself."

His eyes were on her. "I never knew I had guts

until that night I told you the whole mess. I thought it would mean curtains for me with you but there had been compulsion in me all along to tell you. The worst as well as the best."

"For better or for worst," Con said.

"Yes." But Dare was solemn.

Con turned to Griselda. "Well, I was wrong, baby, usually am. But I thought Kew was hanging onto you to get dope on me."

Kew broke in, "I was. I had to get to you before you started running around loose again. Albert George was going to kill you. He'd figured even if you didn't know it all, you knew too much. And I didn't know but what he might strike through Griselda. The safest bet was to stick with her. You'd come to her when you could. Dare didn't tell me she was in touch with you."

She said, "I couldn't. I was pledged on that. And I actually wasn't. Con came to me but I didn't know where he was."

"It wasn't safe for anyone to know, except Chang. He likes me. He'd cut folks up into little pieces for me. Anyone else might give it away by error, or compulsion."

Griselda wanted all the loose ends tied. Then the others could go and leave her with Con again. She asked Dare, "How did you happen to find Walker Travis?"

Dare said, "I want a drink first."

Con gathered the glasses.

Kew employed the interlude. "You'll marry me now, won't you? Don't you think I've waited long enough?"

Dare began to tally years on her fingers. She spoke flippantly, "You need someone to take care of you, keep you on the right side of things."

"You'll have to give up your career."

"Good Lord, you don't think I'd make a career of matching thread, do you, darling? That was Garth's bright idea when Con sent me to him this spring, a way to put me in with the Navy where the secret agents were boring. You see I was already on the ground before Albert George met the Admiral."

He kept his voice steady, "I don't exactly like that career. You might get hurt. Maybe you could train me to take your place with Garth."

Griselda whispered, "Don't let him do it, Dare." He was too brave, recklessly brave as Con was. Women couldn't rest and their men in danger.

Con handed the glasses around. "Let's get back to Walker Travis. I suppose the omniscient Mrs. Crandall guessed right off that Kathie had struck again. He couldn't have left Huntington Beach with her that night. Someone would have seen him return to the hotel. The car had sped away before the guards were aware. In the heavy mist they couldn't know if two persons were in it. Whatever had happened to him, it happened before Kathie raced back to the hotel. No wonder she was hysterical the next day. She didn't know where he was or what he would say."

"Walker told me the whole story when I found him," said Dare.

"Where did you find him?"

"Walking back from his ride. Skulking along the beach, afraid she might be cruising the highway looking for him. He'd hidden out all day. Didn't have the nerve to ask to phone anywhere looking as he did. And he didn't dare go back to their cottage; he didn't know but she might be there waiting for him. He was plenty scared of her; he saw it clear then. He'd missed a gun from his collection—all Service men collect guns. He remembered he'd been asking her about that, if she'd seen it. She probably thought he suspected her too. Although he didn't until he nipped out the window and ran for it."

Con asked, "How did you know where to look for him?"

"I did have a hunch there. After I'd examined their cottage and the near ones, I found where he'd hidden under a porch until she left. I drove back and started walking from this end. I found him, and believe me, he was glad to see me. He was about done in." She shook her head. "Con, she'll deny everything and there's no proof. Can they hold her?"

"She'll break." Con's mouth was grim. "If she doesn't, the wheel of Mannie's launch is going to show up in court with her fingerprints all over it."

He looked at Griselda and then at the others. "Why don't you two run along to Yuma and get married tonight? No, Griselda and I are going to bed, but they keep witnesses on order. You'd better do it before you remember to start fighting again."

Dare stood up. "We'll get out of here anyway. See you tomorrow."

Con walked up to her. They looked at each other in silence. He ordered, "Don't come back without a ring on your finger." And then he bent suddenly and kissed her. "Thanks for everything, angel."

He stood at the door watching until they were gone. Griselda wondered if there were regret in him mingling with satisfaction of a good deed done.

He was yawning when he returned to the couch. "Well, I'm home, baby. With the home fires burning."

"What next?" she asked lightly.

"Now we'll have a honeymoon." He traced the shape of her face with his forefinger. "I wish I'd been

here when the major barged in tonight. I'd have
killed him."

"No." She moved close to him. "No. I'm glad you
didn't come. You wouldn't have had a chance." She
wouldn't think of that again. "Con, were you looking
for Shelley that first night at the Bamboo?"

"I wasn't. I knew she was in town. Dare had told
me that. But I hadn't ever laid eyes on her. I didn't
see Pembrooke there and I didn't connect Kew with
her. I'd heard of Kew and Kathie—she was searching
for him that same night, of course, not for her husband—but not Kew and Shelley. I knew he was playing a dangerous game. I didn't trust him; that's why
I didn't want him around where he might find out
my business. And my poor Dare trying to whitewash
him and keep him out of it until he could clear up his
mistake."

He yawned again. "Think I'll have another little
drink before we turn in."

She spoke out of habit. "You don't need it." He
could have anything he wanted, tonight or any night.
She'd never again question anything he did.

He began to pour it but wheeled suddenly. "Baby,
I got a wonderful idea!"

She waited.

"Soon as this thing is in the bag, we'll go to
Niagara Falls and have a real honeymoon." At her
lack of response, his enthusiasm faltered. "What do
you say?"

She smiled. "I looove honeymoons." And then she
laughed. "What does Barjon Garth want us to do
there?"

CPSIA information can be obtained
at www.ICGtesting.com
Printed in the USA
FSHW022002160820
73027FS